I0740296

Mary Homes

A wreath of rhymes

Mary Homes

A wreath of rhymes

ISBN/EAN: 9783337273408

Printed in Europe, USA, Canada, Australia, Japan

Cover: Foto ©Andreas Hilbeck / pixelio.de

More available books at **www.hansebooks.com**

A WREATH OF RHYMES.

A

WREATH OF RHYMES.

BY

MILLIE MAYFIELD.

" Written with little skill of song-craft,
Homely phrases, but each letter
Full of hope, and yet of heart-break."
LONGFELLOW.

PHILADELPHIA
J. B. LIPPINCOTT & CO.
1869.

Entered according to Act of Congress, in the year 1869, by

J. B. LIPPINCOTT & CO.,

In the Clerk's Office of the District Court of the United States, for the Eastern
District of Pennsylvania.

LIPPINCOTT'S PRESS,
PHILADELPHIA.

CONTENTS.

CONTENTS.

	PAGE
Night	101
Half-mast	103
Spring	105
"Hic Jacet."	107
Homely Hetty Gray	109
Contentment	111
A Lay for the Ladye Moon	113
The Wind Spirit	114
The Song of Life	116
Unrest	119
Weary	121
Life	122
Let us Forget	126
The Song of Other Years	129
Dying	129
Inconstancy	131
'Gainst Wind and Tide	133
The Mystic Land	134
The Beautiful	136
Daylight	138
The Angel Monitor	139
Midsummer's Eve	144
The Norse Queen's Ride	146
Once Upon a Time	149
The Loved and Lost	151
My Birth-day	152
A Little While	154
Heaven	156
Bessie Bell	158
Hesperus	161
My Bird	163
The Penitent Mary	165
An Album Dedication	166

CONTENTS.

A WREATH OF RHYMES.

FAME.

A FAINT, low breath o'er the sea of Life—
  And a little bubble's born;
Onward it floats, through the whirlwind's strife,
  Or the hush of midsummer's morn,
Riding the top of the stormiest wave
  The distant goal to gain—
A golden strand, where no tempests rave
  To toss the silvery main.

Where the bay tree bends o'er the jeweled beach,
  And murmuring myrtles near
Are weaving crowns for the daring reach
  Of those who were born to wear!
And the painted bubble, with pride inflate,
  Has kissed the shore, so gay—
When lo! it bursts, and its empty state
  Has passed, with a breath, away!

THE BATTLE OF LIFE.

MORN'S jeweled fingers
  Roll up the mist-shadows
From pearl-beaded rivulets,
  Emerald-crown'd meadows—
And crystallized mirrors
  Of sky and of lakelet
Gleam blue as the violet's
  Eye in the brakelet.

Out of the purpling
  Haze of the mountain,
And clear thro' the silvery
  Spray of the fountain—
Over the glass of the
  Serpentine river,
And up from deep Ocean's
  Light wavelets, that quiver—

Are earth's ringing pæans
  All grandly ascending,
The while the old Day-Star
  His lustre is lending
To light up the great
  Panorama, where Strife
With the Angel of Peace
  Fights the Battle of Life!

Arm for the contest,
  O mortal! how glorious

The morning shall redden
  That finds thee victorious!
Man! tho' the field may be
  Bloodless, the struggle
With Evil's wild army
  Asks strength of thee double.

First—tho' the hosts that
  Beset thee are legion—
Look down in thy heart's
  Secret, shadowy region,
And there, to entrap thee,
  A foeman is nestling,
The whom to subdue takes
  Thy mightiest wrestling.

Buckle the breastplate
  Of truth to thy bosom—
Let Faith be thy banner—
  And twine with the blossom
Of Reason, the soft buds
  Of Love and Forbearance;
Then off with the veil of
  The senses—the clearance

Shall show thee, that light
  Is the cause of the shadow;
And from old decay springs
  The green of the meadow;
That what we call "right"
  Has evolved from the Wrong—
And when ye discern this,
  Your armor is strong!

Fight the good fight,
　And your courage make known
When asking for bread
　Ye are tendered a stone.
For Nature harmoniously
　Singeth one song,
And Man shall its burthen
　Triumphant prolong !

Type of the Being
　Who made thee ! no trembling
When facing the ill ; it
　Is useless, dissembling
That sin, sorrow, *self* must
　Be conquered, ere glorious
That morrow shall dawn that will
　Find thee victorious !

These are the evils
　Foreshadowing the good—
Battle *one* bravely,
　Away flies the brood—
Down with strong SELF
　In the troublous strife,
And the conquest is gained
　In the Battle of Life !

KING FROST.

B Y the red brand on the sunset hill,
   And Dian's burnished horn,
Gleaming o'er twilight's purple rill—
   The King will ride ere morn !
His herald, the North wind, a blast has blown
   For a full score of hours,
And the chilled blood has curdling flown
   From the lips of the frightened flowers.

There's a weird glare in each lamp afar
   That's lit in the burnished blue,
Which only burns when the grim King's car
   Is rolling night's arches through ;
And a hush in the woodlands and on the plain,
   As his chariot's wheels draw nigh
And scatter white spray, in an icy rain,
   Unheeding the daisy's sigh.

Oh the pale-cheeked morn will beckon the sun
   To view a desolate sight—
To see how the tyrant's hand has undone
   The summer's work in a night !
How the forest lords have doffed their green
   To don his yellow suit—
How the grasses fade 'neath his glittering sheen—
   How his sword has cleft the fruit !

And the crimson spots on each rifted leaf
   Will tell of the darker deed,

Of midnight struggle fierce, tho' brief,
  And the conqueror's bloody meed !
Oh ring your bugles shrill and clear,
  Winds—pipe aloud your glee ;
For your King, in his ermine robes, so fair,
  Has led to victory !

Yea, toss the withered leaves on high,
  Make sport where you've ruin brought ;
A few brief days, and sweet April's eye
  Will weep o'er the wrong you've wrought ;
And the gentle drops, as they softly fall,
  Will waken hope anew
In each trodden heart, till the sombre pall
  Rolls back from the violet's blue.

The crocus her starry glance will raise
  At sympathy's sweet tear,
And mountain-pinks blush forth their praise
  When her tender tones they hear ;
And from its emerald tent of leaves
  Each bud, at the call, will spring,
And with dainty hues hang its fairy caves,
  And its sweetest perfume bring

To greet the victor, now, who comes,
  Not with the flashing sword
To mark a track thro' desolate homes—
  But with power of *a gentle word !*—
The magic power of a kindly smile,
  The eloquence of tears
That fall on the bruisèd heart, the while,
  And heal the wounds of years.

O power of kindness! April's smiles,
    Alternate with her tears,
That work their sweet and winning wiles,
    Till every nook appears
Clothed with a splendor Solomon,
    In all his glorious state,
Could not compete with—show to one
    That thou, of all, art great!

Brute force may tread with an iron heel,
    And rule with despotic rod;
But gentleness will softly steal
    Round the heart, for it comes from God!—
For while devastation marketh all
    Oppression's ruthless deeds,
The flowers of hope at a tender call
    Spring up, and bear goodly seeds!

PEARLS.

AN anguish-drop, 'tis said, is the pearl,
    A tear by the shell-fish shed—
That the glistening gem in beauty's curl
    Is a drop that its heart has bled.

So pearls of feeling, and gems of thought,
    Are the products oft of pain,
In sorrow's alchemy purely wrought
    Till they shine without a stain!

WRECKS.

STREWN o'er Ocean's "Place of Skulls,"
  Where the wave the petrel lulls,
Lie the missing spars and hulls.

Crystallized upon the shore
Of icy-jeweled Labrador,
Are staved life-boat and broken oar.

Where the storm-fiend holds the pass
Of tempest-ridden Hatteras,
Have noble barks gone down, alas!

Not a foam-wreathed lip of land—
Not a beach of golden sand—
Not a shell-enameled strand—

Nor a rock where breakers boom
Minute guns through midnight gloom,
But has sounded notes of doom

To some fated ship the gale—
That pirate grim!—has shorn of sail,
And reft of rigging, rope and rail!

Ah! woeful wrecks the eyes of night,
With their lightning gleams bedight,
Glare down upon in ghastly light!

And the deep sea's coral caves
Are but gem-bespangled graves,
O'er whose uncoffined dead the waves

Will dance and leap and joyous play—
Tho' tearful eyes watch, night and day,
For the ships that went away.

Tide of Time ! that drifteth now
Laden with each gladsome prow
That tempts thy waves—how like art thou

To yon restless flood, that sings
The same old song, tho' priceless things
Are buried in its hidden springs !

Thou hast borne our hopes and fears,
The garnered joys of early years—
And o'er their wrecks have fallen our tears ;

To thy billows we have given
The trust our childhood brought from Heaven
To see its white sail soiled and riven !

Yet thou flowest careless by—
Tho' on the strand of Ages lie
Wrecks that would wake an angel's sigh !

CHARITY.

HE sang of Love :—The lady turned,
　　Her lip was curled in cold disdain,
And in her eyes' dark centres burned
　　Those lights, scarce scorn, nor wholly pain,

But compound of the heart's intense
Enlightener—Experience !
And Time's all-potent, powerful test,
That probes the strength of every breast.

" Love ! 'tis a weird, deceitful glare,
    Hiding the marsh from which it sprung—
A meteor gleaming in the air—
    A bubble on life's streamlet flung !
O minstrel ! strike again the chord,
But let it thrill to nobler word—
For tho' Love like a seraph sings,
His earthly bondage soils his wings."

He tuned again his lyre ; and now
    Of Friendship—she of placid mien—
He sang ; he praised her thoughtful brow,
    Her smiling lips and eyes serene.—
" Cease, cease !" the lady cried, " there lies
Cold calculation in her eyes ;
For Friendship may be bought and sold,
She is not proof 'gainst shining gold !

" I'll give thee theme for noble song,
    To thrill upon thy harp-strings free
And echo all the spheres among—
    O minstrel, sing of Charity !
Long suffering is she, yet she's kind–
Thinketh no evil, and is blind
To her own merits.—Envieth not
The good that is another's lot :

" Beareth all things unto the end—
    Hopeth all things—endureth all ;

Seeking the injured to defend—
　Knowing man's weakness, by his fall.
Faith may lift up its eyes on high ;
Hope may aspire to reach the sky ;
But loving arms round *earth* throws she,
To hide its faults—sweet Charity !"

THE GLEANER.

WHERE`the sunset fields are overlaid
　　With ridges of yellow grain,
The dark-eyed Night, like the Moab maid,
　Follows the reaper's train—
Old Day, with his sickle and stores of light,
　Letting down Eve's golden bars—
And out of the chaff the gleaner, Night,
　Brings her apron full of stars.

Then, thus on the world, go forth, O Soul !
　If not as a reaper—glean
The little seeds that unnoticed roll
　The stubble-mounds between ;
And thine may be a crown, forsooth,
　Like that which the midnight weaves—
For oh there are golden grains of truth
　Underlying all fallen sheaves !

BACKWARD AND FORWARD.

OVER what mountain ranges,
   In the mystical dream-light,
Thro' lonely, rain-steep'd valleys,
   Hath my soul gone forth to-night !
O'er meadows grim with hoarfrost ;
   By silent founts and rills ;
Thro' forests whirling dead leaves
   All over the barren hills—

Until my feet have trodden
   The shore of a tideless sea,
Whose blackened beach is strewn with
   Ashen apples for me ;
With glittering barks dismantled,
   Riven and sullied sails,
That once flashed bright in the freshness
   Of promise-breathing gales.

The white fog lies on the water
   Like a shroud o'er the sheeted dead,
And the stars look out of a vapor
   Of tears, o'er my bended head ;
While dim, in the mist-stained heavens,
   The moon like a tombstone gleams
Cold and white, and lettered
   All o'er with my early dreams.

I would not dream them over,
   For the wealth of the golden stars—

Not for the diamonds of Venus—
  Nor the rubies red of Mars!
Not again would I grasp the rainbow
  To find its brightness fled—
Thank God! they lie in the chancel
  Withered and cold and dead!

Thank God! for the eye that can fathom
  The depths of the fleshy coil—
Thank God! for the heart that can battle
  With this earthly state's turmoil ;—
For thus the red wine is gathered
  From the crushing press of Life,
When the spark divine within us
  Ignites from the friction—Strife !

'Tis true, in the vaulted chambers
  Of the ruins of the Past,
Covered with rust and mildew,
  Lie things too bright to last ;
But out of their dust and ashes,
  On some resurrection-morn,
They will spring like the meadow daisy
  From last year's mould re-born !

And tho' by a tideless ocean,
  With no returning wave,
I stand to-night in the blackness
  And find no jewel to save
From the wrecks that in pride once bore me—
  I know in the depths of that sea
There are priceless pearls awaiting
  The diving—ay, PEARLS FOR ME !

3

So, welcome, the rack of feeling—
  Welcome the scourge of years—
Welcome, the Stygian billow
  That crystallizes tears!
Forward! forward! *my jewels*
  (Each glittering tear I've shed)
I'll gather in untold brightness
  When the sea gives up its dead!

THOUGHTS.

COMING, going, in the twilight,
  In the morning, noon and night,
Wingèd shapes are flitting past me,
  But the brightest ne'er alight.

Never one with golden sunshine
  Meshed within its radiant wing,
But it mocks me—fluttering ever
  Where I cannot hear it sing.

I would charm the warbler, knew I
  Lure to catch the bright-wing'd thing,
While I'm flooded with the glitter
  That its waving pinions bring—

But my reach can never grasp it;
  Never unto durance bring
One of all the bright-plumed creatures
  That come near, but never sing!

SUNSHINE.

TELL me not of moonbeams gleaming,
  Far too death-like are their rays;
Give me the merry sunshine beaming
  Thro' the golden summer days.

The bright sun comes like Hope, to lighten
  Weary pilgrims on life's road—
The earth's green livery seems to brighten,
  And fruit and flowers before him nod.

The birds break forth in joyous measure;
  All Nature sings a song of praise—
The tiniest mote will dance with pleasure
  Within his warm, inspiring rays!

While cold and pale the moonbeams quiver—
  The white-faced planet's tithes are tears!
'Tis only in the rushing river
  Reflected, her dim face appears.

Her satellite, the tided Ocean,
  Pays watery tribute to her power;
Her wan smile wakes but sad emotion,
  And tears beseem the moonlit bower.

But give me smiles instead of teardrops—
  I love the daisy more than rue;
Life is too short—its wear and tear stops
  Mirth too soon—despair to woo.

WAIT PATIENTLY.

"To everything beneath the sun there cometh a last day."

DROOP not, Brother, in the valley
   Roofed with tears and bridged with sighs—
Far above thee, o'er the mountain,
   See the bow of promise rise !
Plume thy soul to struggle bravely
   With its fetters made of clay ;
For, be sure, to all earth's sorrows
   That there cometh a last day.

Weary Sister, wounded sorely
   By a harsh, unfeeling world—
Courage ! tho' the shaft of slander
   With its venom's at thee hurled ;
Virtue wears a charmèd mantle,
   Which repels the dart's dark way—
Time alone will test its merits,
   And to thy wrongs bring a last day.

Child of Pleasure ! gayly chasing
   Phantoms, fading in thy clasp—
Plucking gilded fruit, which ever
   Turns to ashes in thy grasp !
Pause ! and think of moments wasted,
   Of time which speedeth fast away,
Yet unimproved—for, oh believe it,
   To thy joys comes a last day.

And cheerful one, who thro' life's changes
   Seeks in all some good to find—

And bears both well and ill together
  With a calm, contented mind—
Oh, thou art blest! for naught can turn thee
  From the bright, the upward way!
Thro' joy's glad smiles, or sorrow's wailing,
  Thou'rt still prepared for the last day.

O mortal! read aright the lesson
  'Graved on Nature's tablets deep!
The bright leaf withers—where the rock rose
  Proudly, now the billows leap!
Star by star, from yon blue heaven,
  Silently hath passed away,
The fate of worlds must still be ours—
  And to each, and all, comes a last day!

Then faint not when the burden's heavy,
  Time will surely make it light;
Hope, thro' all things, for the morrow
  Which must dawn o'er darkest night!
And, thro' all life's ills, remember
  The years still roll their ceaseless way,
Shaking from thy glass the moments
  Till there's left but THY last day.

So live that when that day's declining,
  And ushers in the night of death,
Its shadow will for thee no terrors
  Have, as flees thy latest breath;
But, brightly o'er the hills celestial,
  As streams the never-dying ray,
Thy soul will soar on wings immortal
  To bask in Heaven's Eternal day!

3 *

RETROSPECTION.

WASTED years! O wasted years!
    Your pallid faces gleam to-night
From Memory's surging sea of tears,
O'er whose up-heaving flood appears
    No ray of friendly light.
Down, ghosts! unto your watery graves!
Sink, spectres! deep, beneath the waves!
Ye stretch your withered hands in vain,
I cannot bring ye back again.

I cannot give ye back the truth,
    The hope and trust of life's young day—
The fresh, warm impulses of youth—
The friendliness, that poison-tooth
    Of falsehood wore away.
I may not string again such pearls
For careworn brow and faded curls—
Then, why, why call ye from the dark?
Why fan to flames the Past's low spark?

Phantom fingers on the wall.
    Of old Remembrance, wherefore trace
The golden moments, squandered all
At folly's shrine—at pleasure's call—
    In lines tears can't efface?
In characters of fire, that burn
The deeper as the path we turn
Whose marble guide-post 'neath the yew
Is lettered—" The Dark Valley to!"—

It may be, that, like him, the Seer
  Of Patmos' isle—(who ate the book
The angel gave, which did appear
As honey to the taste, but ere
    The thunders ceased, which shook
The rainbow-girdled firmament,
Had turned to bitter streams, which sent
The life-drops of experience
His prophecies to tincture hence,)—

That we must turn life's honeyed page,
  And drink its cup of sweetness dry.
To find within the lees the sage,
Tho' bitter, wholesome truths of age,
    Ere we can prophesy ;
And if the chalice we have drained
Before life's noontide hill we've gained,
The tangled path will not seem long—
We've learned to suffer and be strong !

FORGIVE.

OH, never think the rankling seeds
    Of dark revenge, will ere
Spring aught but bitter, noisome weeds,
  To put forth buds of care.

Then tear them quickly from the heart—
  Once rooted there, they'll live—
And choose the nobler, better part—
  Be God-like, and forgive !

A BROKEN FRIENDSHIP.

'TWAS a fleeting, waking vision,
    False as dreams of night could be—
Yet I thought it no illusion
    When as *friend* I pictured thee !

Pure as snow-flakes seemed the promise
    (Ah ! I've found it was as cold !)
Of the white bud friendship grafted
    On my heart in days of old.

But the canker there was feeding,
    Tho' soft petals hid the sight ;
Now, the withered leaves are telling,
    Ceaseless gnawing ends in blight !

Yet the tree it sought to cling to
    Still puts forth its loving arms—
'Twould have sheltered the fair blossom
    From all ills, all vain alarms,

Had the poison-worm not entered—
    Sapped the fountain of all bliss—
And with venom'd lip betrayed it
    With a treacherous, Judas kiss !

When thou said'st " my friend !" I deemed thee
    Truthful, and I clasped thy hand—
Thinking that such seal was lasting
    As German love for Fatherland !

Like a beatific vision
   Was the whitened shrine I reared ;
But the altar-flame was lighted
   Too near earth—and now, 'tis charred.

Yet the ashes I have gathered,
   In my heart to be inurned,
Remnant of a plighted friendship
   All too holy to be spurned !

For tho' thou so desecrated
   The pure temple, still, to me,
It was the fane where I enshrinèd
   A true heart's idolatry—

And so fair the whited sculpture,
   That I scarce could think it clay—
And I mourn that hand of *thine* should
   E'er have roll'd the stone away !

"BLESSINGS BRIGHTEN AS THEY TAKE THEIR FLIGHT."

'TIS the *last* flash of day's departing splendor,
   Lighting its funeral pyre on night's dark bier,
That glows with greatest radiance, yet more tender,
   Because the brooding darkness is so near !
And thus the blessings, o'er our pathway scattered,
   By daily use lose their intrinsic light—
But when they leave us, by some rude blow shattered,
   They grow the brighter as they take their flight.

LITTLE ALLIE.

L IKE a star-eyed daisy
    Brightening the valley,
With a smile of gladness
  Cometh little Allie;
All her hopeful glances
  To the heart appealing,
As if angel pinions
  Stirred our depths of feeling!

Little wandering sunbeam,
  In the shady places
Where life's clouds have darkened
  Many weary faces—
What may be thy mission
  He, alone, knows best
Who took dear little children
  Within His arms, and bless'd!

And He hath said, " Their angels
  My Father's face do see :—
Of such is heaven's kingdom !"—
  Then, Allie, dear, in thee
We may be entertaining
  An angel, unaware—
For God has set His signet
  Upon thy golden hair!

And if thy spirit standeth
  Beside the great White Throne,

Then we poor earth-stained pilgrims
  Thy ministry should own;
Nor spurn the Infant Teacher—
  Remembering *our* need,
When lions shall lie down with lambs
  And a little child shall lead!

THE MOON'S JOURNEY.

ROYALLY rose the queenly Moon,
  Refreshed from her ocean bath,
Which sweetly flowed 'neath the ides of June—
  And up the crystal path
That wound to the silver heights afar,
  Where the glittering tower of night
Hung out a flashing, signal star,
  She floated in liquid light.

Out from the darkness the roses came
  And raised their drooping heads,
The peony bared its heart of flame,
  And daisies kissed the meads;
And many a thing that the thoughtful night
  Had veiled—not a whit too soon—
Now broke on the placid eyes of light
  Of the calm, unruffled Moon.

On many a scene of sweet content,
  And many a deed of ill,

Fell her glances, as she slowly went
 From starry hill to hill.
Now, where the pulse of the city bounds
 With life, shone her full, bright eye ;
And now, on the hallow'd, grassy mounds
 Where the silent sleepers lie !

Over the billows, where sea-weeds wave
 Around some seaman's tomb,
And a coral branch marks the watery grave
 Of manhood's stricken bloom,
She lettered with silver the rolling wave,
 And wrote on the sparkling tide,
That, " He who once walked its breast to save,
 Was near when the sailor died !"

She saw the mother lay her child
 To rest, in its coffin bed—
And brighter grew her eye, as the wild
 Grief broke o'er the waxen dead.
For she caught the ray from the golden wing
 Of the angel as he passed
With the soul of the sweet, seraphic thing
 That its earthly crust had cast !

And wherever the seed of sorrow fell
 She smiled with a brighter ray,
For she knew the germ in that darken'd shell
 Sprang goodly fruit alway,—
That the sunlight of pleasure dries the heart,
 And sterile makes its sod ;
But chastening drops that in anguish start
 Are the streams that lead to God !

Oh, many a golden lesson she
   Inscribed on her silver page ;
And many a quaint old homily,
   Taught her by Nature sage !
She learned from the trampled, bruisèd flower
   That had but a breath to live,
Yet yielded its sweets in its dying hour—
   'Tis blessed to forgive !

And she learned from the little shoot that sprang
   A slender thread in the dew,
Then budded and leafed, till its branches rang
   With a tune that is always new—
That the veriest atom its fruit will bring,
   Each grain is with impulse rife—
And *little things* are the germs whence spring
   The evil or good of life.

Oh, here a voice and there a breath
   Came up from the brown old earth,
Whispering the secrets of Life and Death
   And holier spirit birth !
And ever her brow with more glory shone,
   While her cheek with awe grew white,
As she listed the cadences 'round her throne
   Chiming deep thro' the solemn night !

4

LENA LEE.

HAST thou seen the merry bee,
　　When the floweret dozes,
Humming gayly o'er the lea
　　Kissing up the roses?
Hast thou heard the tuneful breeze,
　　While the day reposes,
Sigh soft music thro' the trees,
　　Like rhymes with sweetest closes?
　　　　Then thou'st seen my Lena Lee—
　　　　Tuneful breeze, and busy bee!

Hast thou mark'd the roving bird
　　Bending o'er the blossom
With the same soft, witching word
　　That's thrilled another's bosom?—
Hast thou watch'd the flirting wind
　　Kiss the dimpling lakelet,
Then whisper to the tendrils twined
　　In the leafy brakelet?
　　　　Roving bird—my Lena Lee—
　　　　Whisp'ring, flirting wind, is she.

Didst ever note the changing moon
　　Flushing red, then paling,
When the fiery sighs of June
　　Pierce her silver veiling?
Hast thou mark'd the blushes bright
　　On the playful billow,

When the sunset's eyes of light
  Glitter thro' the willow?
      Changing moon—my Lena Lee—
      Blushing billow, bounding free !

Hast thou seen the angler sit
  Where in streamlet flowing
Silver perch and sunfish flit,
  As the tide is going?
Hast thou mark'd his coaxing bait
  Flung to catch a nibble—
And the wily fish still grate
  Low down o'er the pebble?
      Angler, with the bait—poor me !
      Golden sunfish—Lena Lee !

HOPE.

SONGSTER ! that trills a soft lay—
    A matin in life's morning hours—
And tells of the splendors that wait the fair day,
  Shining glorious in manhood's far bowers !

Syren ! that strings a wild lyre
  O'er the far-sweeping billows of time—
And sings of a name ringing higher and higher
  In fame's thrilling anthem sublime !

Seraph ! that bends o'er the tomb,
  And murmurs of error.forgiven—
Of flowers perennial adorning its gloom,
  And gently points upward to heaven !

THE RAINY DAY.

THERE is a wail in the wind's low sough,
    And a moan that the sea hath made;
The morn has a black band over her brow,
    For the sun in his shroud is laid.

Oh put his golden curls away
    'Neath the cloud-scarf fringed with white,
And sit by his bier and weep, O Day!
    And waves, at the piteous sight,

Hide all your treasures in the sands—
    For he cannot see the shells
You've brought in your jewel-girdled hands
    From the crimson coral cells.

And drop the leaf-veil over the heart
    Of the rose, for her love is dead;
She sits in her widowhood apart,
    With the thorny crown on her head—

And cannot read the message sweet,
    That the velvet leaves unfold,
Which the little pansy lays at her feet
    In purple, blue and gold!

And watch the lily while she bends
    Her pale cheek over the brook,
And stooping lower, lower, sends
    A sadly-searching look

For the one bright face, that ever gave
    Her answering glances sweet
From the blue mirror of the wave—
    And is now in its winding sheet.

Oh, watch her well, for the weight of tears
    Bows down her beautiful head,
As the tramp of the mourning rain she hears,
    And knows that her sweetheart's dead.

And, "Come, come, come," says the tempting brook;
    "We will wander out to the sea,
And down in the amber caverns look
    For the eyes so dear to thee!

"I knew, last night, as his golden boat
    Went out at the twilight bars,
And I saw the ghostly mist-shapes float
    Over the pallid stars—

"That the morn would rise from a troubled sleep
    To a legacy of tears;
For that boat went down to a stormy deep,
    And the wind its requiem bears!

"But, come, come, come, we will wander where
    The billows sparkle up
To fill with nectar, rich and rare,
    Thy creamy porcelain cup;

"And pledge thy sweetheart 'neath the waves;
    We will meet him there to-night,
As he seeks the flaming opal caves
    With his ringlets streaming bright.
    4 *

"He is not dead; he is hid away,
  To shun the pleading eyes
Of his old love, weary-hearted Day,
  Plodding the pathless skies.

"And he longs to kiss the pearly rim
  Of the chalice, to your name;
Oh we'll fill, fill high to the golden brim,
  If we find him still the same!"

Oh watch her well, for tear-drops bead
  Her lids with a weight of pain,
As she hears the hollow sigh of the reed
  And the tramp of the mourning rain.

O heart, bowed down with a tearful woe,
  How like to the lily thou—
Listing a brook with a wily flow
  Singing, murmuring now,

"Come, come, come, there is rest for thee
  In oblivion's dreamy cave—
Over the tide of Life's rough sea
  Oh seek the placid wave!"

How like to the mourning rose, obscure
  'Neath grief's all-clouded sky—
No eyes for the golden lessons pure
  That at thy feet may lie.

Oh up from the depths! shake off the rain
  Of slowly-dropping sorrow;
Or bravely bear its weight of pain—
  For the sun may shine to-morrow!

THY MEMORY.

THERE is a green spot in the waste,
   The desert drear of Life —for me ;
A sunbeam in each shady place—
   It is thy memory !

There is a lone star struggling thro'
   The darkness, that envelops me
And shuts out Heaven's kind eyes of blue—
   It is thy memory !

There is a beacon beaming bright
   As lighthouse lamp o'er surging sea,
For me—thro' sorrow's stormy night—
   It is thy memory.

There is a steady flame that burns
   Where distance shuts cold gate on thee,
Which fell Despair's chill breath ne'er turns—
   It is thy memory !

There is a priceless gem which glows
   In Grief's dark mine all radiantly,
Till all the gloom with glory flows—
   It is thy memory !

There is a voice, with cheering tone,
   That's ever fondly whispering me,
" We'll meet again !"   Till then, mine own,
   I'll keep thy memory.

WHITHER?

WHITHER, Life,
　　　　Swift current—densely freighted
With barks, where joy and grief are strangely mated—
O turbid, rushing stream, whither away?
What ending is ordained thy April day,
　　　　　　　　O Life?

Whither, Heart—
　　　　　Compound of wrath and meekness,
Angelic strength and erring mortal weakness—
O human heart, where are thy pulses leading?
Whither thy aim, and whence thy bitter bleeding,
　　　　　　　　O Heart?

Whither, Mind—
　　　　　Thou gleaming spark electric!
Sun, that illumes mortality's ecliptic!—
Whither, fine essence, will thy perfume float,
When in Death's gulf is moored our fragile boat,
　　　　　　　　O Mind?

Whither, Soul,—
　　　　　In transient storms controlling
The waves o'er Life's tempestuous ocean rolling—
When the Great Captain bids us furl our sail,
Where will your wing find rest, as swells *that* gale,
　　　　　　　　O Soul?

Whither? where?
　　　　　Life, Heart, Mind, Soul?—Oh ask not!
Thy poor, weak, *finite* comprehension task not:—

Be sure that He who wills the sparrow's fall
Will find a haven for each bark, where all
                          Is fair !

ECHO.

MOCKING fairy, tattling Sprite !
   Where mak'st thou thy dwelling?
Is earth thy home, or cloudlets bright,
That thus, for aye, by day or night,
   What others say, thou'rt telling?

We know that thou wert doomed to lie
   In hopeless love's embraces,
Till thy frail form didst pine and die,
And but thy voice was left to sigh
   In solitary places.

Didst turn thy spirit's sweets to gall?
   And is't revenge thou'rt seeking—
By list'ning, mocking, telling all
Which mortal lips may chance let fall
   When near thy dwelling speaking?

A weary lot is thine, poor Sprite !
   A tattler's doom, remember—
Dwindles fair form to spectres quite,
But leaves the *tongue* inflamed with spite,
   The only active member !

THE MIDNIGHT HOUR.

THE whisp'rings of the midnight hour !
  The broken cadences
That chime from every star-lit tower
  Or float on every breeze,
When noon of night with ebon key
  Unlocks her sheeted dead,
Tombed in the vault of memory—
    The ghosts of pleasures fled :
      How dreamily, how tenderly,
        Upon the heart they fall,
      Like strains of some old melody
        We only half recall !

The anthems of the midnight hour !
  The fingers stilled by day,
That hold the heart-strings in their power
  And on them grandly play
A thrilling sweep of chords, to blend
  With tones long passed away ;
When angels thro' the darkness send
  Songs never heard by day !—
      How gloriously, sublimely,
        From the blue heights they fall ;
      Like the pæans ever sounding from
        Some mighty waterfall !

The sermons of the midnight hour !
  The voices from the mount,
That tranquillize, with spirit power,
  The waters of the fount

Within each breast—that speak to each,
  And murmur, " Peace, be still !"
The seraph voices clear, that teach
  Obedience to His will !—
    How holily, impressively,
      Upon the soul they fall ;
    Like those grand strains old masters' hands
      Could from the harp-strings call !

The echoes of the midnight hour !
  The sounds from long ago,
That touch our bosom's rock of power
  And bid its waters flow !
The echoes from the far-off time—
  The songs of youth and spring,
Ere Happiness had lost its chime
  Or Joy had found its wing.
    How mournfully, how vaguely,
      Those sweet, sad echoes fall ;
    Like the ghostly sounds old ruins give
      In answer to our call.

The promises of midnight's hour !
  The starry stretch of blue
Where God has writ, " Tho' darkness lower,
  The day will burst anew !
So, from the midnight of the tomb,
  Glowing with new-born light,
Thy soul will break the bonds of gloom,
  Triumphant o'er Death's night !"
    How eagerly, how hopefully
      We listen as they fall ;
    Like " the good tidings of great joy,"
      Once said, " shall be for all !"

FORGETFULNESS.

MOTHER FAIRIE, boon I crave !
   Lave me in the Lethean wave ;
Bind my brow with poppy leaves,
And lay me 'neath the primrose eaves,
Pillowed on the violets ;
Where the cooling, silvery jets
Of a crystal fountain near
Murmur softly on the ear.
I would dream a pleasant dream,
Could I stop the rushing stream
Of saddest memory, this eve,
With the mellow moon to weave
Silver tissue in the grass ;
And the wooing wind to pass
Yon queenly dahlia's coronet,
To kiss the lowly mignonette.

I would tell how modest worth
Needs no tinsel'd gaud of earth
To adorn its loveliness—
For the sweetest blooms that bless
The mossy, green retreats of Flora
With most fragrant, purest aura,
Wear the least attractive hues—
Hyacinths, steeped in the dews,
Heliotropes and scented broom,
Ambrosia-laden with perfume,
Eglantine and sweet acacia,
Have no colors to abash you

Like the gaudy, scentless tulip,
Or the china-aster's blue lip
Where no perfumed breath e'er lingers;
And the golden ringèd fingers
Of the stately peony
Ne'er were kissed by fragrancy,
As is the calycanthus simple
Peering 'neath its russet wimple.

See yon flaunting hollyhock,
Boldly glaring from its stalk—
Would you place it in your bosom
Sooner than this tender blossom
Sending modest looks between
Leafy folds of curtains green,
Amethyst in emerald set—
Dewy, glistening violet?

Ah! I would forget a while
Stony heart and hollow smile,
Treacherous show of friendliness—
Lips that *seemed* born but to bless—
Eyes of beauty, brow of light,
That covered purpose dark as night.
Come, oh come, Forgetfulness!
Bring poppy wreaths my brow to press,
And lay me in the garden haunts,
With their bright-wing'd habitants;
Let me dream a while that worth
Shall acknowledged be on earth;
Let me gather buds as fair
As the campac blossoms are
That ope their sweets in Paradise!
Let me peer in the bright eyes

Looking out from leaf and bower,
And place each unpretending flower
Where its sweets, thus brought to light,
Will shame each gaudy stamen bright,
That with a meretricious glare
Flaunts gay petals to the air.

I will dream that this may be,
If the wreath you bring to me,
Mother Fairie !—Bind my brow
With the crimson poppies' blow,
That forgetfulness of ill
May my heart with bright dreams fill.

NOTHING NEW.

THERE is nothing new under the sun,
   The preacher saith to the stars' amen !
The rivers unto the sea have run
   But to return again.

And where it listeth the wild wind blows—
   Over the tropic belt rides forth—
Unto the far south region goes,
   And back to the frozen north.

The sun completes his fiery span,
   And still again in his circuit burns ;
And faithfully the dust, called man,
   Unto the dust returns !

Oh nothing new ! Oh nothing new !
    But ah ! for us all, there is something *old*—
Some starry moments, tho’ may be few,
    Like pictures set in gold.

They sparkle once, but not again—
    Only in visions of the night,
Like bright-plumed birds, they sing a strain
    Of wild but lost delight :

’Tis, “ Oh for the smile on a sweet young face,
    And oh for the days that return no more,—
For the shadowy foot-prints we faintly trace
    Upon that wave-wash’d shore !”

Oh nothing new ! Oh nothing new !
    There is nothing new can charm us now,
When on the heart falls Time’s mildew,
    His rust upon the brow.

But something old ! Ah ! something OLD !
    That we hide for aye from mortal eyes,
As the miser does his cherished gold—
    Within our bosom lies ;

That we turn to when the evil years,
    That bow the strong man down, draw nigh ;
And the sun of Hope has set in tears
    Upon a darken’d sky.

Oh something old ! an unspoken word,
    That thrilleth anew the fainting soul—
Tho’ loosened be the silver cord,
    And broken the golden bowl !

LOOKING IN THE FIRE.

IN a robe of misty gray,
    Down the sunset river,
Goes the weary boatman, Day,
    With a sigh and shiver;
For the red-eyed March, with gun
    And baying bloodhound, lingers
The fading western hill upon,
    And blows his purple fingers.

All along my chamber creep
    Dim and ghostly shadows,
And the light has gone to sleep
    On the fog-stain'd meadows;
Sweeping thro' the leafless trees
    Comes the dark night nigher—
But my soul feels none of these,
    Looking in the fire!

Looking in the fire, I see
    The shining pathway whither
The sainted go—and lo! to me
    A voice says, "Come up hither."
And far away above the clouds
    My daring reach goes higher,
Beyond the gloom that earth enshrouds—
    While looking in the fire.

Gazing thro' the vistas bright
    At the City Golden—

Jasper, topaz, chrysolite,
  Its foundations olden—
And beside its Gates of Pearl
  Sit the watching Angels,
On each base of sapphire, beryl,
  Writing blest evangels!

Neither sun nor moon there shine,
  For the glory brightens
From the Throne—the Lamp Divine
  All the city lightens!
And the Tree of Life bends low
  To the Gracious Giver,
Who set the Morning Star aglow
  Above the crystal river!

Piping loud, old March may blow
  His jubilant symphony,
While silver-shod my soul doth go
  O'er streets of chalcedony!
And upon Night's viol Time
  May set the key-note higher—
I harken a celestial chime,
  Looking in the fire.

Winds may sweep this nether world,
  Tempests rave and rattle;
And the storm-fiend's flag unfurled
  Call aloud to battle.
And the cold white moon may mount
  ·The ashen cloud-rack higher—
I only hear a silvery fount,
  Looking in the fire.

5 *

When, O tardy boatman Day,
　Will thy white sail shiver
In a wan and misty ray
　To row *me* o'er the river?—
To walk that shining, golden way,
　And draw me nigher, nigher
Such radiant gates as gleam and play,
　When looking in the fire!

MEMORY.

THERE is, on each heart's shelf,
　A treasured tome, filled with recordings brief—
A volume opened only by one's self
　At many a folded leaf.

Some pages lettered light,
Traced by joy's pencil in fair childhood's years;
But these are few—for every one that's bright
　There's tenfold dim with tears!

A volume gray with mould—
Where oft in turning some forgotten page,
We shake the mildew from its surface old
　To read a lesson sage!

On many a leaf appears
Dark records; this we may not pause to doubt—
Oh bless'd are they whose soft, repentant tears
　Blot such impressions out!

THE POET'S HOME.

THE insect dwells in her silken house,
    The polypus in its cell—
A grassy bower has the wild field-mouse,
    And the oyster a pearly shell;
The butterfly's roof is of sweet rose leaves—
    The seal has a crystal dome;
And the swallow builds her nest in the eaves—
    But where is the Poet's home?

The eye cannot compass his wide domain;
    'Tis spread to the outer bars
Of the universe's circling plain,
    Rayed by the countless stars!
From lowest depths of the rolling sea
    To the firmament's jeweled dome—
In the cavern's gloom, 'neath the greenwood tree,
    Behold the Poet's home!

A tissue web for her fairy eaves
    Has the patient spider spun—
But, to gild his tower, the poet weaves
    The golden threads of the sun!
And makes of the rainbow a tinted woof
    And warp for his cunning loom,
To fashion a richly-frescoed roof
    To cover his princely home!

The coral-worker, grain by grain,
    Has a solid structure wrought—

But the sparkling waves of the Poet's brain
  Hold the mighty reefs of Thought
That underlie the depths of Mind,
  And gleam 'neath the silvery foam
With the grains of Beauty and Truth combined,
  The base of his precious home !

The hind and stag but the covert see
  As a shield from the hunter's ball ;
But the Poet paints the greenwood tree,
  To hang on his Memory's wall ;
And pictures the leafy emerald glade—
  The river's sparkling foam—
The sunny beam and the sombre shade
  To deck his gorgeous home !

The shell-fish, in lethargic sleep,
  Sees not his tinted roof—
But pearl and fire, in the " upper deep"
  (With the Poet's eyes aloof)
Gleam in the moony layers that lie
  Upon the azure dome,
That rears its burnished rafters high
  Above the Poet's home.

And not more sweet is the rosy sheet
  Of the butterfly's fragrant bed,
Than the wingèd thoughts that glowingly meet,
  With perfume round them shed,
When Poesy lights her nuptial torch
  Beneath her bridegroom's dome,
And hangs her garland upon the couch
  In the Poet's sylvan home.

O'er Arctic skies the auroral arch
  Glitters with rockets red,
To light the seal on his chilling march
  To his cheerless, icy bed ;
But the shimmering sheen of the weird North-light,
  Hath not more flaming plume
Than Inspiration's fires ignite
  To flash from the Poet's home !

The twit'ring bird 'neath the sheltering eaves
  Has woven her cozy nest—
But *his* birdlings the poet-songster leaves
  In the hearts that love him best !
He drops his seeds in the wayside's weeds—
  His pearls in the ocean's foam—
And finds, in their spring, meed for his needs,
  And in every heart a home !

HIS OWN WORKS.

"What profit hath a man of all his labor which he taketh under the sun ?"—ECCLESIASTES i. 3.

AS well may ye ask what profit hath God
  For forming this beautiful world we see,
With yon firmament fair, the stars' abode,
  And setting bounds to the rolling sea !
As types of His power do they not stand?
  And man (tho' last of His works) is great !
And the promise to him is, " The fruits of his hand
  And *his own works* shall praise him in the gate."

TO-MORROW.

WHAT a world of gloom and glory,
    What a web of joy and sorrow,
Night throws from her shuttle hoary
    In the loom that weaves the morrow!
        Hopes for ever on the wing,
            To that Land of Promise flying—
        Shadowy fingers beckoning
            Where its honeyed fruit is lying.

And a tangled skein we ever
    Give its willing hands to ravel—
Good resolve and pure endeavor
    Still unto its portals travel!
        Weakness ever whispering, " Wait,
            We from Time a day will borrow"—
        But, alas! how oft " too late"
            The duty banished to the morrow!

Waiting, waiting for to-morrow,
    While to-day unheeded passes;
Always satisfied to borrow
    Futurity's prospective glasses.
        Thus we go, from youth to age,
            All unmindful of the present;
        For the days " to come" engage
            Alike the pauper, prince and peasant.

Ah! that morrow for the many
    Ne'er may dawn upon Life's ocean—

Scarce a bubble breaks, of any
  Rising in the wild commotion,
    But a life the tide still swells
      Onward to the glorious Giver,
      Where souls are crowned with asphodels
        Beside the great eternal River.

Time's a linkèd chain of morrows
  Leading on to the Immortal!
And *each day's* well-battled sorrows
  Are our passports at that portal.
    The " to-day" alone is ours
      To temper joy and hallow sorrow,
    That we may wear a crown of flowers
      When Death's night breaks a glorious Morrow!

A CHILD SLEEPING.

HE sleeps the sleep of childhood,
    The soft, balm-breathing sleep,
That floats from out the wildwood
  Where buds their vigils keep—

And falls as falls the dew-drop
  Upon the drowsy flower,
Seeking its mossy leaf-prop
  In evening's starlit bower.

The rosy sleep, that glowing
  With heavenly radiance seems—

With seraph music flowing,
And angel-peopled dreams !

———

CONVALESCENT.

THE surging fever-tide ebbs low,
And softer pulses warm,
Till on my cheek breaks health's bright glow,
Like sunshine after storm !

For scorching fingers seared my brain,
And branded deep my brow,
And hotly held each throbbing vein,
So mildly beating now—

Till, ring'd with fire, my sleepless eyes
With aching gaze, would pierce
Some wondrous overarching skies
Of a new universe,

Myth-peopled, goblin-tenanted—
No silver gleaming stars
A tender, tranquil radiance shed
Between the glowing bars

Of that red molten firmament ;
But comets, at white heat,
Across its brazen surface went
With burning, blistering feet !

And over arid wastes of sand,
    In the dim even-tide,
The fierce simoon of Afric's land
    Would pestilential ride ;

While in vast circles, round and round,
    Unceasing sailed my soul,
Nearing, but reaching not, the bound
    ·Of flame, that either pole

Shot upward toward the zenith, where
    A meteoric host
Seemed battling with the friends of air,
    And neither won nor lost.

O weary soul !   O sleepless eyes !
    What angel of the night
Led thee where coolest shadow lies,
    And quenched the baleful light,

And tuned anew sweet Nature's lyre ?—
    Till on my charmèd ear
An anthem from the feathery choir
    Seems softly floating near ;

And whispering grasses murmur low,
    Fresh with the breath of woods
Where humble-bees, buff-coated, go
    In honey-laden broods ;

·And silver-sounding surf seems near,
    Complaining to the shore ;
Till dreamy languor seals mine ear
    And steals mine eyelids o'er.

O ransomed soul! freed from the dark
　Where fever-demons keep—
Give morning praises with the lark,
　Thank God for health and sleep!

A THOUGHT.

DEEP in the knotted meshes of my heart
　　A shadowy thought lieth,
And sometimes from the tangled web 'twill start
　When the eve sigheth;
'Tis of my very self a formless part
　That never dieth—
But shape it I may not with all the art
　That my soul trieth.

Like song-sprite, prisoned in the pearl sea-shell,
　It singeth ever
A nameless melody, whose secret spell
　I fathom never.
A strain that strives, like mighty ocean's swell,
　In vain endeavor
To reach those purple isles where radiant dwell
　The bless'd, for ever!

'Tis blended with all things of beauty fair,
　An Omnipresence—
The soul that gives the morning's dusky air
　Rejuvenescence—

The Magian's cup, fill'd with a subtle, rare,
  Immortal essence—
The Master Hand, that gives brown branches bare
  Full efflorescence!

I *know*, that when, unstrung, life's golden bow
  Is loosed and aimless—
This pulsing heart, so wildly throbbing now,
  Is silent, blameless—
That, silver-shafted then, that thought will go,
  Untiring, tameless,
Where the sweet, holy songs of seraphs flow—
  No longer nameless!

GOOD-NIGHT.

THE Spirit of sleep is descending
  In vapory dream-light,
Thro' star-beams and clouds softly wending—
  Good-night, love, good-night!

Good-night! there's a lullaby humming
  In every breeze from the hill—
A murm'ring refrain lightly coming
  From lakelet and silvery rill;
And off, where the wizard Eve heapeth
  Its dun pile of clouds (ashes gray
On day's fading ember), there sleepeth
  Soft mist-shapes, that dreamingly say,
    Good-night, love, good-night!

Good-night! there's a drowsy-toned ripple
    Comes up thro' the scattered rose leaves,
That are folding soft coverlets, triple,
    Beneath the oak's sheltering eaves,
O'er yon fount, to its shelly bed bending,
    The moon, too, has pillowed her cheek
On the white arm the cloud is extending;
    And sleepy stars wink as they speak,
        Good-night, love, good-night!

FAITH.

OH come with me in the mellow light
        Of a young harvest moon,
And I'll sing you a simple song to-night,
    To an old, familiar tune—
A song that I learned ere I found a blight
    At the core of the ripening June,
And the silver disk of my soul was bright
    As night's star-dial'd noon.

For I've bared in my heart a treasured page
    That was hidden from sight away—
You'd little dream 'mong the leaflets sage
    That one could breathe of May;
But I folded it down in the golden age
    When life was a summer's day,
And not a war that Time can wage
    Can make the record gray!

It is not years, oh no! not years,
  That unlink youth's trusting chain,
Tho' we drain to the lees the cup of tears
  And the poison draught of pain—
Some green spot 'mid the waste appears
  If the heart has a sunny vein,
And the true soul still in life's winter hears
  Spring's promise-breathing strain.

Then come with me; I've a cozy crypt
  Far down in secret bowers
Where buds may grow, and bees have sipp'd
  Not the sweets of the hidden flowers,
Whose velvet petals all are tipp'd
  With the bloom of my morning hours,
Which never a breath of despair has nipp'd,
  Tho' a storm-cloud round me lowers.

But I only enter this charmèd sphere
  When my spirit's light and free;
And shining ones sometimes draw near
  And walk its aisles with me,
And point me out each anguish-tear
  On life's wayside dropp'd—to be
The wholesome dew to nourish and rear
  Some fruit-dispensing tree!

And over the hedges wild, that screen
  This rosy solitude,
A line is traced in starry sheen,
  Which I read when in the mood—
A mystic sentence, that comes between
  The doubts that would intrude—

6 *   E

'Tis " the evidence of things unseen !"--
  And my soul says, " It is good !"

Then sing with me ; oh sing the song
  Of the trusting time of life !
When the haggard cares were hidden that throng
  The crowded mart of strife,
Where boldly battles the giant, Wrong,
  'Gainst Truth's two-edgèd knife—
For trumpet notes to it belong,
  With prophecy full rife !

Oh sing ! and ye'll see the sunshine burst
  From out the cloud-rack wild ;
Sing ! and sweet flowers, that your heart once nursed
  When your golden summers smiled,
Will lift their rosy faces, as erst
  Thou didst to thy mother's mild—
Have faith, such faith as was thine at first—
  The faith of a little child !—

The faith for whose sake hath the poet striven,
  In earth-encrusted gloom,
To prove him heir to a crown God-given
  Beneath a jeweled dome !—
The faith that sees in the light of even
  The gates of the starry home,
And the shining ladder from earth to heaven,
  Where angels go and come !

WHY IS IT?

" Why is it that some seem fated, while others, not half so deserving, pass on with more of this world's goods than their share—with no cares or afflictions to crush the heart—why is it ?"—*Extract from a Letter.*

WHY was the sorrowing Hagar sent
　　To tread Beersheba's wild?
As outcast from the patriarch's tent
　　She clasp'd her sinless child,
And called aloud, in her despair,
　　" Let me not see him die !"
Ah ! was it not her anguished prayer
　　That drew the angel nigh?

Why was the Israelitish flock
　　Led thro' the desert drear,
To reach at last a barren rock
　　With not a fountain near,
Nor vine nor fig leaf from the sod,
　　The arid sod, could grow?
Ah ! was it not the smiting rod
　　That bade the waters flow?

And when the Babylonian king
　　His impious wrath did show
To those who, at the sackbut's ring,
　　Refused the knee to bow
Unto the golden image—and
　　Would slay them, in his ire ;
Did not God's angel by them stand,
　　And walk with them the fire?

We may not question His decree
  Who from the whirlwind spake
To that poor son of misery,
  And bade him answer make—
Saying, "Who darkeneth counsel by
  Words, without knowledge fraught?"
Ah! what *seems* ill to mortal eye,
  Hath often blessings wrought.

'Tis not the sunshine and soft breeze
  Our life-boat's strength may test,
Floating adown the tide of ease
  To royal port of rest—
But, buffeting the thund'ring gale,
  Breasting the surges' roar,
Well done, good bark, with tattered sail,
  If *thou* canst reach the shore!

Life without trials?—Who would give
  The cares that make him wise,
To be the useless drone that hives
  No honey as he flies?
Why, Nature, in her mighty book,
  This wholesome truth still shows,
That even the thistle's thorny crook
  Can blossom as the rose.

And Night unfolds her glowing page
  For Faith's all-earnest eye
To profit by the lesson sage,
  It may alone descry—
That fortune's sun, like to the day,
  Hides many an orb of light,

That never gleams upon life's way
Till sorrow's hallowing night!

Why is it that the bruisèd flower
Is sweeter for the wound?
Why is it that the darkest hour
Is nearest morning's round?
Ah! these are mysteries which God
To solve, our soul invites—
When done, we'll bless the chastening rod,
And kiss the hand that smites!

FRIENDSHIP.

"He is a happy man that hath no need of his friends."—*Arab
Proverb.*

OH, call it not friendship—the hollow professions
That's made to your station, your wealth and
your name;
That man's friends are "legion" who boasts of pos-
sessions,
Of titles, and lands, and a loud-ringing fame!
Ye'll prove it—as Time, to Eternity stealing,
The clear-sighted eye of Experience lends—
That that man is blest, beyond earthly revealing,
Who can say that he never had need of his friends.

Ah! Friendship's a bird of most delicate feather,
That plumes its soft wing in prosperity's ray—

But when storms of adversity gloomily gather,
  The light-pinion'd warbler is off and away!
Oh count not on friendship in dark hour of trouble—
  The stream takes a turn where the jutting rock
      bends;
The least chilling breeze breaks the gay, painted
      bubble—
  Ah! happy's the man who'th no need of his friends!

But why sound the warning so oft vainly spoken?
  'Tis experience alone the sad lesson can teach;
For all wish to prove that those vows can be broken
  Before they'll! believe—so, 'tis folly to preach.
They'll hug the delusion that flatters their weakness,
  And follow the spectre wherever it wends;
So let them—the wise can but bow them with meek-
      ness,
  And pray *they may never have need of their
      friends!*

THE SONG SPIRIT.

I WING my way from my starry home,
  Where the moon-beams play and the zephyrs
      roam,

As the golden jets from the sunset rill
Ripple and flash o'er the western hill.

Ye may catch my cadences on the breeze
When its old-time music is thrilling the trees;

Harps of a thousand strings are there—
Incantations of earth and air—

And every rustling leaf has a tone
So very like to my dreamy own,

That I claim as my sylvan dwelling-place
The greenwood's radiant halls of grace.

And then on the deep, where the billows play
New melodies ever from day to day,

Ye may hear my voice, now low, now loud,
Hum with the wave to the bending cloud—

Or roar with the thunder-drums that beat
The march of the storm, when wild winds meet

To war on the plain of midnight black—
And then, in the morning's golden track,

I call to the lark that the night is done,
Bidding her up to hail the sun !

My mournful numbers, low and clear,
In December's wail for the dying year,

Float o'er the snowy winding-sheet,
And sob with the rain and the driving sleet ;

Yet scarce hath the first bud kissed the May,
Ere I fill the woodlands with warblings gay,

And out of the rosy heart of June
Awaken summer's sweet bridal tune.

There's a drowning buzz on the drowsy air—
I have roused the bee from his flowery lair!

There's a gush of song in the maple grove—
I have sounded the key-note attuned to love!

And mine is the music that evermore
Is hymning along the reedy shore,

Where the wavelets scatter their diamond rain,
And the pink-lipp'd shells sound a low refrain

From old Ocean's tender symphonies,
To blend with my ceaseless melodies.

And saintly Night, from her cloister cell,
Echoes my psalms in their choral swell—

My deep hosannas, as they rise
To the gilded dome of the far-off skies,

Where seraph harpists catch the strains,
And golden lyres, on celestial plains,

Reverberate thro' rolling spheres,
The grand old anthem of the years!

Till Lyra tunes her harp anew,
And every orb that gilds the blue,

Sends pæans back, with sweet accord,
Of " Holy, holy, holy Lord !"

ZOE.

GONE to rest !
 As some pale light in the golden West
Melts in the flood of glory there,
  So hath fled
The soul of her, whom we call dead,
  She of the sunny hair !
Her earth-light faded away, away,
To lose itself in the shining day
  That knows not night or care.

  Sweet wild flower !
Fragile bloom of a tropic hour,
Folding all its beauteous leaves
  When the dark
Lighted the glow-worm's tiny spark
  Under the lily-eaves !

I dreamed that the Flower Sprite came down
And wanted buds for an Angel's crown—
Crimson banners and purple wings
Fluttered over the fairy rings
  In the garden shade,
  Where peonies play'd
And golden-coated butterflies stray'd ;

And down in the hollows the yellow eyes
Of marigolds look'd a glad surprise—
And dewy mirrors glistened where
Soft winds comb'd the aster's beautiful hair—
　　But—ah me!
Not of these could the bright crown be;
Past them all the spirit flew,
To pluck from our darling's tender eyes
The light of stars in cloudless skies,
　　The dreamy hue
　　And deep'ning blue
Of the nestling hare-bells looking thro'—
And to bear off the peach-blossom's velvet leaf,
That lay on her cheek in slumber brief;
And the crimson heart of the wild musk-rose,
That puls'd her lips in fragrant throes;
And the beaded moisture of her breath,
To coat each bud with a crystal sheath—
All these he gathered, the envious Sprite
(Alas! 'twas more than a dream of night),
And entered with them the golden gate,
And left our garden desolate!

MAGNANIMITY.

WHEN Summer's gilt index
　　Has circled the hours,
And told o'er the moments
　　On dials of flowers—

And Spring, dying early,
   Bequeaths her, in tears,
·All April's sweet nurslings
   To rear as her heirs ;
When close her charm'd girdle
   She clasps round the earth—
Which, like cestus of Venus,
   Gives loveliness birth—
What wonder that beauty
   And grace should appear,
To crown with their glory
   The queen of the year?

But when from his ice-girdled
   Fastness, rides forth
The hoary old monarch
   That ruleth the North—
And not a gold king-cup
   That pledged the sweet May,
But has hidden its chalice
   'Neath brown leaves away—
It is then, when all nature
   Is barren and sear,
That the meek little snow-drop's
   White bell, ringing clear
(To the ear tuned to hear it),
   With silver tongue says,
" I keep my sweet music
   To cheer the dark days !"

It is true, that the red rose
   Will blush when gay June

Is singing her praises
  In many a soft tune ;
And princely young Daffodil
  Loveth dear May,
Whose hands 'mid his yellow curls
  Timidly stray ;
And Daisy has dreamed
  O'er the bright golden ring
She got from the rover,
  The green-coated Spring ;
And Sweet-William smiles
  When soft zephyr is near,
And sings the low ditty
  He best loves to hear ;

And Lily will bend her
  Pale cheek to the kiss
Of the fountain that murmurs,
  "None fairer than this !"
But they, like their prototype,
  Man, do but give
Love for love, as the Publican—
  Selfishly live.   .
" For if ye love them that
  Love you, what reward
Will ye have ?" says the Book
  Ye profess to regard—
Ah ! would ye be like to
  Your Father in heaven,
Return good for evil—
  Put out the old leaven !

For he is untrue to
  The angel within,

Unworthy the crown 'tis
  His birth-right to win,
Who nurses the asp of
  Revenge in his breast
To gnaw at his happiness—
  Rob him of rest!
Brood not o'er the wrong
  Ye have met in the strife—
If ye slight it, ye've learned
  A good lesson in life;
Turn another bright page
  And forgive, would ye know
The joy that is purest
  Above or below!

And like the wee snow-drop
  That singeth her tune
To bleak winds, as tho' they were
  Breathing of June—
Greet thou icy neglect
  With a song as she goes,
And you'll not feel the chill
  Of her merciless snows.
E'en Enmity's winter
  May circle you round,
If the sweet bud of kindliness
  With you is found,
No storm from that quarter
  Can break your repose—
And 'mong your heart's flowers
  You'll not miss the rose!

"AFTER THE DARKNESS COMES THE MORNING."

UP from the depths of a brooding sorrow,
 Soul, arise, and arm anew!
So, from the night's dark side, the morrow
 Bounds with a smile o'er the trackless blue.

Sit not drooping with folded pinions—
 Up! and plume for a higher flight;
Pass, with a sweep, to the stars' dominions
 Up from the gloom of Despair's dark night!

Life is just what we choose to make it;
 Joy or sorrow, pleasure, pain,
Each its mark makes, as we take it—
 Hug it close, you'll its stamp retain.

Oh, then, treasure the joyful only,
 Lay the sad with the day to rest,
With eve's pale star for a headstone lonely,
 To mark its grave in the fading West.

And, free from care as the lark—that, scorning
 Sadness, sings as it mounts from the sod,
" After the darkness comes the morning"—
 Up, O soul, and trust to God!

THE PRINCE OF WOOERS.

A ROYAL wooer is the Wind!
   He comes from his palace of pearl and fire
Thro' the morning gates, where the mist-shapes bind
   A silver wreath on the day's gold spire—
He comes from roving in Araby,
   And brings me sweets from that blest strand,
And spicy odors from Indian sea,
   And dewy gems from the far cloud-land.

He kisses my cheek, and leaves the stain
   Of the rose's lips that he press'd last night—
He fans my brow, and the fever-pain
   Is stilled beneath his breathing light;
I almost hear the waves at play,
   As he whispers low of a reedy shore;
And I catch a scent of new-mown hay
   As he tells of the meadows he's wandered o'er.

A golden woof in the web of dreams
   I weave, as he gently toys with my hair—
I seem to stand by those mystic streams
   Where light is born of light, mid-air;
And over a sea prismatic start
   The diamond shafts of each gorgeous ray,
Till every quivering, changing part
   Is blended in all-perfect day!

He tells me tales of Fairy-land,
   Of elves and fays in the acorn bowers

Where he waved at eve his magic wand,
  And pilfered the perfume of slumb'ring flowers.
But he murmurs oft, in a softer tone,
  Of the pale cheek'd moon that he left in her shroud,
With none to list his prayerful moan
  But the leaden-eyed and tearful cloud.

And then he sings a dirge-like strain,
  Tho' a harvest song, to a saddened tune,
That blends with the chime of the yellow grain
  Tolling the age of the dead young June.
But I tremble when in his wrath he tells
  Of the mountain waves that come at his call,
When the mighty heart of Ocean swells
  And the giant strides from his Amber Hall.

I love him best when I weary wait
  In the moonlit aisles of sleep, and moan
While my soul lies down at the trembling gate,
  But cannot cross the threshold stone—
Oh then he comes, with an angel's wing,
  To waft me on to the Isle of Rest,
Singing the song that seraphs sing—
  'Tis then, 'tis then, that I love him best!

His voice has a music unto mine ear,
  An undertone, maybe lost to thee—
For it is only the charm'd ones hear
  The sweet old ditties he sings to me.
But this Prince of Wooers is all mine own,
  Tho' he roams the world and sings in each bower,
Yet he keeps for me his tenderest tone,
  And I give him my heart's perennial flower!

GARLANDS.

ROSES, red roses are
   Tempting my fingers—
Scarlet auriculas,
   Purple syringas—
Crimson japonicas,
   Pearl-cheek'd camellias,
Yellow laburnums, and
   Ruby-lipp'd dahlias;
I'll bind me a coronet,
   Regal and royal,
Of these for the brow of
   The true and the loyal!

Then for the conqueror,
   Laurel and holly—
Poppies for him steep'd in
   Deep melancholy;
For all who foul slander's
   Dark waters unsettle,
I'll pluck fell lobelia,
   Night-shade and nettle,
Hemlock and hellebore,
   Rank aconitum,
For tongues that can venom
   Distill *ad-libitum!*

Dancing young blue-bells I'll
   Cull for the cheery ones—
Flowering almonds for
   Hopeless and weary ones—

Pansies, to strew where the
    Night-dews are weeping
O'er the green mound where some
    Loved one lies sleeping—
Faithful " forget-me-nots,"
    Green arbor-vitæ,
To tell, as time passes,
    Remembrance grows brighter.

Then the meek lilies that
    Bloom in the valley
I'll twine where contentment
    Best loveth to dally ;
And with them sweet daisy
    And daffodowndilly,
That crouched 'neath the hedge
    In their frost mantles chilly
When wild winds went wailing
    Their sorrowful dirges,
And ocean kept time with
    His dead-march of surges.

Oh, thanks for your casket
    Of jewels, fair Flora !
I kneel in your parterre
    An humble adorer,
Not crown'd with your bay-wreath—
    The ivy that's clinging
Around me is sapping
    The life whence 'tis springing—
But thanks, that I gather
    Such garlands as these,
If within them I find but
    A leaf of " heart's-ease !"

APRIL.

"If a man die, shall he live again?"

THE dying March, with a stifled sigh,
   Kissed the young April's brow—
"Go forth! fair Sprite of the tearful eye,"
   He said—"'tis thy mission now,
With the smile of faith, to unseal the tomb
   Of each slumb'ring bud and grain;
That man may see, in their risen bloom,
   "Tho' he die he shall live again!"

If a man die, shall he live again?—
   Hark! as a thousand tones,
From mountain, valley, hill-side, plain,
   The truthful answer owns.
A voice floats up with the fountain's play,
   Loos'd from the ice-king's reign—
Saying, "Death's night hath pass'd away,
   I'm free, I live again!"

The daisy's gentle glances light,
   On its resurrection morn,
Where the snowy garments flutter bright,
   Of the sweetly flowering thorn;
And each with sighs of perfume greet
   The gentle April rain,
That opes their lids with kisses sweet,
   Bidding them live again!

If a man die, shall he live again?
   List! comes there not a sound
From the acorns and the buried grain
   In their graves in the dark ground?
For see—the quickening germs have sprung
   To the surface of the plain,
To take their places earth's hosts among,
   Saying, " We live again !"

Shall earth in her brown bosom nurse
   Blest immortality
For flower and fruit—yet man so curse
   That a partaker he
May be not?—Perish the thought !—A voice
   Sings in each heart one strain ;
'Tis Nature's, bidding man rejoice !
   Telling, " He'll live again !"

If a man die, shall he live again?
   Ah ! trust the secret sense
That whispers thee—sin, sorrow, pain,
   Shall cease when we go hence ;
That death is no December night
   Dark'ning life's every gain—
But April's sunny smile of light,
   Bidding us live again !

STORM.

A FLYING moon in a scarf of white
  Is driving the mists along;
The witch-elms wave in the ghostly light
  To the thunder's muttering song,
And over the hollow arch of night
  The sheeted lightnings throng.
    But sing, sing lullaby,
    Skies weep and wild winds sigh
      Over the rocking earth!
    Lullaby, lullaby,
    Calms come when tempests fly,
      Clouds give the rainbow birth!

I knew a heart where pleasure made
  For itself a golden nest—
And all day long, like a sunny glade
  That a rain-drop never press'd,
The verdure sickened for want of shade
  Till a desert grew that breast.
    But storm, storm came one night,
    Wild floods put out the light,
      Steeping the arid sod;
    Then came a fresher morn—
    Lo! of its tear-drops born,
      Sweet flowers look'd up to God!

Oh, the sunlight is a joyous thing,
  But the sun may shine too long;
For the earth, like the heart, needs chastening
  To purge it of ancient wrong:

And shine and shade in turn must sing,
To make harmonious song!
Ring, ring, ye thunder bells,
Sing, sing, ye sounding shells,
Over the roaring sea;
Winds, pipe your loudest strain—
Sweet calms *must* come again,
And earth the brighter be!

FORGET ME NOT.

Written on finding a blue "forget-me-not" pressed within the leaves of a book belonging to a deceased friend.

FLOWER of the blue eye's tender beaming!
What sweet, pale face met thy last life-gleaming?
What tender orbs of thine own soft hue,
Gazed into thy chalice of morning dew—
What rosy lips sipped the moisture up
As they kissed the brim of thy golden cup?
Ah! to fade and die hath been their lot—
Like unto thine, forget-me-not.

The cold, white stone is laid on that brow,
As this snowy page press'd thee ere now;
And mould has gathered o'er those eyes,
Like the dust that on thy soft leaf lies;
From her lip and thy bosom the dewy spray
Has passed with thy tender lives away—
But her spirit voice, pale flower, thou'st got,
And my soul hears it murm'ring, "Forget me not!"

DREAMING.

MY soul is dreaming to-night, Nellie,
    Dreaming under the stars—
And a wondrous strain of delight, Nellie,
    Floats down thro' the silver bars;
And over the grand old sea afar
    There cometh the solemn calls
Of deep unto deep—and the echoes
    Of musical waterfalls.

Red were the eyes of day, Nellie,
    Red, as she went to rest;
For she laid sweet summer away, Nellie,
    With a faded rose on her breast,
And folded her up in a fleecy mist—
    While his crown of gold to hide,
The kingly sun sank, mourning
    His beautiful, lost young bride.

But not of that crown of gold, Nellie,
    And not of the summer gone,
Do I dream, in the starlight old, Nellie,
    And catch the monotone
Of silvery dropping founts and rills,
    Like those enchanted streams
That spake to the fairy—yea, I hear
    Them whisp'ring in my dreams!

From the mountain's purple heart, Nellie,
    Cometh a gladsome voice,

Where mighty rivers start, Nellie,
  Saying, Rejoice! rejoice!
And the pulsing arteries leap and run
  To the great broad arms of the sea
Singing the song of Life!—Do you hear
  The " wonderful melody?"

You tell me I but dream, Nellie—
  And what is life but a dream?
To some, less tangible, my Nellie,
  Than yonder singing stream.
But ah! 'tis much to live, tho' life
  May be not what it seems,
And we be only " made of such stuff'
  As dreams," my Nellie, dreams!

Much, much might the dreamer tell, Nellie,
  Of the *real* aim of life,
Were his tones not drown'd in the swell, Nellie,
  The harsher roar of strife—
For every leaf in the forest glade,
  Each blade of grass by the stream,
Holds a psalm which he reads by the mystical light
  That comes to him in a dream!

Creation's a beautiful dream, Nellie,
  Lighting an Infinite mind!
And Love-Divine is the theme, Nellie,
  That its spirit hath enshrined.
And talking waters, and whispering trees,
  But echo the holy strain
That floats for aye thro' the marvelous depths
  Of the Omniscient brain!

Then leave me to my dreams, Nellie,
  My soul hath a lesson to learn
From the wonderful singing streams, Nellie,
  That man in his pride would spurn.
I love to read great Nature's book
  By the light of the shining stars,
And hearken the wondrous melody
  Floating down thro' the silver bars !

WE MISS THEE!

WE miss thee in the morning
    And in the evening hour—
Our daily paths are desolate
  Without our household flower,
Our pure and spotless lily
  That gave its sweetest bloom
To grace the fireside circle
  In the sacred wreath of Home !

But in that land where sorrow
  And parting are unknown,
Another angel standeth
  Beside the great White Throne !
And while we bow in anguish
  Beneath the smiting rod—
She softly whispers—" Weep not,
  It is the hand of God !"

8 *

THE SOUL'S HOPE.

O'ER the swiftly-flowing river
　　Of our lives, there floats a haze
Thro' whose veil the dim " Forever"
　　Comes in visions to our gaze—
Comes in visions of the twilight, shadowing out our
　　　　future days
　　In the land of the Immortal,
　　When the Spirit at Death's portal
Sings its last of earthly lays!

Like an eve of tropic splendor,
　　Where the dew in silver showers
Drops, from moonlit fountains tender,
　　On the brows of sleeping flowers,
Wak'ning fragrance as it slumbers in the starry jasmine
　　　　bowers—
　　Comes this twilight calm, distilling
　　Perfume from our souls, and filling
Full of hope our mortal hours.

While the tidal waves of feeling
　　And the surging seas of crime
Bear us earthward, still come (stealing
　　Like the echoes of a chime)
Dreamy whispers of a heritage so holy and sublime,
　　That the Spirit's folded pinions
　　Seek escape to those dominions
From the leashes laid by time.

There—beyond the sparkling reaches,
  Dimmed by Saturn, fired by Mars—
Our inner vision boldly stretches
  Outward, o'er its finite bars,
Far beyond the farthest limits of the constellated stars—
  Upward, where the iridescent
  Brightness of the Omnipresent
Pales the glory of the stars !

And, with an immortal longing,
  Look we thro' the radiant line
Where the white-winged hosts are thronging—
  And we see the glittering shine
Of their waving pinions, gleaming o'er us as they loving
      twine
  When a good deed is recorded,
  And the doer is awarded
One claim more to realms divine !

Body, perishing twin brother
  Of a deathless Soul !—why tempt
With thy poor pottage so the other
  That its higher hope's besprent,
With the anguish-droppings glittering when the angels'
      hearts are rent
  To see a mortal sell his dower,
  His heavenly birthright, for one hour
In vain earthly pleasures spent?

Soul ! white doveling, downward driven
  From the radiant silver cot—
Seek some branch, by Seraph riven
  From the Tree whose leaves fade not,

And sent earthward for the shelter of those birdlings,
       whose sad lot,
  Exiled from their spirit bowers,
  'Tis to pine in realms like ours,
Caged in flesh, and death, and rot!

O'er the stellar heights are streaming,
  Up among the sunset hills,
Beacons, on the road-side beaming,
  Safe to guide thee through all ills;
And along the golden pathway that the glowing ether
      fills,
  Walk sweet Holiness and Faith,
  Through the sombre gate of Death
Him to pilot, who so wills!

THE NEW YEAR.

LAY the dead old year away,
  Toll the bell and heap the clay,
And leave it in its winding sheet
Where ghosts of joys in graveyards meet.

Many an idol turned to clay
By its side must mouldering lay—
Many a rifted leaf of trust
Will mingle with its silent dust,

And dearer buds of love and bloom
Will wither with it in the tomb—

Not alone the gray old year
Lies upon its icy bier!

But the gate is closed upon
The fading spectres, one by one,
And pale Remembrance dries her tear
As laughing comes the glad New Year!

Like a bride on wedding morn,
Snowy wreaths her brow adorn,
And old Winter's diamond zone
Is reset for the favored one.

Hope is whispering again
In her ear the same old strain;
Pointing to the birds of spring,
But telling not they're on the wing—

Painting Summer's roses fair,
But not the thorns that hide them there—
And on Autumn's withered lip
Laying a soft crimson tip,

To hide the wrinkled seal of age.
'Tis a bright, bewitching page
Unsullied by a single tear,
That meets the eye of the New Year.

Unsuspicious let her go
From May's bloom to December's snow;
Never cloud the brow of youth—
Time will teach full soon the truth!

When her hand plucks Pleasure's fruit
And finds it ashes—be thou mute ;—
With its dust she'll surely find
Wisdom's precious grains combined.

When Love's golden links she'd clasp
And sees them loosen in her grasp,
The parting chain will lead her on
The upward path it winds upon !

And every seedling she may sow
Must sweet or bitter herbage grow—
But all will bear the selfsame flower,
Experience—'tis a goodly dower !

Then leave her to her heritage—
The lessons that will make her sage,
And fit her for a higher birth
Above the training-school of earth ;

So may she join the thronging years,
Wandering 'mid unnumbered spheres,
And filling all the aisles of Time
With teachings holy and sublime !

LOVE.

A FITFUL light, whose luring flame
   We foolish moths pursue,
Until a scorched and wingless frame
   Shows what a fire we woo !

THE CENTENNIAL BIRTH-DAY OF RO-
BERT BURNS.

FORGET him not—the bard who trill'd
  A lay for Auld Lang Syne,
And touched a chord whose tones have thrill'd
  Where'er Love's tendrils twine ;
Who wrought for Age's " frosty pow,"
  With song's sweet, silver flow,
That halo that adorns it now—
  "John Anderson, my Joe !"

And gave to immortality
  The modest daisy's name,
Weaving for meek humility
  A never-dying fame !—
And sweetly told of lover's faith
  O'er Highland Mary's grave—
Oh, honor him, for Poet saith
  The loving are the brave !

Shall he who sang the praise of Doon,
  And Devon's banks, and Clyde's,
Not reap the myrtle's fadeless boon
  O'er Mississippi's tides ?
Yea, rolling seas have borne his songs,
  And sunny climes have heard,
And to all lands his fame belongs
  Where thrills an English word.

All, all must own the magic spell
  Of each old melody—

For childhood's pitying heart will swell
  At Mallie's Elegy ;
And maid, whose sire for worldly store
  Would barter her away,
Grows pale when warbling sadly o'er
  The suit of Robin Gray.

E'en soldier lips will wreath a smile
  For him, whose cheery fancy
Brings back again the banks o' Coil
  And some sweet, witching Nancy.
And graver wights to mirth give way
  While following Tam O'Shanter
By haunted auld Kirk Alloway,
  As he frae Ayr did canter.

And many a heart, in which still sings
  In whispers, low and deep,
The angel—tho' its prisoned wings
  Seem furled in dreamless sleep—
Flutters with inborn, pure delight,
  Above the simple page
That stamps the humble Cotter's Night
  With precepts holy, sage !

Then fill a " cup o' kindness" to
  The memory of Burns—
Tho' Caledonian breezes blow
  Where flowery heath inurns
Sweet Nature's Child !—Ay, stretch the hand
  Of fellowship sincere,
Across the wave to Scotia's land
  And wreathe his honored bier !

NEW ORLEANS, *January* 25, 1859.

A-MAYING

SING, O heart! for a low, sweet strain
   The wind-harp's softly playing;
The lily bells ring a chime again—
   O heart, we'll go a-Maying!

We will not pause to seek a thorn
   Where a bud of hope is peeping;
Nor watch o'er the sun-illumin'd lawn
   The stealthy shadow creeping.

But while the sparkling sands of Day,
   So radiantly golden,
Fall from her crystal glass—our May
   We'll keep, as in times olden.

When every harebell on the heath,
   Or daisy in the dingle,
Had some sweet message in its breath
   With our young hopes to mingle;

When Nature op'd to us her heart,
   And from its tinted pages
Some wondrous lessons would impart,
   Undreamed of by the sages.

Oh yes, we'll keep a bright May-day—
   And should we fail to gather
Dear buds of promise on the way,
   But flowers of feeling, rather—

We'll read the precious leaflets o'er,
　Our later May adorning
With such a page of tender lore
　As we found not in life's morning—

Until, O heart, a flood of song
　Thou'lt send where the leaves are playing;
Then come from the gloom where spectres throng,
　Poor heart—and go a-Maying.

A QUESTION.

"Why art thou sad?"

OH never ask why tears oft start
　　And from the cheek blot out the rose;
There is a page within the heart,
　A careless hand may ne'er unclose—
Writ in the pictur'd "long ago,"
　And only read thro' Memory's glass
When lengthening shadows come and go,
　As hopes, long buried, dimly pass
Along the vista'd light that streams
　Down the worn path where plod the years—
The misty shapes, that filled our dreams
　Ere we had drunk the cup of tears!
And when upon this leaf we gaze,
　See life's great loss—its meagre gain—
What wonder Memory's gathering haze
　Should fall in sad Regret's wild rain?

MY MOTHER'S PORTRAIT.

SOFTLY the love-lighted eyes look down
    From the canvas, as look none other
Upon me, with never the shade of a frown—
    Mother, my beautiful mother!

Goldenly brown fall the sunny curls
    On the peachy cheek's soft roses;
And the parted lips have the smile of a girl's
    When her heart's wealth she uncloses.

Just the same eyes that kept watch and ward
    O'er my childhood's wayward fancies—
Just the same lips that bade me guard
    Against youth's extravagancies!

All are there, save the loving tone
    Attuned to motherly sweetness:—
Speak to me, speak! mine own, mine own,
    And show me thy completeness!

Hushed—hushed—hushed! The willow hath waved
    Long years in the summer even,
And the searching wintry tempest braved,
    Since thou returned to heaven!

And cold, cold, cold are the voices now,
    And stony hard the faces
That earth upturns—no mother's brow
    With its soft, expressive graces;

No mother's hand, with a gentle touch,
   To soothe world-weary anguish ;
O stricken ones ! for such, for such,
   How vain do ye pine and languish.

Pine for " mother love," pine for all
   That ye'll never find in another—
Only a pictured face on the wall,
   Of mother, beautiful mother !

Beautiful eyes and lips and cheeks,
   Beautiful hair—and fingers
Whose tender pressure your cold hand seeks
   In a dream that lovingly lingers ;

In a rosy dream of your childhood's days,
   When those fond eyes watched your slumber ;
And a mother's smile was your dearest praise,
   Her song, your sweetest number—

Her knee, your shrine when you lisp'd the prayer
   In the softened light of even—
Her arms your refuge in every care,
   Her face the star of your heaven !

Just such a face as now looks on me
   From the canvas, as looks none other,
Tenderly thoughtful, and lovingly—
   Mother, my beautiful mother !

NIGHT.

NIGHT o'er the hill-side,
    Night o'er the wold—
Night, with her shining hair
    Wrapt in the fold
Of a mist-veil, is telling
    Her rosary o'er
Where the white foam-flake
    Is wreathing the shore—
Where the young willow
    Bends low to the rover,
The west wind, all fragrant
    With kissing the clover—
Where the tares meet
    O'er the mossy head-stone
That watches the sleeper
    Who never makes moan—
Where the great heart
    Of the city is beating—
Where on the green sward
    The fairies are greeting—
Over the mountain-top,
    Over the wold,
Counting her rosary
    Silver and gold,
The Nun, Night, is doing
    Her penances old.

Oh breathe me an *Avé*
    Most merciful Night!

Like thee I am ever
  Pursuing the light,
And counting MY rosary's
  Bead-gems and crosses,
Whose decades are numbered
  In blisses and losses:
Breathe me an *Avé*,
  O holy-brow'd Night!
Earth and its palaces
  Fade from my sight—
Only those mythic
  Air-temples arise,
Whose shadowy towers
  Are lost in the skies;
While parting the veil
  Of the mystic " To-come,"
My soul is a-tremble,
  Awestricken and dumb—
As wave after wave
  Of life's billows ebb low,
Stranding each fallacy,
  Joy-dream or woe.
Over the grave
  Of a dead world I roam
Homeless, yet seeking
  A far-vision'd home,
Where the Spirit of Beauty
  Reigns ever a queen,
And gilds the dark waters
  That still intervene—
While helpless I wander
  The ghost-crowded shore,

And reach for the gleam
  That recedes evermore.
Oh breathe me an *Avé*,
  Dear saint, in your cell—
A soft *Pater-noster*,
  Whose musical swell
The sweet chords of Truth
  'Mongst my heart's strings shall test,
'Till a star, like to Bethlehem's,
  Shines in my East,
And a *Gloria Patri*
  Thrills in my breast!

HALF-MAST.

DRIFTING out on the rising tide
    Of memory, away—
And the gladsome waters laugh and lift
  Sweet kisses to the day,
As the buoyant billows bear me back
  O'er childhood's sparkling bay.

Oh, royal barks with silken sails
  I launched upon that sea ;
How grandly loomed the distant shore,
  The fancy-wrought " To-be !"
The phantom shapes that steered each helm
  Were hidden all from me.

I only saw thro' purpling haze
  The future's glowing strand ;

The shimmering prows by hope upheld
　Bearing me to the land—
No rude gales lashed the rippling waves
　Or stirred the silver sand ;

While tropic birds of thought would skim
　Across the waters bright,
To warble of spice islands set
　In seas of liquid light,
Of gardens of Hesperian fruit,
　The dragon out of sight !

My Argonautic fleet was bound
　Unto that Euxine Sea,
Whose golden fleece still lured me on—
　But, ah ! I could not see
The hosts of ill I must subdue,
　Springing, armed men, at me.

For morning rosy made my East
　With flush of promise gay—
How proudly from each spar I flung
　Out pennons to the day,
As each bright bark of hope was launched
　Upon that sparkling bay.

But, one by one, those barks went down ;
　Some in that summer sea—
Some stranded on a barren beach—
　Some struggling manfully
'Gainst wind and tide and whirling wave,
　So bravely, hopefully ;

To sink, at last, from weariness,
  When lashing storms were sped.—
And now, but one poor battered hulk
  Remains, that fleet that led,
With drooping colors at half-mast
  For those royal hopes all dead !

SPRING.

’TIS the sly green-slippered Fay
    Thro’ the woodland noiseless stealing
Dropping wild-flowers by the way
All this loving, sunny day,
  Her bright presence thus revealing ;
And I far with her would flee,
Like some honey-seeking bee,
Hiving purer, sweeter store
Than the cells of Hybla bore—
Did I not, ’neath blossoms fair,
See ghostly branches wan and bare !

Could I from my vision part
  The ray, that ever sees the shadow
Stealing spectrally athwart
The sunniest vistas of the heart
  In youth’s hope-illumined meadow—
Yonder thorn tree, white with bloom,
Would not gleam a ghastly tomb—
That wild warbler would not sing
“ Bright I am, but on the wing”—

But, beneath the blooming tree,
I'd trill with bird and hum with bee !

From the grass-enameled hill
    I would call unto the daisy,
Whisper to the daffodil,
Where the mist-inviting rill
    Makes the verdant valley hazy—
Saying, " Pretty ones, arise !
Open all your golden eyes ;
Crocus, with the yellow hair,
Cowslips, from thy leafy lair,
Up, and strew with sweets the way
Of the blossom-girdled May !

" For the spring has come again,
    With her dainty fingers stringing
All her gems of April rain,
To glitter in the Iris train
    That the flower-sprites are bringing
From the white gates of the morn,
    Where the perfume censers swing,
Whose rich incense downward borne
    On the zephyr's viewless wing,
Fills each little azure cup
That the violets hold up.

" And the young moon weds the eve
    With a silver ring so slender,
That I fain would have you leave
Your low, grassy beds, to weave
    Garlands for the bridal tender."—
But round me swart shadows lie,
Deep'ning as the years go by,

Till my heart knows no more spring:
Yet I'd have each bright-brow'd thing
Happy, joyous in its May,
Ere the radiance fades away!

Ah! the songster on the thorn
  Has no merry lay to sing me;
And the spring-time's leafy morn,
Tho' with greenest promise born—
  Has no opening bud to bring me;
For the flower that crown'd my life
Perished when the May was rife—
  And the Spring's sweet floral chimes
Teach me but the mournful art
  Of twining simple wreaths of rhymes
From the leaflets of my heart!

"HIC JACET."

BURIED deep, "full fathom five,"
  In an unmarked grave it lies—
You would never find it, strive
  As you might with mortal eyes;
For the mournful years have paced,
  With their solemn steps and slow,
Over it, and all erased
  The wild marks of long-ago.

'Twas a simple, careless word,
  When at first it saw the light;

Many such may still be heard
  When the young moon woos the night.
'Twas a word—but ah ! how fraught
  With good or ill, you'll never know ;
Only soon a grave it sought
  Somewhere in the long-ago.

Lowly grave—how long kept green
  With the secret tears of pride,
Falling when the silver sheen
  Of the starlight's veil could hide.
Now—'tis covered with dead leaves—
  O'er it moss and lichens grow ;
And on ghostliest of eves
  There roam shades of long-ago—

Spectres from the misty shore,
  From whose livid lips *one word*
Is repeated o'er and o'er,
  Faintly in the gloaming heard ;
And upon the haunted tide
  Rushing memories ebb and flow,
Wrecking many a bark of pride
  On that strand of long-ago.

He is bless'd who never stands
  By some secret grave and sighs,
And must wring no tell-tale hands,
  Breathe no audible " Here lies !"—
But above his dead may weep
  Tears that give relief to woe,
Where the loved ones fell asleep,
  In a peaceful long-ago.

But for that unlettered mound
    Where a budding hope lies crush'd—
Is it not unhallow'd ground,
    That no prayerful knee has brush'd?
Lonely, flower-forsaken tomb,
    Not a healthful shrub may grow
Where, like mildew, hangs the gloom
    Of that fruitless long-ago!

HOMELY HETTY GRAY.

HOMELY Hetty Gray!
    Never beauty wooed her tresses,
Touched her lip with soft caresses;
All the beauty of her nature
Fled each inexpressive feature—
    Shunned the light of day—
To illume the inner portal
Of the soul; a light immortal,
    Never to decay!

    Sought ye Hetty Gray?
Not in lighted halls of pleasure,—
Where, to music's jocund measure,
Dancing feet and pulses beating,
Glances fond, fond glances meeting,
    Youth turned night to-day—
Would ye find the little maiden;
But where want stalk'd, sorrow-laden,
    Should your footsteps stray,

There, where wretchedness transmitted
To its offspring, crime !—unpitied
    In Life's cold affray—
There—beside the fever'd pillow,
Hand extended, from the billow
Of despair, the sinking pauper
To uphold from madness' torpor—
    Found ye Hetty Gray !

    Homely Hetty Gray !
Whoe'er felt thy want of beauty,
As thou trod'st the path of duty,
    Rugged tho' the way ?
Seem'd thou not some straying angel,
Hymning forth a soft evangel
To the outcast, worn and weary
With the world's race, cold and dreary,
    As he wounded lay,
Shunn'd by priest and Levite scorning ?
Ah ! as bright-brow'd as the morning
    Leading forth the day,
Shone thy face of tender pity ;
Lark ne'er carol'd sweeter ditty
Than thy lips, which told of heaven !
Of error past and sin forgiven—
    Homely Hetty Gray !

    Saintly Hetty Gray !
Calmly 'neath thy green roof sleeping,
Where the robin watch is keeping,
    And the zephyrs play,
Now thine endless rest thou'rt taking
From all earthly duties—waking

Where the skies are softer, fairer,
And thine eyes are brighter, clearer
  Than the new-born day!
And thy soul—which earthly feature
Hid—shines far excelling creature
Beauty, as the radiant sunbeam
Pales the stars' faint, twinkling white gleam—
Shines with holiness supernal,
In the realms of light, eternal,
  Glorious, Hetty Gray!

CONTENTMENT.

IN the garden of the heart,
  If ye part the weeds—ye'll see,
Standing from the paths apart,
  A firm, thrifty little tree,
That your slightest care repays,
  Bearing golden fruit the while,
Thro' the cloudiest autumn days
  As in summer's sunniest smile.

Storms of sorrow may assail,
  But its leaves are ever green,
Lifting to the rudest gale
  Still their glittering emerald sheen.
Sit beneath its spreading limbs,
  If you'd 'scape life's fever-heat—
Listen to the ceaseless hymns
  Floating 'mong its branches sweet.

Down yon tangled avenue
   Bloom the amaranth buds of Fame—
But the thorns ye'll journey thro'
   Write in blood the empty name !
On yon mound Ambition rears
   Laurel, pointing to the sky—
Watered by the anguish-tears
   Wrung from trampled Nature's eye.

Flowery ways lie all around
   Tempting thee to farther stray,
But Love's roses on the ground
   Scattered are ere fall of day.
Friendship's buds are rudely nipt
   By the first chill wintry wind—
And the golden bowl once sipt,
   Leaves its bitter dregs behind.

Pleasure, with her phantom train,
   Twines her fading garlands there,
Hanging on the brow of pain
   Mocking wreaths to hide despair.
Hope flaunts petals painted bright
   By the magic hand that weaves
The mountain's azure veil of light
   Which in distance still deceives.

And a ghostly band appears
   When Remembrance beckons, too,
Water-lilies, dropping tears,
   Where low bends that mournful yew.
But the garden runs to waste
   As the sands of life wax low,

And the foot-prints are effaced
That you counted long ago.

Tares and brambles rudely climb
Where the trellised arbors stood;
And the paths are gray with time—
Moss and ivy crown the wood.
But Contentment's sturdy tree,
If ye prune in Life's young spring,
Still in age will shelter thee,
And birds in its branches sing!

A LAY FOR THE LADYE MOON.

THERE'S a white-brow'd maiden up in the sky,
Pale is her cheek, but bright her eye;
She is the Ladye of my love!
She comes at eve when all is still,
And naught is heard save the whippoorwill
In the leafy linden grove—
Ah! with her I love to rove!

Her air is modest, her smile is pure,
She is welcome ever at cottage door
Or palace portal grand;
She smiles on the prisoner in his cell,
Or glides thro' the green and mossy dell,
With a silvery lamp in hand—
And her looks are ever bland.

10 *   H

She sends a glance o'er the rippling tide,
And the mighty billows swell with pride
  As they rise to kiss her feet;
She lingers soft in the jasmine bower,
And with white fingers points the hour
  When lovers there may meet,
  And she guides their willing feet.

Oh, this Ladye of my love, you see,
Hath no fonder, dearer smile for me
  Than for other weary wights;
But I worship her, as one may a star
Sparkling bright where a thousand are
  Thro' the dreamy summer nights,
  When elfins dance and sprites!

I love her for her gentle wiles,
Her tender glances and loving smiles,
  Her brow of purity!
Her cheek's soft white, which never flushes
At silly praise; her heart, which gushes
  With love for all, so free!—
  Ah! she's my loved Ladye!

THE WIND SPIRIT.

OH, a tricksy sprite! a mad, mad sprite!
  Roameth abroad the livelong night—
Up and down,
Up and down,
Over the woodlands and thro' the town;

Now tossing in air a mountain billow—
Now whisp'ring soft sighs round a lady's pillow—
    In and out,
    Round about,
With deafening clamor and boisterous shout!
Down the chimney he wildly rushes,
Out at the keyhole he shrilly gushes;
Then rattles the door with mocking glee,
Holding his breath till you come to see
    Who knocketh without—
    When, with a wild shout,
He puffs in your face and your light puts out.

Now he is off, with a whistle shrill,
Piping away o'er the distant hill;
    Now up on high,
    Over the sky,
Where the frightened clouds before him fly:
    Down again
    He seeketh the main—
And the straining cordage groans with pain,
As it vainly tries in its clasp to hold
The restive sail, which this trickster bold
    Is coaxing away,
    In his frolic gay,
To join him in his frantic play.
Now he has gained his point at last—
Upward and onward it speedeth fast,
    Flapping white wings,
    Splitting in strings,
And dancing along with the crazy blast!

You cannot see this gleesome elf,
Tho' all around you he whirls himself;

But you feel his might
In the chilly night
When he twirls your hat clear out of sight :—
The crackling branches own his sway,
As he scatters them over the broad highway—
　　While the aching bones
　　Of ancient crones
Feel the approach of his faintest moans.
When we hear of shipwrecks and storms without,
We know that the elfin has been about ;
'Tis then that he screeches and howls with pain,
As he looks on the victims his sport has slain ;
　　And his grief-stricken sighs
　　Wail over the skies
As he hides his face in a cloud, and flies !

THE SONG OF LIFE.

WHAT a wondrous volume,
　　Bound in blue and gold,
Hath the hand of spring-time
　　Tremblingly unrolled !
Turn its gilded pages—
　　Every one is rife
With the rhythmic measure
　　Of the Song of Life !

Where bare branches rattled,
　　See—the poison-thorn
Hath a flowery mantle
　　Milk-white as the morn ;

Sunshine brought the blossoms
  From a heart of guile—
As wrathful natures sometimes
  Are conquered by a smile !

Hark ! what busy murmurs
  Float upon the air,
As the wild bee poises
  O'er his dainty fare ;
Catch the breath of fragrance
  Stealing down the trees,
As the pine is tossing
  Kisses to the breeze.

List ! what strains of music
  Faintly come and go
Where the brooklet's dimples
  Were hid beneath the snow :—
All are bringing, bringing
  Their armor to the strife ;
All are singing, singing
  The stirring Song of Life !

Delicate peach-blossoms,
  With promise on their lips—
Greenest blades, with plenty
  On their finger-tips—
Point to the coming harvest
  Of fruitage and of grain,
Whose sheaves can but be garnered
  By toil, perchance by pain.

And what a meek rejoinder
  The daisy offers up,

And the crocus pledges softly
  In her golden cup—
" We'll leave the favor'd blossoms
  To bear of fruit the birth ;
If we cannot be useful,
  We'll beautify the earth."

Read the wondrous Poem,
  Till every line's retold—
God hath writ the volume
  Bound in blue and gold !
Read it on the mountain,
  Read it by the sea,
Every rhythmic measure
  Hath been set for thee.

Learn the mystic meaning
  Of the bud and fruit,
And the tender lesson
  The daisy offers mute ;
Let thy soul interpret
  Why the thistle bears
A beauteous purple flower
  Amid its thorns and tares.

Not a tuft of mosses,
  Not a lace-wing'd fly,
Not a world of glory
  Sparkling in yon sky,
But hath an evangel,
  Whether great or small—
Seek thou out the meaning
  Of the Hand upon the wall !

Then thou canst join the anthem,
  The thrilling, glorious lay
That open lies before thee
  In God's own Book to-day!
And all thy soul grow stronger
  To battle with the strife—
For Angel Hosts are singing
  The grand old Song of Life!

UNREST.

DEATH-DAMPS gather and pallors rest
  On the clay-cold cheek of the moon,
And the cloudy winding-sheet is prest
By the grieving wind, on her waxen breast,
  As he moans a hollow tune.

Afar the sea is wailing low
  Its sad, complaining song,
As Ocean's ghosts glide to and fro,
In dripping cerements of woe,
  Trailing white locks along.

And naught is out on venturous wing
  Save churchyard bat and owl;
The woods with elfin laughter ring,
As from fay-man wild, and eldritch thing,
  From goblin, gnome and ghoul!

While o'er the welkin sounds a bell,
    Now far off and now near;
It comes with weirdest of spell,
As though the sexton, Night, would tell
    The dead Day's age in fear.

And now the waves of troubled thought
    Are rising in their might,
To sweep the gauzy barriers wrought
By pale Philosophy, to naught—
    As wind-swept films of night.

Beat on, vexed waters, in my breast,
    And lash the wreck-strewn shore;
Ye bear to me, in your unrest,
Some olden wrong to be redressed,
    To grieve me nevermore!

Some memories wakened from the sleep,
    The Dead Sea calm of old,
To bubble up the stagnant deep
In widening circles, till they sweep
    The distant strand of gold,

Where every wrong will be made right,
    And every tear's a gem:
O wondrous gift of second-sight!
Ye come to me this storm-swept night
    That I its force may stem.

For it was not a sky of light
    That showed the Promised Land—

A pillar'd cloud, by day and night,
O'er wilderness and waves of might,
  Led to its silver strand !

And thus, on sorrow's Pisgah mound,
  I stand, like one of old—
And see the spice trees waving round,
The palms and purple fruit beyond
  The grain-clad fields of gold !

Oh be thou brave and true, my heart !
  There is the waiting shore—
Turn not to right or left, but start
In strength, and the wild waves will part
  And bear thee safely o'er

WEARY.

OVER the purpling sea
  The day goes down to the dark—
And the hope again is wrecked for me
  That shone with her golden bark !

I call to the ships of Morn,
  " What cheer from the Isle of Shade ?"
And whispered tones, like echoes born
  Of a faith that is half afraid—

Come back—" The tide sets in
  Where black and bare lies the sand ;

Take heart! there's a haven of peace to win
  Beyond the wreck-strewn strand!"

But, alas! on the shore I wait,
  Where the waves once frolick'd free,
But no bark draws near with a golden freight
  Of love and trust for me.

The royal fleet of days
  With the wealth of worlds floats by
Unheeding the trembling hands I raise
  Or my low, despairing cry.

I am weary of the strife
  Of angry waters near—
For I hear the roar of the waves of Life
  From a strand so bleak and bare—

That I long for the flood-tide now,
  To hail the phantom bark
With its misty sails and skeleton prow
  Bearing away for the dark!

LIFE.

ON midnight's arch, to gild the gloom,
    Are richly frescoed golden spheres,
Brought from nonentity's dark doom
  To being—tho' its price be tears!

In every shimmering gleam of light
    Wand'ring adown the misty blue
Of the old aisles of solemn night,
    Some world's great eye is looking thro'.

Some world's great pulse, in every ray
    Quivering among the faintest stars
That pale when Hesper's watch-fires play,
    Or the red beacon's blaze of Mars—
Is thrilling thro' the azure veins
    Of space, and pulsates Nature's heart;
And life, mayhap, is there—its pains
    And joys and hopes may all have part.

And martyrs in some far-off sphere
    Perchance have stood the torturing stake
Without the palm of glory there,
    Where hearts, as here, in silence break.
And patient ones, who've borne the cross,
    Tho' all-deserving of the crown;
Who cheerful wait, come gain, come loss,
    And give a smile for every frown.

And some whose lives are like the brook
    Winding its gleesome way along
O'er sunny mead, thro' leafy nook,
    Singing a low, perpetual song
To starry flowers that crown its banks,
    And fling love-kisses to its lip—
Ah! well may choral hymns of thanks
    Float o'er the golden bowl they sip!

But Life to some—like torrent wild
    That thro' the gaping chasm pours,

Where light amid the gloom ne'er smiled,
  Nor verdure clothes the rocky shores—
May sterile be, and bleak and bare,
  And green spot in the waste be none :
Forgive *them*, Father, if the prayer
  Should falter, that " Thy will be done !"

And some be there, whose Hope's low tide
  Is like the sea's in Arctic zone—
Whose waves of trust have flow'd in pride,
  To turn on the cold shore to stone.
But if above the glacier strays
  A slanting sunbeam's golden plume,
How soon the auroral arch of rays
  Shows fire still smoulders 'mid the gloom.

And sadder lives be onward driven,
  Like oarless boats with rudders lost,
When o'er the pilot star of heaven
  The cloud-surf is all wildly toss'd—
No beacon light amid the foam
  To lead to refuge and relief,
They drift away from God and home
  To strand upon Sin's treacherous reef !

While other lives leap 'mid the strife,
  Like the bold cataract, fierce and free,
Roaring along the rocks of Life
  Unto its ever-restless sea ;
No time to note the blessed peace
  That in the flowery valleys lie—
In thunder tones that never cease
  Ambition calls them and they fly !

But gentler lives, unknown to fame,
  Like the sweet fountain in the glade
To which the thirsty traveler came
  And found the ever-friendly aid—
May flow, as in our nether sphere,
  Whose never-failing streams suffice
All pain and woe to soothe and cheer—
  Their depths conceal the " Pearl of Price !"

For meek Humility's the gem
  That crown'd with light the Nazarene,
More glorious than the diadem
  That graced the brow of Egypt's queen !
And sparkles not a jeweled prow
  In all night's shining argosy
Of worlds—so bright as streams that flow
  From the deep well of sympathy.

All, waifs upon the tide, we float
  Upon creation's mystic sea—
It matters not if golden boat
  Is yours, and a frail plank for me—
We're steering for that Icy Strand
  To join a goodly company,
Who ask not how we gain the land
  Where pride is wrecked and souls are free !

'Tis much to live, but more to die,
  For Death unseals Life's mystery ;
We've but to close the weary eye
  To learn our Being's history—
To see the mighty wheel that turns
  Its labyrinth of worlds along

Where the great central sun still burns—
And hearken the Archangel's song !

LET US FORGET.

WHAT do the early-blown
      Violets say ?
What chime the lily bells
      Forth to the May ?
What murmurs the stream 'neath
      The spring-time's sweet kiss,
That has warmed its chill'd lips
      Back to life and to bliss ?—
" Let us forget in the
      Smiles of to-day,
Old Winter's bleak frowns—"
      Is their blithe roundelay.

What saith each diamond-crown'd
      Star of the night,
On its silvery throne
      Holding sceptre of light—
Shining more glorious,
      As deeper the gloom
Shrouds the dun earth like a
      Pall o'er a tomb ?
" Let us forget," says each
      Shimmering ray—
" That our light was obscur'd
      When shone the dead day."

What is the burden of
   Every tune,
Whose rhythmical measure
   Makes vocal sweet June—
Rolling in billowy
   Surges of song
The purpling hill-tops and
   Green meads along?—
" Let us forget we are
   Creatures of Time,
But rejoice while we may—"
   Is the ring of each chime.

What is the carol on
   Wingèd winds borne,
That progress is sounding
   From watch-tower of morn—
Rolling in echoes o'er
   Mountain and plain,
Trilling a cheering,
   Soul-wakening strain?—
" Let us forget, in bright
   Truth's dawning ray,
The gloomy surroundings
   Of Error's dark day."

What is the anthem that
   Seraphs above
Are chanting with tender
   And pitying love—
Each angel-chorister,
   Veiling his brow,

While in that blest Presence
　　To which all things bow?—
" Let us forget"—is their
　　Merciful lay—
" And forgive mortal's failings—
　　We're wiser than they!"

What is the wisdom that
　　Reason should give,
To teach us to truly
　　And happily live—
That we all the roses
　　May cull in our path,
Leaving the thorns for the
　　Black brow of wrath?
'Tis to cherish all kindliness
　　We may have met—
But the wrongs and oppressions
　　Let us forget!

What is the whisper the
　　Monitor blest
Is breathing in secret
　　Recess of the breast—
Pointing to Him, who, though
　　Scorned and reviled,
Upon His inhuman
　　Betrayers still smiled?—
" Let us forget—'tis the
　　Motto of Heaven—
And forgive, as we all
　　Hope to be forgiven!"

THE SONG OF OTHER YEARS.

WHEN the heart, no longer flushed
　　With hope, ás in its sweet spring-tide,
Has put its dreams away, and hushed
　　The golden chords once struck with pride—
A fitful breeze of memory may
Sweep o'er its strings an olden lay—
But ah ! the song of other years,
Tho' woke in glee, will end in tears !

We may not sing the tender strain
　　That's hallow'd to the peaceful dead !
Its notes of love, its low refrain,
　　Would rouse but ghosts of pleasures fled—
We lay it on the heart away,
A never-sung but cherished lay—
That sweet old song of other years,
Baptized in joy—embalmed in tears !

DYING.

POOR heart ! she says her boat of life
　　Is drifting down a darkling sea !
And all the golden beaches fade
　　Where the old landmarks used to be.

And then unto the crimson lips
　　Of a sea-shell she bends, all pale,

I

To hearken—how one night it fled
  In terror from the murderous gale,

That shook the solid oaken hearts
  Out of the iron-girdled barks,
And hurled the shrieking seamen down
  Where gaped the jaws of hungry sharks.

And then, a loosened chord vibrates
  On Memory's rifted lute a while,
To tell of one beneath the wave,
  Who robbed her young lip of its smile.

Poor heart! poor broken lute! a thrill
  Is all that's left for either now—
Darker and deeper grows the wave,
  While swifter goes the reeling prow.

'Tis cold, she says, oh very cold!
  And the frail boat is shivering o'er,
As out of time on seas unknown
  An icy hand leads from the shore.

But when the lighthouse warden, Night,
  Set all his lamps in starry towers,
And a low moon with slanting rays
  Made lengthened shadows 'mong the flowers—

She said, sweet sounds came o'er the deep,
  Soft ripples as of singing streams—
And the low whispers that once made
  The music of her childhood's dreams;

That a faint light was on the wave,
  Like that of skies that breathe of morn ;
The sea was placid now—her boat
  Seemed on some angel's pinions borne—

While far, and yet how near, a line
  Of silver haze hung o'er a strand,
That something in her spirit ear
  Was breathing, was the Better Land !

Oh, Boat of Life ! that moon went out
  The purple gateway of the West,
But not until thy quivering prow
  Had touched the sacred port of Rest !

INCONSTANCY.

SIGH not for vows broken—
    They were not made to last ;
Weep not o'er words spoken
  In the unreturning past !
Mutable, by nature,
  All things are below,
From man, the lordly creature,
  To waves that ebb and flow :
Moving, changing seasons,
  Rising, falling sea,
Are as many reasons
  For inconstancy.

Dunner the leaf groweth
  In the autumn brown—
'Swifter the stream floweth
  When stern Winter's flown ;
Rounded moons are waning
  Even while we gaze—
And the sunshine gaining
  Lengthens summer days ;
Panoramic visions—
  Rolling clouds we see
In the stellar regions,
  Paint inconstancy.

Hope not that Love's bubble
  Will its hues retain ;
Vapor is Life's trouble—
  Mist, its joy or pain !
Naught that's human's lasting—
  Pleasure findeth wings ;
And even grief is casting
  Moulds in short-liv'd things !
Fading, changing, passing—
  All things that we see
Are mirrors fairly glassing
  Forth Inconstancy.

'GAINST WIND AND TIDE.

> " I cannot hide that some have striven,
> Achieving calm, to whom was given
> The joy that mixes man with heaven ;
>
> " Who, rowing hard against the stream,
> Saw distant gates of Eden gleam,
> And did not dream it was a dream."—TENNYSON.

NO dream—no dream :—If fearless hand
  And steadfast will but guide,
Thy boat may reach that Eden land,
  'Gainst stubborn wind and tide.

I've seen the young moon's pilot bark
  Float down a sunset sea,
And in her wake, where skies grew dark,
  A sparkling argosy

Of jeweled prows, on Night's blue wave,
  Which to my questioning " Hail !"
A wondrous page of wisdom gave
  On every silver sail—

Telling, that holy midnight came
  Like sorrow, softly down,
To hide the fiery sun's fierce flame
  With a mild, starry crown,

Such as our daylight may not bring
  In pride for us to wear ;

As nightingales the sweetest sing
    When darkest hours draw near.

It may be that the cloud that brings
    A shadow o'er thy sky,
Folds blessings in its dewy wings,
    That missed, thy flowers would die !

It may be that the gathering gale
    That threatens wreck to thee
Is sent in love to speed thy sail
    Unto a tranquil sea,

Whose crystal waters, calm and bright,
    Might never meet thy gaze,
If never lower'd the angry night,
    Or broke the cheerless days.

Then shrink not, when wild waves advance,
    And look not backward then ;
For know—" In the reproof of chance
    Lies the true proof of men !"

THE MYSTIC LAND.

I LIVE in a world of my own,
    Where tear-drops and laughter are brothers ;
'Tis a mystical clime, in a sun-lighted zone,
    Outshining the cold world of others !

'Tis peopled by elfins and sprites,
  That dance to my harp's trembling measures—
And wingèd thoughts wander to taste the delights
  Of fancy's most exquisite pleasures.

Far away in the regions of space
  Is this magical land of my dreaming—
Where, tired of earth and its feverish race,
  I turn from the torment of *seeming!*

Its sunlight can dry up the tears
  Which falsehood and coldness have started;
And the spirit of childhood there radiant appears
  As when pure, in lost Eden, we parted.

I sit in this rainbow-propp'd clime
  And forget the dull earth 'neath me turning;
I hear not its jarrings of strife as they chime—
  I feel not its heart-scalds and burning!

Alone!—I am *never* alone!
  For I beg not from others my pleasures;
My heart holds the key to a magical zone,
  Whose caverns are sparkling with treasures.

O beautiful land of my dreams!
  I enter thy mystical portal,
And drink of thy fount of oblivion that streams
  To banish the sorrow that's mortal

Oh, lonely and sad on the earth
  I should wander all hopeless and weary—
Could I not at the shrine where my spirit had birth
  Arm my soul for the journey so dreary!

THE BEAUTIFUL.

O POET'S dream of old delight!
　　O master-chord of Nature's lyre!
O charm! that haloes dark-brow'd night
With holy radiance—whence, the light
　　Of thy mysterious fire?

O Beauty, thou art everywhere,
　　Thou chalice of enchantment, bliss!
Do we not quaff' thee in the air
We breathe—as thy gold nectar there
　　Rolls sparkling to our kiss?

Thou'rt limned upon the blushing face
　　Of youthful, blue-eyed morning gay;
And 'tis thy cunning hand we trace
Touching the faded locks with grace,
　　Of ancient evening gray.

And when the withered boughs let fall
　　Their last pale yellow leaves—'tis thine,
With snowy shroud and glistening pall
To drape the branches bare, till all
　　The woodlands radiant shine!

Over the blue wave with a wing
　　Of fire, thou gildest Ocean's surge!
On Alpine heights thou'lt grandly sing,
Or in the vale, with lowliest thing,
　　Warble a plaintive dirge.

The tiniest streams that find their way,
  Singing and laughing, to the sea—
The mightiest cataracts that play
Triumphal marches to the day,
  Alike, are tuned by thee.

And when the purple storm-cloud rears
  Its crystal jets in yonder sky—
'Tis thine to catch the jewel tears,
And set the covenant of years,
  A gorgeous bow, on high !

The swelling buds adown the dale,
  The full-blown flowers with golden crowns,
And nun-like lilies, purely pale,
Have wrapped them in thy mystic veil
  To glorify the downs !

And when the red moon sits upon
  December's cold and barren hill,
Thy master-hand has belted on
The snowy mound, a diamond zone
  Of shimmering icicle.

And when the wayward human heart
  Once owns thy spell, there's not a thrill
Of Nature's pulse—a quivering start—
That has not magic power to part
  The filmy folds of ill !

O witchery ! O vision wove
  In realms of high Infinity,

To show to man (by wakening love
For all things lovely here—above—)
His Immortality !

DAYLIGHT.

MORN, on the mountain-top,
    Misty and gray,
Heralds the coming of
    Beautiful day—
Chasing the night from its
    Leafy-crown'd nest,
Who in the vale lingers
    A moment to rest.

But day, like a conqueror,
    Marshals his hosts—
And forests and meadows
    Assist in his boasts ;
His clarion-voiced trumpeter
    Crows from the corn,
And shrilly-pip'd choristers
    Sing from the thorn.

All nature shakes off the dark
    Chains of the night,
As nations from bondage hail
    Liberty's light !
The beauties which darkness with
    Sable wings hid,

Shine forth as the day-god's bright
Hand lifts the lid.

For night, like the pall which
Oppression doth fling,
Conceals with dark foldings
Each glorious thing—
Till day, with glad anthems
Of freedom, doth give
A tinge from its bright wing
To all things that live.

THE ANGEL MONITOR.

MIDNIGHT broodeth, hushed and dreamy,
Over sleeping earth's expanse,
Folding in her star-gemm'd garments
Myriads, in a death-like trance.
Scarce a ripple stirs the ocean,
Wind and wave have sunk to rest—
" Tired Nature's sweet restorer "
Claspeth all things to her breast.

Angels now their watch are keeping,
Softly from their golden home,
With the dews of night descending—
Lo ! in bright-robed throngs they come !
Circling downward—nearer, nearer,
Poising now on radiant wings,
Soon the sounding arch of heaven
With their choral anthem rings !

Now the chorus dies in echoes—
　While from out the brilliant throngs
One with brow serene and holy,
　Still a softened note prolongs;
Love with gentle pity blending
　In her voice persuasive, mild—
Welling from her heart's deep fountain,
　Tender, pure and undefiled.

Mortal—wouldst thou wisdom borrow!
　Learn the secret whilst thou can?
How thou may'st with skill supernal
　Blend the angel with the man!
Waken thee from sleep's embraces,
　Leave the shadow of her wings;
Mortal, lend thine ear and listen,
　Listen—while the angel sings!—

" From the far abode of glory,
　Where the white-wing'd cherubs stand
Chanting with celestial praises
　All the wonders of His hand
At whose word, from realms of darkness,
　Countless worlds have bright'ning smiled—
Lo! to erring man I hasten—
　Man—the restless, wayward child,

" From the Father's house still wandering
　On the broad and open way;
Ever plucking fruit forbidden—
　Still the wily Serpent's prey!
Yet not wholly unprotected,
　Heavenly guards upon him wait :—

Man ! wouldst thou but list their teachings
   Thou wouldst cease to rail at fate.

" In thy heart's most secret chamber,
   There a seraph folds its wings ;
Hearken to its gentle warnings—
   List the ' still small voice' that sings !
Through the flowery fields of pleasure,
   Down the steeps that lead to crime—
Still may'st hear the whisp'ring measure,
   Still may'st list the dreamy chime.

" When the siren beckons onward,
   Warbling liquid notes of love ;
Pointing with a taper finger
   To the garlands she has wove,
Covering with their fragrant blossoms
   All the thorns that hide them there—-
Comes not *then* the whispered warning,
   ' Touch not—taste not—oh beware !'

" Oh there breathes not human bosom
   But hath room for angel guest !
List its pleadings, it will lead thee
   Gently thro' the paths of rest ;
It will point the shoals and quicksands,
   Hidden by the treacherous wave,
In whose depths poor, sin-drawn mortals
   Madly rush and fearless lave.

" It will bid thee help each other,
   Soothing earthly cares to rest ;

Then thy sin-benighted brother
  Thou wilt fold unto thy breast,
Saying—‘*I, too,* wandered weary,
  Groping in the darkness drear,
Till I heard the angel singing
  Bidding me my brother cheer !’

“ Once you list its gentle breathings,
  Heed this angel monitor,
You will learn a truth immortal—
  It will teach you what you are!
Show how prone to do the evil
  Which you feel you should not do ;
How your sin-entrammeled spirit
  Shuns the good it would pursue.

“ Thus with new-born, mental vision,
  Your own weakness you will see ;
Then you’ll feel, and feeling show it,
  For your brother—charity !
Charity, which beareth all things,
  Is long-suffering and is kind ;
Evil thinks not—hoping ever
  In all hearts some good to find.

“ Some little seedling, which, with culture,
  Yet will bloom a goodly tree,—
Warmed to bearing fruit perennial
  By thy smile, sweet charity !—
Which distrust’s cold breath had blighted,
  Dark suspicion’s tares had curst,
Calumny’s foul sneer had withered
  Ere the germ to life had burst.

"Man! thy erring brother judge not,
　　Thanking God you're not as he!
Ah! you know not what temptations
　　Made him such as now you see.
Pitying angels round him cluster—
　　God, the Father, loves him still;
And shall fellow-mortals spurn him,
　　As if *they* could do no ill?

"Ah! you know not when the moment
　　You may slip upon the road,
Over whose uneven surface
　　Thus far you have safely trod;
Then, with wild, despairing glances,
　　Seeking succor far and wide,
Pained—you'll see some scorning Levite
　　Passing on the other side.

"Rouse thee, Man! be up and doing!
　　For the morrow draweth near,
When to serve thy fallen brother
　　Thou no longer may'st be here.
Hearken to the voice of warning,
　　To the counsel which it brings;
Mortal, lend thine ear and listen—
　　Listen while the angel sings!"

Now the morn with rosy lustre
　.Trembles in the Orient gates,
Like a bride all bathed in blushes,
　　For the sun, her bridegroom, waits.
Day, with busy step advances
　　Bringing earthly toil and care—

Angel hosts withdraw their pinions,
  Fading into upper air.

Still soft tones, like dropping waters,
  Through the morning twilight come,
While in distance melt their voices
  As they seek their heavenly home:—
Hear ye not the dying cadence?
  Now it louder swells again—
Hark! the burden of the measure—
  "Peace on earth—good-will to men!"

MIDSUMMER'S EVE.

DAY has burned away to embers
  On the hearthstone of the West,
But grave twilight still remembers
  His warm lips her cheeks have prest,
And within her purple chambers
  Flushes with a sweet unrest.

Rustling leaves and buds are pealing
  Low-toned chimes within the dell—
Nature's vesper songs—that stealing
  O'er the spirit with a spell,
Waken all the chords of feeling
  In the heaven-tuned heart that dwell.

'Tis the witching hour for dreaming—
  Rest, my soul, from earthly strife!

Let the waifs float past, that streaming
  From the wild flood-gates of life,
With its bitterness are teeming—
  With its treachery are rife :—

And upon yon sea of amber,
  In the young moon's silver boat,
Off to some star-lighted chamber
  Of the blue vault, lightly float
Past the will-o'-wisps that clamber
  Where the meteor lanterns shoot,

Ere the dying eve is shrouded
  In her misty robe of white ;
Ere the coming damps have clouded
  O'er yon azure mirror bright ;
Ere sad memory's ghosts have crowded
  All those halls of golden light !

Up ! where asphodels are blooming
  By some silver-crested spring—
For the shadowy past is coming,
  All his phantom shapes to bring,
As the dark-plum'd night is looming
  Like a bird of evil wing.

Off—and tread the white and azure
  Of the tessellated floor,
Where each crystal-lined embrasure
  Holds a crown of worlds, or more,
With the constellated treasure
  Of the monarchies of yore !

Bear me softly, tide of even !
  On thy rippling billows, where
All these sceptred kings of heaven
  Hold their courts in golden air—
For I dream, to crush the leaven
  Of the bitter loaf—despair !

THE NORSE QUEEN'S RIDE.

A FANTASIE.

BLOOD-RED glows the starry palace
    Of the Norse Queen, Borealis,
Golden-haired, pale-cheeked Aurora,
Of the Halls of Cynosura !
There ten thousand lights are glancing,
And blue signal-fires are dancing—
Purple plumes and banners streaming,
Crimson rockets weirdly gleaming
In fantastic corruscations,
Sparkling jets and radiations,
Diamonding the icy towers
Where the beetling glacier lowers
O'er the battlemented sweep,
Frozen moat and donjon keep—
Till each vapory tide that darkles
O'er the sea-cerulean, sparkles,
Limned in colors emerald, yellow ;
Golden rose or orange mellow,
Steely gray or greenish azure,
In a starry-ray'd embrasure,

Waving with a tremulous motion
Like the pulses of old ocean.

For the bold Norsemen are met,
With glittering spear and bayonet,
Gilded barb and lance and crescent,
Paley-tinted phosphorescent—
To attend their queen, Aurora,
To the sweet domain of Flora.

She had heard, cold Borealis,
Of the wonders of that palace
In the far-off Tropic seas,
Fabled as Hesperides
For their luscious fruitage golden—
And, until she had beholden
All the curious devices
That the flower sprite entices
Bright-plumed creatures with, her pinions
Could not rest in her dominions.
She must see the beauteous queen
On her throne of emerald green,
With her handmaids so enchanting
That the words will ere be wanting
That can paint the porcelain tinting
Of their cheeks and lips—no printing
Of the poet's pen can blazon
Forth the charms she fain would gaze on !

*   *   *   *   *

Now, behold, the pale Aurora
Sees her rival lie before her,
Azure-eyed, rose-lipp'd young Flora !

In her fragrant jasmine bower
Sipping sweets at midnight's hour;
While the silver winds are stooping
O'er her perfumed tresses, drooping
In a shower of glistening rain—
And an Iris-banded train
Of bright-plumed creatures flutter by
To catch entranced her balmy sigh,
And Zephyr fans the heat away
Left by the fiery-footed Day—
While all the garden sylphs are wreathing
Fresher coronals, and breathing
Odors o'er the couch of sheen,
To lull the slumbers of their Queen—
And Peace sits brooding like a dove
Above these realms of happy love!

From her chariot in the skies
The cold Queen sees, with glistening eyes—
Till a flush, a quivering glow
Reddens o'er her brow of snow:
True, she has her morris dancers,
Her bold spearmen and her lancers,
Archers, meteor-forgers, all
To ride forth if she but call—
Thor, the bravest son of Odin,
Points the lightnings at her noddin',
And the old god at her call
Waits in his Valhalla Hall,
All his ruby wine to pour
Over heaven's starry floor!
Yes, she feels it, she has POWER!
But love ne'er points one golden hour

For her, upon the dial's round—
And woman should be but love-crown'd!
For what is power, but the cold light
That bristles o'er the Arctic night
In spears and lances, 'mid the gloom,
Like death-lights dancing o'er a tomb?
But love is the warm Tropic's sigh
That fills with dew the violet's eye,
Throbs in the wild carnation's heart,
And sweetest fragrancy will start
From the young herb's deep bruisèd leaf—
Ah! question not the pale Queen's grief,
The world hath many a chill'd Aurora
As well as love-crown'd, blessed Flora!
And many a richly gilded palace
Has some pale, spectral Borealis,
Watching with a glistening eye
A flower-crown'd rival passing by
To happy home 'neath green-wood shades
Which power's cold death-light ne'er invades!

NEW ORLEANS, *September* 1, 1859.

ONCE UPON A TIME.

'TIS the wind, the same old, restless wind,
   That in tuneful numbers thrill'd the pine
Upon the hillside, where the willows twined
   Above the brooklet in days o' lang syne.
How it murmurs *now* of wasted years,
   Scattered like the leaves in autumn's prime—

13 *

Ah! they were not washed away in tears
    Once upon a time!

'Tis the wind, the ever-moaning wind,
    Like a wand'ring spirit, sad, unblest—
Ever seeking what it may not find,
    Shelter where its weary wing may rest.
It ne'er sang us such a solemn strain
    When to youth's joy-bells it lent a chime—
From our hearts it caught the glad refrain
    Once upon a time!

'Tis the wind, it calls us from afar
    With a blended tone, half mirth, half tears,
Like a cadence some vibrating bar
    Sends from the past adown our later years.
Ah! its melody once sweetly trilled,
    But the measure long has ceased to chime;
Only echoes fall where music thrilled
    Once upon a time!

'Tis the wind, it waileth evermore
    Plaintive dirges for the buried hours;
And we hear it on Time's star-lit shore
    Calling spectres from the misty bowers;
Trooping ghosts they come, as gray-eyed Eve
    Lights her watch-fire after curfew chime,
But such visions ne'er caused us to grieve
    Once upon a time!

Then the breeze at rainbow-tinted Morn
    Brought glad promise of most golden Noon!

Short-lived glory—better far unborn,
    Than upon our pathway pale so soon !—
Tone by tone, as all those splendors dimmed,
    Sank the sweet breeze to a sadder chime ;
Till the heart forgets the lay it hymned
    Once upon a time !

Weird wind, cease, cease your mournful song !
    See, the gray mists at thy bidding come,
Putting out the lights that shine along
    The blue aisles of the far-off starry home.
And thy chilling breath has blown the flame
    Of many a hope out, with its churchyard chime,
Never in our hearts to burn the same
    As once upon a time !

THE LOVED AND LOST.

LOVED and lost ! O loved and lost !
    And will the May put on
Her rosy scarf and gay green hood,
    When our pale Lily's gone ?
Will the shy bluebird seek its home
    Across the wind-rock'd main,
And our dear nursling nevermore
    Come back to us again ?

I marvel how the breeze can toy
    With the wild willow's hair,

When sunny tresses all unstirred
  Lie 'neath the daisies there ;
Or how the careless day can turn
  Her empty glass again,
And all the golden sands run on
  Unmindful of our pain.

Oh, night of sorrow ! may there come
  A mist-dispelling morn
Across our shrouded household skies,
  Of faith and mercy born—
When looking o'er the grave, we'll see,
  What bids our anguish cease—
A white-robed Pilgrim enter at
  The pearly gates of peace !

MY BIRTH-DAY.

ANOTHER leaf to-day laid bare
  By Time's untiring wing !
Another page, perchance, for care
  To leave a blotted thing—
Or angels make a record where
  Their shining feet may ring !

By my heart's ocean's wind-swept shore
  In my life-boat I stand,
The while the waves come rolling o'er
  Unto the lonely strand,

Some freighted with the trust they bore
  When first they left the land—

Some muttering of an angry gale,
  Of strife and thunder-guns—
Some strewn with wrecks and corses pale—
  Some radiant, shining ones,
Tinged with the glory (soon to pale)
  Of bright but setting suns !

Some murmuring of amaranth bowers
  And golden asphodel,
Of isles where Fame's white buds and flowers,
  Like Ocean's foam-wreaths swell—
But ah ! the temple of the hours
  Sends forth a muffled knell.

For every wave that seeks the strand,
  Laden with song or roar,
Breaks, like the tides of Arctic land,
  Upon an icy shore—
Their white lips parting where I stand,
  To whisper low, " No more !"

How can I give a bark of hope
  Unto that darkling tide?
Is it but wayward Fancy's scope
  That low distrust would hide—
That thus I feel my soul doth ope
  To day her portals wide?—

Wind music, I may not shut out,
  Comes up through withered leaves,

Singing of spring-time—how can Doubt
  Garner her dusky sheaves,
When promise-breathing seedlings sprout
  'Neath grand old forest eaves?

Away, away before the gale,
  Under bare poles I'll go—
I'll reef my breeze-inviting sail
  When tempests rudely blow
Or spread it when a tender tale
  The south wind whispers low.

With the dead past beneath my keel,
  My log-book turned anew ;
A steadfast purpose—true as steel—
  Shall guide me safely through !
So now, the helm—thro' woe or weal,
  Stand Pilot, firm and true !

February 12, 1861.

A LITTLE WHILE.

DAY adown the golden stair
  Has turned the hinge of Sunset's gate :
A ghostly mist is waiting there,
  To rob her of her glorious state.
See ! upon her brow of light
  Its chilling, death-damp folds are hung,
While from the silver bells of night
  A low-toned dirge is softly rung.

Close your waxen lids so meek,
  Lily, pining in the glen;
She who kissed your pallid cheek
  Ne'er will praise its pearl again.
When the fickle sun smiles on
  The younger buds the morrow brings,
Thy beauty, with the day that's gone,
  Shall too have flown—like all bright things!

Passing thus away, the while,
  Other days will bloom and fade—
Other sunny hours will smile
  Above the dun old churchyard shade
That wraps the tomb where mouldering lies
  All that once sprang from quick'ning germ—
Will smile—tho' kindly hearts and eyes
  Are left to darkness and the worm!

A little while, and we shall lay
  Us down to rest, with folded hands;
While the great world its mystic way
  Will circle on—tho' as the sands
That pave the desert are its graves—
  What recks it that our little breath
Should pass upon the breeze that waves
  Our new-found wings o'er gulf of death?

The rolling earth must still fulfill
  Its mission; and, like bird of Spring,
That droops its old, worn plumage, will
  Renew its crests tho' on the wing:
Other feet shall press its sod—
  Other hopeful hearts will beat—

Other weary ones shall plod
　　Toward that goal where all must meet.

A little while, a little while,
　　And each his burden will lay down ;
And he who sorrows now, will smile
　　To find his cross hath won a crown !
A little while, ye weary wait—
　　Some pitying Day will beckon you
To enter at the golden gate
　　Life's thorny path hath led you to.

———

HEAVEN.

IS it where the spiral stairway,
　　Set with gems, leads up the blue ?
Are the gleams that pierce the ether,
　　Eyes of angels looking thro' ?
Is that great white road that stretches,
　　Paved with stars, across the skies,
The way—beyond poor mortal reaches—
　　That the ransom'd spirit flies ?

Is that land of wondrous glory
　　Undivined by human sight ?
Like creation's mystic story,
　　Hieroglyphed on scroll of Night.
Ah ! not so ; faint heart, despair not—
　　Heaven is very near to you ;

Tho' thy burden weighs, yet, fear not,
  With the Father's house in view !

For, without the prophet's vision,
  The mysterious lines to read,
That God for man's blest intuition
  Writes in every guileless deed—
Ye may see—if not foul fettered
  By the blinding bands of sin—
Thy soul's wall all sublimely lettered,
  " Heaven's kingdom is within !"

If within be peace and gladness—
  Love for all things, great and small—
Pity, nigh akin to sadness,
  For an erring brother's fall ;
For enemies a meek prayer, rather
  Than revenge's fiendish due—
Lowly breathed, " Forgive them, Father,
  For they know not what they do !"

Humility, when wreath of laurel
  Crowns thee conqueror in a field,
Where self stood trembling in the quarrel,
  Urging thee to dastard yield ;
But martyr firmness, when thy spirit
  At life's fiery stake is tried,
Tho' no palm awards the merit
  That has stemmed the raging tide.

And, withal, a hopeful nature
  Sifting out the grain of good,

14

The one redeeming, better feature
  Found in every evil brood,—
Feeding hate and falsehood only
  With the sweet fruit of the True !
Loving, tho' unloved and lonely—
  Say, can heaven be far from you ?

Ah ! nearer, nearer for the crosses
  That have strewn thy way of life ;
Nearer for the hallowing losses—
  Nearer, for the conquered strife !
Nearer, for the wise ordeal
  That leads thee rough-shod o'er the stone,
Till thou canst bravely bear the real,
  And trusting say, " Thy will be done !"

Never upward look for Heaven,
  If no Heaven's begun below ;
Never onward look for Heaven,
  For you pass it as you go.
Never outward look for Heaven,
  Outward lies the slough of sin,
The old corrupt, fermenting leaven—
  Look for Heaven alone within !

BESSIE BELL.

I BREATHE thy name in sorrow,
  Bessie Bell ;
There cometh no glad morrow
  My grief to quell—

Night's breezes softly sighing,
  Sadly tell,
That thy head is lowly lying,
  Bessie Bell !

The whisp'ring prairie grasses
  Lightly wave,
And the West wind softly passes
  O'er thy grave !
By the sunset's golden glory
  Angels tell
Thy young love's mournful story,
  Bessie Bell !

And to me the angels bear it
  O'er the lea—
And in my home I hear it,
  By the sea ;
When the evening's purple splendor
  Crowns the dell,
I hear their voices tender,
  Bessie Bell.

I grieve for young buds gathered
  Ere their bloom—
For flowers of feeling withered
  In the tomb ;
But those angel sounds at even
  Softly tell
Of transplanted flowers in heaven,
  Bessie Bell !

And I listen as their voices
  Come and go ;
And my bleeding heart rejoices
  That 'tis so.
But still there comes a feeling
  Hard to quell—
A wild thought o'er me stealing—
  Bessie Bell :

I wonder if to mortals
  Loved like thee,
There is bliss when Heaven's portals
  Open free?
For thine eyes must see mine anguish,
  Thy heart swell,
As for thee I sadly languish,
  Bessie Bell.

But I vainly tell my sorrow
  To the sea ;
From its blue arms springs the morrow—
  But not thee !
Oh ! when will sounds at even
  Softly tell,
That I've follow'd thee to heaven,
  Bessie Bell?

HESPERUS.

LAMP of twilight!   Hesper, Venus,
   Silver censer, swung between us
And the dazzling altar golden,
Where the day burns as of olden—
Art thou myth, or art thou real?
World of beauty, or ideal
Bark of fable—ship of Argo,
With the golden fleece for cargo?

Never in the darkling midnight
Catch we glimpses of thy hid light—
Tho' upon night's glinting stars' height
Burns the fiery shield of Mars, bright—
Tho' thro' the silvery horns of Taurus
Saturn's white lamp glimmers o'er us,
And to Lyra's tinkling tunes
Dance Jupiter and all his moons
In circling changes zodiacal—
Thou, as ruler hierarchal,
Seekest ministering angels,
Whispering their blest evangels,
Till the rosy morn is stealing
In light ripples o'er that ceiling
Bending its blue folds above us
Like soft azure eyes that love us—
Sometimes, then, we catch thy glances
Where the Orient's bright wave dances.

Beacon light of purest argent,
Lapis-lazuli for margent—

Hanging half-way 'twixt nocturnal
Realms and climes of light supernal—
Hesperus or Vesper, Venus,
Is there aught in kind between us?

Plodder in the fields of science,
Off—I set thee at defiance!—
Tell me not, the planet's orbit
Lies within ours—to absorb it
So completely in the sun's light
That our zenith thus it shuns quite—
(Seemingly, at least,) 'tis so
Hidden in the day-beam's glow;
Off! nor mar my bright ideal
With cold glimpses of the real.

Let me thro' the twilight vapor
Watch the lighting of the taper
On the cloud-land shores of heaven,
Past the sunset tides of even—
Watch—as mariner the glimmer
Of the lighthouse lamp's soft shimmer!

To my life-boat it is gleaming
With an incandescent beaming,
That has burned the grosser fires
Of this mortal state's desires,
To pale Purity's white ashes—
And upon the silver flashes
Rises (phœnix-like) the dove
Of a deathless, holy love
For the beautiful—the golden
Age, we have not yet beholden—

When the morning stars again
Shall take up the glad refrain
They chanted when the Word was spoken,
" Let there be light !"—and night was broken.

Then, O Hesper, Vesper, Venus,
Then the lay we'll chant between us !

MY BIRD.

A DOWNY shape, half moulded,
   With shadowy pinions folded,
Comes to me—a presence felt, scarce seen—as spirit
   wings that glance
   Thro' the starlight calm and holy,
   When the prayerful heart bows lowly,
And the upturned eye is startled by a passing radiance,
   It pales and gleams, like light in dreams,
     The moonlight of a trance !

   And I cannot give expression
   To the strangely sweet depression
Stealing o'er my being, dreamily, until my soul unbars
   The gates of sense that bind it,
   And, without a look behind it,
Takes the flood-tide that will bear it to its home among
   the stars—
   To regions bright, in-isled in light,
     Above earth's leaden jars !

Then my bird of beauty, showing
All its golden plumage—glowing
Like the tropic tints that brighten where the fragrant
　　　spice trees grow—
Sings to me the holy numbers,
Such as lulled my infant slumbers,
When the angel-watchers sung them in the blessed
　　　long-ago—
While far away Life's billows play
　In noisy ebb and flow.

Thro' the sunshine glancing brightly,
And the star-gems flashing nightly,
In the summer's golden prime as in the ermined Ice-
　　　king's reign—
Comes this nestling of my bosom
Lighting on some folded blossom
In my heart, that gladly opens all its leaves into her
　　　strain ;
Like the rose whose lips unclose
　When the bulbul tells his pain.

Ah ! my doveling, none may prison
The far-reachings of my vision
When thy spirit tones I hear, and catch the gleaming
　　　of thy wings ;
And cold earth can never bind me
Where thy soft call may not find me,
For I cast its shackles easily when thy dear music
　　　rings—
Ah ! bird of mine, unto thy shrine
　My heart its tribute brings !

THE PENITENT MARY.

SHE kneels, while from her downcast eyes
    Fast fall the blinding tears—
As thro' her soul remorseful rise
    The sins of former years.

With tears she bathes the Saviour's feet,
    And wipes them with her hair,
Anoints with precious ointment sweet,
    And scatters perfume there!

The Pharisee, with scornful eye
    And proud, self-righteous thought,
Scoffs to himself, and asketh, Why
    Such sacrifice is brought?

But Jesus read his thoughts—and said,
    " Such offerings are sweet;
Thou never didst anoint my head,
    While she doth kiss my feet!

" Her sins are many, but the tears
    Her broken heart lets fall,
Doth wash away the guilt of years—
    Make pure her offerings all!

" Her deep transgressions I erase,
    Because she loveth much :
O ye who need not pardoning grace
    Can never love as such!"

Then to the woman kneeling low—
  " Arise ! thy woes are o'er ;
Depart in peace ! thy faith I know—
  Go thou, and sin no more !"

AN ALBUM DEDICATION.

THINE are leaflets of the heart,
    Album—bound in Friendship's name—
Tho' no shrinking one hath part
  In the flaunting wreath of fame !
Yet like that sweet, modest flower
  Nestling in its leafy cot,
Fidelity its blessed dower—
  They will breathe " Forget-me-not."

Memory's tender buds will blend
  With the flowerets garnered here,
Sealed in the pure name of " friend,"
  With a smile and with a tear ;
Whispering of some dear one still
  Tho' the turf lies on his breast,
Causing plaintive chords to thrill
  In the hearts that loved him best.

Youth and hope and happy love
  Here will tell their rosy dreams ;
And faith will paint some silvery grove
  In-isled amid celestial streams !
Book ! may thy leaves be overblown
  By precepts pure as breath of even,

And in them may such seeds be sown
As bear immortal fruit in heaven!

KINDNESS.

O WHITE-WINGED angel,
   That holds the bright key
Of the heart—what the tribute
   To offer to thee?
For thine is the wand
   Of the prophet, that brings
From the rock in our bosom
   The deep hidden springs—
Thou seraph, that ever
   Melodiously sings!

Oh life were a desert
   Bleak, dreary and bare,
Whose depths we, tho' bold
   Would all-shrinkingly dare,
Were it not that a green spot
   Now here and there lies—
Sweet kindness! mild beaming
   From soul-lighted eyes,
The golden chain linking
   The earth and the skies?

The pure " *benedicite*"
   Laid on the grass,

When silver dews spread
  Their soft palms as they pass.
The " bread on the waters,"
  That falls in sweet rain
And springs in a green coat
  Of foliage again—
A glorious hosanna
  From hillside and plain !

Oh, forth to the mountain-top,
  Man, when the day
Is driving the shadows
  And mist-shapes away—
And see how new beauties
  Come out of the gloom,
When smiling, sweet sunshine
  Is spreading its bloom—
Like kindness, the one light
  This side of the tomb !

The sunshine we all,
  If we please, can impart,
To chase the dark shadows
  From grief-shrouded heart,
And call back to blossom
  Some fast-fading flower,
That pines for the light
  Of a soft, sunny hour—
O man ! why not cherish
  The heaven-grafted power?

For the scroll of the star-script,
  At night's sparkling noon,

When glinting waves kiss
　　The white sail of the moon,
And silver-linked winds
　　Breathe of flowery June—
In jeweled notes pages
　　A God-given tune,
How His kindness vouchsafes us
　　In darkness, such boon !

CRUSHED.

A TRAMPLED rose-bud—nothing more
　　I found it in a quiet stroll
Where the great city's troubled roar
　　Vexed not the pulses of my soul.
A poor, pale, trodden flower—ah me !
　　Its velvet petals rudely torn,
But keeping still the fragrancy
　　That blessed a happier morn !

Ah ! what a sweet, pathetic psalm
　　Upon its bruisèd leaves I traced,
That shed upon my spirit balm
　　And the deep scars of wrong effaced.
I laid it on my heart, to keep
　　The record fresh with grateful tears—
Its perfume softly, while I weep,
　　Steals upward with my prayers.

For, brooding in a cloud, my soul
　　Sat with a drooping, wounded wing,

15

Where dark Despair's low thunders roll,
　And never comes a bird of spring.
Crushed—crushed—the hope within me fled—
　Till this pale blossom spake so low,
With perfumed lips that softly shed
　Forgiveness for the blow

That left it bleeding!—and I heard
　The anthem on its fragrant breath,
Till all my spirit-pinions stirred
　To its sweet song of Love in death!—
Of love that conquered hate and scorn,
　And gave a sweet return instead—
Oh! a new sunshine lit the morn,
　And to my soul I said:

" If a poor dying flower can give
　Aroma to the passing breeze,
O soul, arise! up, up and live—
　Ye're worth ten thousand such as these!
For ye may soar on pinions bright
　To Saturn's rings of glittering gold—
Orion's jeweled belt of light
　Grasp in thy daring hold—

" Tread the blue fields of space afar—
　Stand even at the jasper door,
That pitying angels leave ajar
　To lure thee heavenward evermore!
Oh what wrong can a fellow-worm
　Inflict to bow thee to the dust,
When in thee lies th' immortal germ
　Of faith and holy trust?

Be sure the rough-shod heel that left
  Its impress deeply, yet was meant
To test thy strength—the rod that cleft
  The rock was in sweet mercy sent!
Then, soul, obey the hest—send forth
  Thy living water's sweet perfume;
Learn of this poor, crushed flower thy worth—
  Thy birth-right, soul, resume!

DEAD LEAVES.

OUT of the **darkness comes a** moan,
    As of one that grieves,
Sighing, in lowest, saddest tone,
  " Dead leaves! dead leaves!"

Cometh it from the pallid lips
  Of the wave that brings
Us tidings of the missing ships
  On its white wings?

There are no tears in **the eyes of** Night,
  And her ebon hair
Is bound with a silver **network bright,**
  Her brow is clear.

I wonder much whence comes the moan
  Under the eaves,
With its mournful, mournful monotone—
  " Dead leaves! dead leaves!"

It cannot be the voice of the wind
  That I heard at play
Where vervain and clematis twined?—
  But then 'twas May!

Ah me! how many hopes have lain
  Them down with the rose,
Under the russet counterpane
  October throws!

I may not wonder, O Autumn wind,
  Why thus thy song grieves—
A human tone in it I find,
  Wailing—"Dead leaves!"

Ashes to ashes and dust to dust,
  Go loves, hopes and fears;
Gay blossoms decay—gold promises rust—
  Rainbows leave tears!

Chant on the refrain, O mournful wind,
  My heart the dirge weaves,
For down in its hollows I only find
  Dead leaves! dead leaves!

FEAR NOT; IT IS I.

"But He saith unto them, It is I ; be not afraid."—St. John vi. 20.

THE tempest unfurls its black wing o'er the wave,
  And rides o'er the billows with glee ;
The winds are let loose, and they franticly rave,
  And toss the white foam of the sea.

A lone, little bark—like a waif on the tide—
  Is lifted a moment in air,
Then gulphed in some monstrous wave's jaws, open
    wide—
  Her crew almost sunk in despair.

They view their rent sails and their rudderless bark,
  And wildly for succor they cry ;
When, lo ! a bright Form walks the waves thro' the
    dark,
  And whispers—"Fear not ; it is I !"

That voice !—Oh what hope in each trembling breast
  Springs up, as its tones greet their ears ;
No longer the tempest can cause them unrest—
  Those words have allayed all their fears.

The winds at His bidding their fury assuage,
  The waters are stilled in their might ;
A mild breeze doth blow—for the tempest's fierce
    rage—
  And anchors their frail bark aright.

15 *

'Tis thus when in life we are thrown on the waves—
  The dark-crested waves of despair;
When rudderless, sailless, the wild billow laves,
  And tosses our life-boat in air—

That we feel all our efforts are fruitless and vain
  The tempest's wild fury to fly,
And we cower 'neath its might—when there cometh
    again
  That soft voice—" Fear not; it is I !"

Yes, 'tis He who hath loosed o'er our wandering path
  The wild winds of passion and grief,
To show us how vain is escape from their wrath
  Till we seek at His hands for relief!

Then lift up your glances, ye grief-stricken ones—
  For can ye not surely descry
That Jesus is near you in sorrow's deep groans,
  And whispers—" Fear not; it is I?"

A DREAM.

I DREAMED :—and the curtain of night,
    With its sombre and cumbersome fold,
Was lifted from off the dingles and dells
    Where the fairies their revels hold.
I stood in the midst of their magic rings,
And caught the buzzing of myriad wings,

As the drowsy elves
Were stirring themselves
From flowery beds,
Where their tiny heads
Had slumbered the glaring day away,
And waited the light of the moon's soft ray.
Springing from rosebuds with frolic glee,
Their fragrant breaths scenting all the lea ;
Lifting the edges of curtains blue,
On their violet couches I saw them too—
Winking their eyes
With pleased surprise
To find that the hours of night had come ;
The mystic time when Fay and Sprite
Meet and mingle in glad delight,
In their leafy forest home.
A lazy glowworm, fat and old,
Was lighting the green sward with sparks of gold,
While every leaflet and tendril near
Supported a fire-fly chandelier ;
The acorn-cups with dew were filled,
And the fragrant balsam was distilled
From every flower,
Which this witching hour
To draw from each blossom has magic power.

But lo ! while I looked, a soft sigh from the hills
Parted the curtains of straw-color pale,
That folded around the velvety bed
Where a spell-bound immortal—a sprite of the vale—
Had lain in a trance through each year's measured
chime
Till fivescore were marked on the dial of Time !

I caught the low whisper that rose
From the flower-decked gentry around.
        And learned that the sprite,
        At noon of the night,
Would awake from her long repose—
Would girdle the earth with sparks of light
Shook from her waving pinions bright,
As forth from her sylvan dwelling-place
A glimpse of the world, and its jostling race,
Would be shown to her gaze thro' dewy tears,
Ere she slept again for a hundred years!
I heard the stroke of the midnight bell—
        · Silvery and clear
        On my dreaming ear
    The mystic numbers fell!
As the ringing chime told the witching hour,
Leaf after leaf of the lovely flower
Oped its silken folds to the night—
And at the last peal, the prisoned sprite
Was borne on a fragrant sigh to earth,
That the flower gave forth in giving her birth.

Then, soft o'er my vision, a misty veil
Curtained the woods and the fairy dale—
And I seemed to be seated within a car
    Drawn by a purple dragon-fly,
Who upward and onward thro' space afar
    Wafted me over the star-gemm'd sky—
        While by my side,
        In fairy pride,
        The tiniest thing,
        On gossamer wing,
    Thro' the blue ether went hovering!

Then round our planet, with speed of thought,
Our magic journey was quickly wrought;
    So swift was our flight
    Thro' the dusky night,
  Leaving behind us a train of light—
    That to mortal eyes,
    That looked with surprise,
  'Twould seem that a meteor had cross'd the skies!
And then, on a silvery cloud,
  That floated above the mossy dell,
We sank again to the fairy haunt
  And alighted upon a grassy fell,
Where the cloud dissolved in a dewy mist,
As our wandering feet the green sward kissed.
    Soon the busy little crew,
    In flowery jackets, pink and blue—
    Gathered round from far and near,
    The wonders of the world to hear.
    Every bush and every twig
    With its swarming life was big;
    Hanging from their cobweb swings
    You might note the tiny things—
    Perched on clover blossoms round,
    Every bud was fairy crown'd,
    Open-mouthed and open-eyed—
    Yet the sprites seemed all tongue-tied;
Silently waiting until the bright Fay
Dropped her pearls of thought by the way—
Seedlings of price, and purchased with tears,
She sowed them but once in a hundred years!

The oracle spoke: " Oh, sister fays!
Our paths have been traced o'er pleasant ways—

M

We have lived in the streamlet, the fount, the grot,
In leafy chamber, or flowery cot;
Our palace columned with mighty trees—
(No sculptor's art ere rivaled these!)
And for carpets the downy moss has been given,
While our dome was the spangled arch of heaven!
Rejoice that from sorrow and pain and strife
We've been free to lead our happy life;
That as the lilies our lot has been—
We have toiled not, neither did we spin,
Yet garments of light we've been clothèd in!
I have flown from the shade of our woody glen
Far over the busy haunts of men—
I have looked deep down in the human heart,
And seen the same warring passions start—
The loves, the hatreds, the hopes, the fears
Have altered not in a hundred years;
Only the actors have passed away
And sleep 'neath the mould of the churchyard clay,
While a new race their places fill,
Grieving, rejoicing and toiling still!
Proud cities have risen where forests stood,
And rivers have swelled with human blood;
The loom and shuttle make music now
Where the herd's boy once led his thirsty cow;
The thundering engines shriek and scream
Where the jolly ploughman drove his team;
And naught is heard but the roar and rattle
Of vast machinery doing battle—
Of whizzing steam, with whoop and hollo—
And the jingling o'er all of the mighty dollar!
'Tis an iron age, and the heart of man
Is turning to iron as fast as it can!

When another century is flown,
And a glimpse of the world I again am shown,
I shall vainly search for some flowery glade
Which the iron heel doth not invade ;
With our woodland haunts we then must part,
And Nature must give place to Art.
     Rejoice while ye may,
     For your happy day
  Is passing away—passing away ;
    No room will there be
    For flower, bush or tree
  For fairies to dwell in, in harmony.
    The petrified lands,
    With their iron bands,
  Will harden and harden as art expands ;
And fairy life will no longer be
Even a tale for the nursery—
    For children then
    Will be miniature men,
And will snap their fingers with mocking glee
At the thought of such little folks as we !
Farewell ! I have warned you, rejoice while you may,
For your happy reign is passing away !"

I, starting, awoke, and still heard the lay—
" Passing away ! passing away !"

SONG OF THE PEN.

A PARODY.

WITH fingers bespattered with ink,
   And stumpy, nibbled pen,
Which flew with his thoughts o'er the paper white,
   And then was nibbled again ;
Surrounded with parchment and " proof,"
   In his literary den—
An editor sat in his easy-chair
   And sang this Song of the Pen.

" Scratch ! scratch ! scratch !
   From dawn till the midnight's chime—
Scratch ! scratch ! scratch !
   Till the day bursts forth in its prime.
And it's oh to drive a quill—
   To flourish and rave and rant ;
To please all tastes with a master's skill,
   And to think for those that can't !

" To wield a magic power,
   More potent than sword or spear—
That charms men's minds with its witchery,
   Or thrills them with its fear.
To breathe a sigh for the sad—
   A roundelay for the gay—
And a mournful dirge for the young and glad
   That have passed in their bloom away.

" Think ! think ! think !
   Tho' the fevered arteries beat ;

And think and write and think,
  Tho' weaving a winding-sheet!
Write! write! write!
  On the rolling years of time,
A sounding name for the trump of fame,
  To echo from clime to clime;

" Scratch! scratch! scratch!
  The paper—then the head,
For a stray idea that is loitering near
  But has to be coaxed ere led!
And it's oh to be a king!
  And an inky sceptre sway,
While lords of the earth and titled ones
  My mystic scratch obey.

" To scorch with the lightning's power,
  Or soothe with soft music's skill—
To light the blaze in rebellion's hour,
  Or the flickering flame to still;
To rule with a sovereign's might,
  ' The camp—the court—the grove—'
Make the sword to leap from its scabbard bright,
  Or attune the heart to love!

" To wave my feathery wand
  O'er the mighty realms of Thought—
And see from the tombs of the past the blooms
  Of forgotten ages brought!
And it's oh for a point of fire!
  To trace o'er heaven's blue scroll
In letters of flame, my well-earned fame
  To blazon from pole to pole!"

With a brow of " D——l-may-care,"
  And a face unlike other men,
The editor sat in his dusty chair
  And sang this Song of the Pen.
Scratch! scratch! scratch!
  There is truth in every word—
For nine out of ten will own that " the Pen
  Is mightier than the Sword!"

SADNESS.

A PARAPHRASE.

PALE spirit of sadness!
  Thou cypress-crown'd and dark-brow'd daughter,
    why
      Dost thou—
   Shadowing our gladness—
Shroud with thy gloomy wings our sunlit sky
    And brow?
   From what cold realm afar,
Linked to our earth by chains of tears and bands
    Of sighs—
  Cometh thy floating car?
Its shadow frightens hope, who waves her hands
    And flies.

   Whether joy smiles around,
Or calm content spreads stores of peace, of bliss,
    And love—
  Sudden there comes a sound,

Booming across our Memory's ocean—this,
Above
The ringing bells of mirth,
The soft, low murmurs of content, and love's
Sweet word—
Comes with the knell of earth,
To tell of parting joys—like mourning doves
'Tis heard.

It is thy voice, O pale
And sorrowing priestess of a shrine whose lamp
In glooms
Thou guardest!   ['Tis a frail
And feeble flame, fed with the mould and damp
Of tombs.]
Our spirit at the sound,
Turns with a shudder from bright, sunny hope,
And hears
Low dirges floating round—
Sees shadows, spectral forms round graves that mope
In tears.

'Tis mystery all, the spell
By which thou hold'st the mirror of our heart,
And by
A little breath can tell
How soon its polished brightness may depart;
A sigh
Can cloud its surface o'er,
Tho' breathed o'er beds of flowers—and thus in halls
Of mirth,
Thou wak'st a thought to soar
And bring us back the past, with all its palls
Of earth!

"MARAH."

SHUT out the sunshine—hide me where
   I cannot see it play:
Low tide has laid the wild rocks bare
   Within my heart to-day!

I would not give the poor return
   Of tears and weary sighs
To the bright lamps of love that burn
   So clear in Day's blue eyes.

For blue and kind her eyes look down
   On all—ay, e'en on me—
But bitter waters welling, drown
   The light I may not see.

And if I sing 'tis but the foam
   That surges o'er the waves
Of deeper feeling as they come
   From Memory's ocean-graves.

I know this tide of bitterness
   Will sweep from off my soul
The chafing waifs of wretchedness,
   That will not brook control.

And then, God's blessed sunshine in
   A golden flood may pour,
And May, with flowery promise, win
   My footsteps to her door;

And peeping from the roses, June
  Will send her humming bees
To sing me many a quaint old tune
  Beneath her spreading trees.

And summer's eve hang in the sky
  A silver-threaded moon—
And starry radiance shine on high
  At midnight's sparkling noon ;

And in my heart of hearts I'll sing
  With Nature, love and praise !
Forgetful of the waves that bring
  Me, sometimes, weary days.

And from my " Marah-fount" I'll stray
  To where the palm trees rise,
And rest me at the close of day
  Beneath peace-whispering skies :

So, shut the sunshine out, and let
  The bitter mood pass by—
The gilded bow of promise yet
  Will span my tearful sky !

BRAVERY.

WHAT is bravery?
  Is it to spurn the yoke, the galling chain
That rusts the eaglet's wings?
  To clip the bonds of slavery?

Ah ! may'st not be Ambition's voice that sings
    The thrilling strain
Which men obey and call it bravery?

    " Liberty or death !"
The hero cries—" we will be free or die !"
    He bursts the fetters, and
    He stands a demigod—the breath
Of acclamation yields to him command;
    He who would fly
From fate (not brave enough to live) to death !

    There's a bravery
Unknown to fame—the courage to endure !
    Hopeless, to live ; when death
    Would end the spirit's slavery.
It is not much to yield a little breath
    Our woes to cure—
But ah ! to face them is true bravery !

    Oh ! call that soul
A hero's which looks mildly on while fate
    Fills high his cup, and sees
    Her bitter drug the golden bowl ;
Then calmly drains the chalice to the lees,
    And with his mate,
Stern, cold Misfortune, smiling goes—Brave soul !

    That is bravery,
Which faces worlds in battling for the right,
    Nor dreads the frown of man—
    Yielding no bigot slavery

To public voice; but, conscience in the van
    And heaven in sight,
Goes firmly on—oh, that is bravery;

TO * * *

"Man is a creature—creatures are thoughts of God."—Mesmeric Revelations: E. A. POE.

IF so, oh what a sweet, quaint thought
    The All-pervading mind
Evolved, and gave it shape in thee;
As in the wild Anemone·
    Embodied is the wind!

The sunny phases of thy heart
    Gleam as a golden ray
Of spring-time, when the red lips part
    Of odor-breathing day,
And on the painted leaves we read
    The message of the May!

And when a mood of sadness vails
    The sunlight of thy song,
The breath of Araby exhales
Less dewy, soft, ambrosial gales
    Than steal its depths along—
Wrapping a silvery mist of tears
    Round paths that angels throng!

For angels are not myths, they wing
  Their viewless way to earth,
And by the hallow'd hearth-stone sing,
  Where such as thee have birth.
They come and ope the new-born eyes
Unto all secrets 'neath the skies—
Unseal the clasp of Nature's book
And bid the favored foundling " Look !"

And thus thy soul's a printed page
Of golden lessons, sweet yet sage ;
A wondrously fashioned thought
Divine, in human semblance, wrought
Of infinite and finite gleams,
Like angel-peopled mortal dreams—
The earth-embodiment we see
Of some seraphic fantasy !

AN EVANGEL.

A RIFTED leaf went quivering by
  Beneath the blue of heaven ;
A yellow leaf—and summer's sigh
  Passed with the breath of even.
It was a weird messenger
  Of darkness and decay—
A lonely, mournful traveler,
  To point the weary way
The sexton wind would surely pass
  To bury all the flowers,

And leave his spade upon the grass,
  His mattock in the bowers.

And still as deeper grew the e'en,
  A blood-red dome raised high
Its disk above the clouds between
  The earth and crimsoned sky ;
And purple floods of glory shone
  Down golden vistas bright,
Till darkness clasped a starry zone
  Around the waist of Night.
And then I knew September kept
  Within her burnished hall
An orgy wild, and never wept
  O'er summer in her pall.

I questioned then the sleepless Night
  Upon her ebon car
Chasing the fiery steeds of light,
  Led by the Vesper star—
And asked, " What meed is to be won
  Within the round of years,
That Summer's golden belt's undone
  When Autumn's finger sears—
And King October's crown of grain
  Falls 'neath old Winter's snows,
That yield when April's tender rain
  Is kissing up the rose ?"

And low and sweet a voice came out
  The starry sweep, and said—
" O man ! the wisdom do not doubt,
  That hath these changes made ;

From evil still evolving good—
  The wholesome lesson see,
And o'er it deeply, humbly brood,
  'Twas written all for thee!
E'en in the storm-cloud's angry din
  A golden page appears—
The prism-bow of promise in
  A baptism of tears!"

REMEMBRANCE.

A DOUBLE chain,
    Linking pleasure fast with pain,
        Remembrance is!
  A mystic web,
That holds of every tide the ebb
        That stranded bliss!

" Ah! I remember, I remember,
  'Twas a bleak and cheerless e'en
When the leaden-eyed December
  Hid the flowers with snowy screen,
That I listed words from Lulie,
  Sitting by the glowing hearth—
That, like the Fairy's words, were truly
  Pearls to me of untold worth.
But midsummer's morn now gleameth
  Cold as ice-belt in December—
Lulie's dead!"   The old man dreameth,
  And his dream is, " I remember!"

A subtle loom,
Weaving churchyard mould to bloom,
Remembrance is—
A soft ray thrown
From that far world beyond our own,
To lighten this!

I remember, I remember,
One pale rosebud bloomed for me ;
But a blast from chill November
Nipt it from the lonely tree ;
And I mourned the tender blossom
Rudely rifted from my love,
Till a chord within my bosom,
Thrilling to a strain above,
Told of buds transplanted, glowing
Far beyond earth's hot-house ember !
Now a thankful song is flowing
From my heart as I remember.

SPACE.

" BLUE mystery"—unfathomed Space !
Suns run their golden rounds,
And silver-girdled planets pace
Upon thy jeweled mounds.
O waveless sea ! whose silent tide
Drifts on, unceasingly—
How lost is pigmy man's poor pride
In thy immensity !

Where lead thy circling aisles?   Where end
   The paths the stars have trod
Since time began?   And where, where wend
   The chargers, silver shod,
Bounding along thy dizzy heights?
   How the soul yearns to cleave
Thy depths, and learn what hand ignites
   The bow the rain-drops weave?

What viewless helmsman steers each bark
   Thy shoreless ocean thro',
And pilots o'er the misty dark
   Of thy unsounded blue?
What mighty arm upholds each prow?
   What magnet o'er the tide
Since first creation dawned, as now,
   Has proved a steadfast guide?

Oh, on ye sweep, ye tireless hosts,
   Thro' the arched halls of night—
And vainly man, tho' loud his boasts,
   Grasps for your crowns of light!
Earth's golden mines beneath his feet
   Have spread their glittering store,
But space has caverns more complete,
   No dross dims their bright ore!

Oh for angelic feet to tread
   Above these mortal bars,
Holding by ether's azure thread
   Strung with the silver stars!
Oh never saint on rosary
   Could tell devouter prayer

Than, jewel-beads, I'd breathe o'er thee,
　A *Gloria Patri* there!

And when the mandate shall go forth
　That from flesh sets me free—
Shall my soul learn the secret birth
　Of worlds?—and space, of thee?
Oh I could rend these fleshy bars,
　If they shut from me these—
And up yon sparkling stair of stars
　Learn all its mysteries!

THE ARCTIC EXPLORERS.

" There must be some warm southern area over which this wind comes—some open water, it may be, that is drawing nearer to us, to minister after a time to our escape. But we must go alone. I have given up all hope of rescuing our little vessel. She has been a safeguard and home for us through many lengthened trials; but her time has come. She can never float above the waves again. How many of us are to be more fortunate?"—DR. KANE'S *Arctic Explorations.*

COLDLY the moon looks down
　On gnarled hills and measureless plains,
On glittering crags where the frost king reigns—
The giant king, whose death-like hand
Fetters alike the sea and land;
Who checks the waves in their maddest race,
And holds them fast in his cold embrace,
　Or curdles them with a frown!

His prototype above—
The ghostly moon, with her chill, pale ray.
Silvers his palace walls so gray—
Gleams o'er his icy-jeweled home,
While the lesser lamps of his azure dome,
The twinkling stars, from the roof on high,
Lend their scintillant brilliancy
    While they look their love.

What venturous foot shall dare
Break the awful silence that reigns around?
Thro' the glittering chambers there comes no sound
To tell of life ; the enchanter's spell
Is breathed o'er all, and it worketh well—
The moaning surf as it nears the shore
Closes white lips o'er the stifled roar,
    As it meets the deadening air.

The very tear-drops shed
By pitying angels for guilty man,
Since first his sin-stained race began—
Which come in the shape of gentlest showers,
And call into life spring's earliest flowers—
Are greeted here by the icy breath
Of the tyrant grim, and a snowy wreath
    They form around his head !

Oh brave must be the heart,
And strong the nerve and firm the will—
The conscience firmer, stronger still—
Of the mortal who, for his fellow-man,
Will come within reach of the giant's span ;

Who for good of his kind will sacrifice self—
Whose soul is not bartered for sordid pelf
  On mammon's crowded mart.

  Can such be found on earth?
Ah yes! Look abroad o'er this icy domain,
Where hummock and ridge and frozen plain
On every side around we view ;
What see we here? 'Tis a gallant crew,
That has stood the storm and braved the gale,
Until spirits, health and resources fail,
  And hope has no longer birth.

  With trusting hearts they sought
This frozen clime, for a purpose high
Shone o'er each brow—flashed from each eye ;
A god-like hope—that to them would be
The fame of solving the mystery,
Shut from man by the ponderous gate,
Upon whose portal the genie sate
  Whose touch had this barrier wrought.

  And also, with manly faith,
They sought for some clue to a brother's path,
Who, like them, had braved the giant's wrath—
Had ventured within the enchanted ring,
Heard the mermaid moan and the siren sing,
But had ne'er returned to repeat the lay
To the anxious ears that far away
  Awaited the faintest breath.

  And now the trusty band,
Their numbers lessened by Death's grim stealth,
With wornout frames and shattered health,

And scarcely enough of remaining life
To brave the last, the final strife—
But with souls still strong in earnest faith,
Look to a mightier Power than Death
　To guide to their native land !

　With thoughtful brows and grave,
They gather to take their last farewell
Of the noble bark that has borne them well
Thro' blinding storm and deafening gale,
O'er bergy seas, where stout hearts would quail—
Their ark of safety thro' trials great ;
But now dismantled and desolate,
　No more can she meet the wave.

　Forgive the starting tear,
That manly cheeks should ne'er blush to own—
Which the long, cold night of this frozen zone
Has failed to chill in its source, the heart !
And moistens the eye when the hour to part
Draws near—With their comrades' graves in view,
And thoughts of the home they are going to,
　And the cheerless home left here.

　No mockery of cheers,
No festal song sped the parting hour—
In silence all felt the Spirit's power !
A whispered prayer from each heart arose
For a safe deliverance from all their woes ;
And the bark is left for good or ill,
With " the same ice around her still"
　That first aroused their fears.

'Twere long to tell the tale
Of the thousand dangers of sea and land,
That around, above them, on every hand
Beset their path, as they sought escape
From icy floe and frozen cape—
Launched their frail boats, with bending forms,
And gave them " to the god of storms,
  The lightning and the gale !"

Heard was the prayer of faith !
The cherub sweet that aloft doth smile,
Watching the life of " poor Jack" the while
Guided the boats thro' tempests drear—
Thro' whirling pool and eddy near—
To the iron-bound steamer's friendly side,
Sent by their brother man, to guide
  From the icy realms of Death.

Let the welkin ring again !—
Ring with the pæans of triumph gay,
That attest the power of that nation's sway,
Whose hardy sons, with a purpose bold,
Have bearded the ice-king in his hold !—
Ring with the praise of the gallant crew,
And their brave commander, staunch and true—
  The noble Doctor Kane !

17 *

THE SIREN'S SONG

UNDER the sea! under the sea!
  Come hither, come hither, and dwell with me!
  Under the wave,
  In a pearly cave,
The sparkling foam thy brow shall lave,
The fever-heat from thy pulse shall fly
Under our crystal canopy—
  While the mossy bed
  For thy weary head
In a rose-tinted shell for thee shall be spread.
Leave to gross mortals the dull, sad earth,
Where sin and sorrow for aye have birth—
  Down in the deep
  Even tears that ye weep
Are turned into pearls 'neath the wave to sleep!

Come away, mariner, come away;
'Neath the green billows our sisters play—
  Their snowy feet
  On the bright sands beat,
Keeping time to the sound of their voices sweet;
O'er their fair bosoms flow locks of gold,
Curtains bright round thy brow to fold,
  When thy weary head,
  On such soft pillows laid,
Is lulled to repose 'neath the wavelet's shade.
An amber couch for thee we'll spread,
With coral branches overhead—

And the moaning shell
Shall softly tell
How 'neath the bright billow thou sleepest well!

Come, my brave! come, my brave!
Fear not to plunge in the dimpling wave—
We've a dolphin near
For thy charioteer,
Thy course to our Opal Halls to steer!
From yon blue heaven, a bashful star
Peeped at itself in our depths afar—
Ere the trembling ray
Could steal away
We caught it, to light thee on thy way!
Diamonds and rubies and sapphires blue,
And emeralds, which tell when a fond heart's true,
Shall mingle their blaze,
With rainbow rays,
To please and delight thy raptured gaze.

Dream no more! dream no more!
Hie thee away from the cold, cold shore,
To our coral cells,
Where love ever dwells—
No sorrows, no sighs, no sad farewells!
What is it the wave doth whisper o'er,
As with dewy lip it kisseth the shore?
Doth it not say—
" Come, come away!
Down in the deep there is peace alway!"
Then come, oh come! to the grottoes deep,
And be lulled to a long and dreamless sleep

> 'Neath a silvery wave
> In an ocean cave—
> Oh sweeter far than an earthly grave!

FRIENDSHIP'S EVENING STAR.

[Dedicated to Mrs. E. G. N.]

I 'D learned to scoff at Friendship's name,
  And call it empty air—
A will-o'-wisp, a churchyard flame,
  A meteoric glare—

A foam-flake on the sea of life—
  A bubble on the wave,
To vanish in the whirling strife
  Where wrecking billows rave ;

For I had launched on Friendship's stream
  Full many a trusting light—
Like those on Ganges' tide that gleam,
  Which Hindoo maids ignite

With trembling hands, and wreathe with flowers,
  And give unto the wave ;
But not one flame my feeble powers
  From currents deep could save.

My sun of favor set at night
  'Mid fierce clouds, lowering dark,

And Hope withdrew her beacon light
   From my dismantled bark.

The storm-fiends held me in their span
   Where wild waves maketh war—
No kindly hand to drowning man
   Would throw a friendly straw.

'Twas then upon my shrouded skies
   A mild beam from afar
Broke cheeringly—my weary eyes
   Hailed it, " Sweet Evening Star !"

It was the smile on thy dear face,
   O friend of darkest days !
The smile of kindness, that can chase
   All demons doubt may raise ;

The holy Power, that lays the ghost
   Of fell Despair to rest—
The leader of the starry host
   Of virtue—Heaven's best !

I hail thee, Hesper of my soul !
   Light sent from realms afar
To gild the waves that round me roll—
   My Friendship's Evening Star !

FAIRY BOUNTIFUL AND LITTLE GRUM-BLER.

(A fairy tale, written for my little Cousin Mary.)

"I HAVE no work and I'm tired of play—
What shall I do with myself to-day?
My doll has a broken arm, and looks
Quite shabby—I've no new story books;
My kitten is cross as cross can be,
And spreads her spiteful claws at me—
And Ponto opens and shuts his eyes
When I pat him, just as he does at the flies—
My birdie's head is under his wing,
A lump of sugar won't make him sing—
Mamma, too, tells me to go away,
She's busy, and I must run and play,
Oh dear! oh dear! what shall I do?
I wish that fairy tales were true,
And then I'd soon have a pumpkin round
Changed to a golden coach, and bound
Away, away, over dale and hill,
And not, with my head on this window-sill,
Sit wearily watching the clouds go by
Like white-wing'd doves o'er the far blue sky;
Or trying to count the motes that run
Like sands of gold in the rays of the sun—
But Ponto, Kitty and little me
Should coachman, footman and princess be;
And when I waved my jeweled hand
We'd off and away to Fairyland,

Where puffy beetles in vests of green
Would hold a leafy fan between
Us and the glaring light of the day—
And when I trod the flowery way,
Upon the grass and the bending twigs,
The lace-wing'd moths, in powdered wigs,
Like courtly pages, should me await—
And butterfly grooms ope the lily gate
Of the bright parterre of the Fairy Queen,
And point to her throne of emerald green,
Where stately dahlias, like courtiers old,
In purple velvet and cloth of gold,
Should nod reproof at the merry trees
Shaking with laughter, when the breeze
Tossed the Peony's fiery hair
Or stirred the bee from his buckwheat lair.
Oh, how I wish it were only so,
And I to those fairy realms could go !
But dear ! oh dear ! it can never be—"

She paused, for a sweet voice said, "Come with
    me !"

And looking up, she saw, with surprise,
A sprite, in a vest made of glow-worms' eyes—
A slender creature with veinèd wings
Like a spider's web of gossamer rings.
A blue inverted harebell made
For her dainty cheek a delicate shade,
And curling tendrils of cypress vine
Round her peach-blossom robe were taught to twine,
While a sparkling dew-drop, *solitaire*,
Gleamed like a star on her forehead fair—

And her eyes, so radiant yet mildly bright,
Shone with the calm of full moonlight.
She held a green witch-hazel wand
In the pearly clasp of her tiny hand,
And with it drew three mystic rings
Round the wondering child, when silken wings
From her shoulders sprang in graceful sweep ;
Then bidding her beside her keep,
Away, away, over hill and plain,
They sought the wealth of the Fay's domain.

"I am the Fairy Bountiful !"
Spake the sprite, " and my ears, not being dull,
To your sad, complaining tone gave heed ;
I've a story-book for you to read,
That, mayhap, you never have read before,
Tho' it was lettered and paged in days of yore ;
And so I have brought you along with me
To read it under the greenwood tree.
'Tis full of riddles and pictures too,
Which, tho' old, still ever seemeth new—
And every lesson will first be plain
To the heart, and then to the duller brain ;
Till at last the scales will fall from the eyes,
That will dance with joy in their glad surprise
To know that they see as fairies can
What is hidden from gross, worldly man.
So, look you first at this dusty page,
And I'll point out its maxim sage.
What do you see?"—
        "Only a roll
Like a withered leaf."
          "We will part the scroll

And look for the treasure that lies within :
Some silken threads that a worm can spin,
Finer than floss and white as the moon,
Wove by a grub in a dim cocoon,
But fit for the royal robe of a queen,
And in kings' palaces may be seen !
And thus saith the picture unto you :
'See what a little worm can do !
I do not fret like you silly things,
But I work in the dark till I find my wings :
Go, little child, and learn of me,
Spin your own cocoon if you would be free !'"

" Here is a riddle we'll pause and read,
On a gay illumined page indeed—
It seemeth a garden fill'd with flowers,
And some are bright as the noontide hours,
And spread their radiant hues to the day
With a flaunting air that seemeth to say,
Who so worthy of praise as they?
While others shrink from the glaring light,
And try to keep quite out of sight,
Drawing green veils o'er their faces meek
That are only lifted to those who seek.
But the gaudy ones are scentless, all,
Tulip, sun-flower, hollyhock tall.
Prince's feather and Guelder rose,
Breathe no balm when their lips unclose—
But under her green leaf the violet sweet
Keeps a choice perfume thy touch to greet ;
This homely little acacia holds
An Eastern odor within the folds
18

Of her yellow hair—and hyacinth true,
Has nectar hid in her cup of blue.
Canst tell what it means?" said the gentle fay.

" No ! read me the riddle, dear fairy, pray !"

" Well, learn of the flowers, my little friend,
That outside show will never lend
The secret spell by which modest worth
Throws fragrance round the lowliest hearth
And charms the proudest of the earth !

" But, come you are tired of riddles, I see—
I heard you a princess wish to be ;
I'll make you one if you promise to use
Aright your powers, and not abuse ;
And handmaids fair shall on you wait,
And porters sit at your royal gate—
But wield your sceptre well, I pray,
Or your palace walls shall fall in a day.
First, I will clothe you in robes of state—
Your crown shall be health, a diadem great !
Your throne, the golden seat of mind !
Your garments, all loyal thoughts and kind ;
Your maids of honor, sweet Patience, Love,
Faith, Hope and Charity, meek-faced dove !
And gentle Mercy, with pleading eyes
Uplifted to her home in the skies ;
And stern-brow'd Duty must have a place,
Tho' harsh the lines of her homely face—
Obey her mandates, tho' seeming hard ;
You'll find they'll bring their own reward.

Then for your guardsmen, good and wise,
Brave Honor, sacred in men's eyes,
And Truth, whose shaft unerring flies,
I'll give—and Justice, and Conscience, too,
And Will, shall be servitors to you—
And your wide domain the World!   Go forth,
And learn therein the wondrous worth
Of the fairy's gifts, O little girl !
Nor waste them—neither play the churl—
But like the little ant, that tills
The golden sand into countless hills,
And hordes her stores for a wintry day—
Oh work, my darling, while yet you may,
Nor spend thy time in repinings vain—
Thy precious time that ne'er comes again.
Life was not meant to be passed in play,
And youth is its golden harvest-day !
Awake ! awake ! you are sleeping still,
With your head on this sunny window-sill
Awake ! O dreamiest of little girls,
For Nature's the fairy that speaks these pearls !"

WOMEN VERSUS LADIES.

FLIRTING a fan or fanning a flirt,
   Lifting the light 'broidered flounce from the
      dirt—
Mincing and tittering, flippant and pert,
Fawning on wealth, but to poverty curt,
      Flits a thing we call " lady !"

Ready to faint when a cut finger bleeds,
But dead to Humanity's deep-wounding needs—
Weeping o'er Fiction's young widow in weeds,
While Reality's mourner too oft vainly pleads
    With the sensitive lady!

Fondling a poodle, or flattering a cur
Of the genus called "*homo*"—(no matter, to her,
If four legs or two legs the creatures transfer
To her presence—all puppies, 'tis well known, confer
    A delight to the lady!)

Leafing the Journal of Fashion, to see
What styles are the latest for breakfast or tea,
In order *au fait* of such mysteries to be,
Is as far as desire for knowledge takes the
    Not over-stock'd lady!

Married or single, the creature we know,
For nothing is like her that we see below!—
Painted and padded, on fantastic toe,
In the vortex of folly to ruin, just so
    Whirls many a lady.

Fathers and brothers and husbands assert—
And swear by the rents in a buttonless shirt!—
That a man should take care how he marries a flirt,
If he would not eat more than his "peck full" of dirt
    With a wife that's a lady!

But who are the honored in Scripture, for all
The blessings conferred upon man since his fall?

Who first at the sepulchre hasted to call,
That they might anoint Him, and saw that the pall
    Was removed?—Who but women?

Who let fall on His feet a meek, penitent tear,
And then wiped it off with her long flowing hair?
A woman!—And to whom did the Saviour appear
When he'd risen?   A woman!—Who, afar off, in fear,
    Looked on when he died?   Women!

For " ladies," if such things existed, did not
Engage in these duties so holy.   The lot
Was cast to dear woman, whose heart selfish blot
Never stains!   In Life's desert the verdure-clad spot
    Is the warm heart of woman!

The heart that with truthfulness throbs for all woe,
And sends from the soft eye sweet sympathy's flow—
The light gliding feet, ever ready to go
Where wretchedness murmurs its agonies low—
    These the dower of women!

As daughter, as sister, as mother, as wife,
In all blest relations that make up her life,
The pleader, the counselor, stayer of strife—
Tho' feeling, perhaps, the sharp edge of the knife
    She has turned—we find woman!

Man's friend from the cradle unto the dark grave—
(Alas! oft his drudge and his badly-used slave!)
Oh, strong in her weakness, how oft does she brave
What heroes would shrink from, her loved ones to save!
    Then most honored be woman!

18 *   O

CONSOLATION.

SHE is dead !
　　Waxen lily, perfume fled,
Lay her in her coffin bed.
　　Mother fair,
Anguished father kneeling there,
Cease your wild, distracted prayer !

　　Angel bands,
Golden harps within their hands,
Wait upon celestial strands,
　　Where the tide,
Rolling o'er Death's ocean wide,
Bears your loved one to their side.

　　" Come away !"
Called they to her, night and day—
" Earth is dark, no longer stay :
　　Here no night
Comes to dim our radiant light—
Here no sin, no sorrows blight.

　　" Come, come now,
While the seal upon thy brow
Radiates how pure art thou !
　　Happier home
Awaits thee 'neath His blessed dome
Who said to little children, ' Come !'"

　　She has passed
The barrier which we all at last
Must leap !　How blest the lot so cast !—

Thus to go,
Without a stain of sin or woe,
From the dark journey here below!

Let no gloom
Shroud her form—from flower-deck'd room
Bear her to no ponderous tomb:
'Neath the sod
Lay her softly—thanking God,
Who spares her from the chast'ning rod!

THE DYING YEAR.

IT matters not the purple pomp
   And gilded state around her spread:
Not all her crimson fires can warm
  The failing year—she's almost dead.
The golden-rod and aster pale
  Are listening 'neath the forest eaves
Unto the death-watch ticking faint
  And low amid the falling leaves.

The blue-eyed gentians meekly lift
  Their fringèd lids unto the sky,
Where mournfully the shortening days
  Are murmuring, She must die, must die!
For see, where flows her deep life-tide
  O'er down and mead, in scarlet dyes,
And all the silken azure stains
  That summer belted o'er the skies.

Fall-roses, children of the wood,
  Chrysanthemums, with yellow hair,
And starry eyes that upward turn
  Enamored of the golden air—
Gather around her couch to bear
  Her last sweet message to the dell,
Where the tall lichens tenderly
  Are waving her a long farewell !

Bring rosemary, the dark and green,
  And set about her place of rest ;
She wore the bridal-saffron once,
  And young moss rosebuds on her breast,
And heart's-ease, and forget-me-nots—
  And tho' hath come her hour of pain,
She still hath smiles with which to tell
  Your kind remembrance is not vain.

And now the long, dark night apace
  Comes with the white frost silently
To drape her glistening bier, and fold
  Her hands and close her glazing eye.
But by the ruined tower uprears
  The lowly wall-flower's humble cross,
To whisper soft, amid our woe,
  Of promised gain for every loss !

COLD BEAUTY.

SHE was fair
    As the calla's petals are
That on a southern cape expand—
    But as cold
As the icy hands that hold
    The tides upon the Arctic strand.

    She was all
Sculptor's vision could recall
    Of the Venus of his dreams;
    But as chill
As the marble goddess still
    Which 'neath his burning chisel gleams.

    And she shone
Brilliant as yon sparkling zone
    That girdles Heaven's mantle blue!
    But no star
Glittering in that belt afar,
    Was more distant still to you.

    Ah! her eye
Was like that magnet in the sky
    To which the earth still turns thro' gloom—
    Attractive still,
It still repels you, with a chill,
    Like some wan meteor o'er a tomb!

    Bloomed her cheek
With that glowing crimson streak
    Seen in heart of moss rosebud;

But it flowed
From a fount where warmth ne'er glow'd—
Like those creatures with cold blood,

Red and cold—
That on land or sea, we're told,
Can live—she seemed amphibian;
Joy could ne'er
Delight, nor throbbed her pulse to fear,
Nor could the wildest grief give pain.

Dead to all—
Her love's white ghost, in memory's hall,
Its silent rounds alone would take—
Now 'tis laid:
That haunting, pallid, restless shade
Sleeps with her, no more to wake!

THE ARCTIC NIGHT.

"At this point one of the guests turned to him and asked,
'What is the most awful thing that you ever experienced?' His
face took a devotionally deep expression, and he answered, 'The
silence of the Arctic night.'"—*Elder's Biography of Kane.*

DARKNESS!—Silence all unbroken
As if God had never spoken!
As if out of chaos, never
Order came, the bands to sever
Which held fast each golden wonder,
Bound the waters over, under,

Worlds and starry systems glorious,
Springing at His call victorious!
As if formless, void and soundless,
Were creation's limits boundless.
  Darkness—silence all unbroken
  As if God had never spoken!

Deep and stilly blackness brooding—
Wild thoughts on the soul intruding,
Of the Scandinavian Niflheim,
Situate beneath the cold beam
Of pale Cynosura's white gleam—
Or the Hades of the Druids,
Region chill of frozen fluids,
Thick-ribb'd ice and cheerless, dark strand,
Called " The Island of the Cold Land."

Ninety rounds the earth must travel
And the sun's gold skein unravel,
Ere the faintest twilight glimmer
Will upon the darkness shimmer:
Seven-score circles, the ecliptic
Under, make she—ere electric
Gleams from Sol will pierce the ice-belt,
Letting warmth be (or e'en life) felt:—
  Darkness—silence all unbroken
  As if God had never spoken!

Such a silence, as 'tis given
Out, that once there fell in heaven
For the space of half an hour!—
Silence—when the Mighty Power,

That the universe still graspeth
In its wondrous hold—unclaspeth
Hidden seeds within the bosom
To put forth their bud and blossom !
  Silence felt, tho' all unbroken,
  To the soul sent as a token
  As if God himself had spoken !

THE SEER.

A LONE, in my palace of dreams !
    An ashen moon in the skies,
Gold-ringed, like unwilling bride, with gleams
  Of tears in her beautiful eyes—
I sit, while the night-winds part
  The silvery mists o'er the lea,
And gaze with a vision from out my heart
  On what you may not see.

As he who stands in a well
  At noonday sees the stars,
I have sounded the depths of life, to tell
  The gold from the leaden bars ;
For not in the dazzling sun
  Of favor, that blinds us so,
Come starry truths out, one by one,
  Like the problems solved by woe.

'Tis a bitter price we pay
  For this power of second-sight,

That bears the rose from the cheek away
  And threads brown locks with white—
But 'tis much to lift the pall
  Of evil, and descry
The wholesome grains of good that all
  Its dark depths underlie.

And much, on Life's mystic wall,
  In characters of light,
To read the lines that ne'er appall
  When interpreted aright—
That the change which we call " death,"
  Is the bloom of a brighter hour,
Of which life is the bud, hanging on a breath,
  And death the full-blown flower !

So, over yon agate sky
  And watery moonbeams cold,
I look with Faith's unclouded eye
  At the city of purple and gold !
And tread the jasper floor
  'Neath the amethystine domes,
Where 'tis written over the crystal door,
  " For him that overcomes !"

MAGIC WINGS.

I 'VE a pair of tiny pinions,
  Where I hide them none may know—
But when they're plumed, the far dominions
  Of the Norland's realms of snow
  Gleam white beneath me, as I go,

19

Spanning seas in my magic flight,
Till by the ghastly, weird, wan light
Of the polar star, the mystery
I solve, of the lonely Arctic sea
Chanting the hymn of eternity!

I've a pair of shadowy pinions,
  You'd scarce notice should you see—
Sweeping the song-enshrined dominions
  Of classic-storied Italy!
  I hear the moan of the grieving sea
    Wailing a dirge for the master hands
    That set on Italia's golden strands
    The dial-plates to mark the hours
    Sacred to fame in those vocal bowers,
    And hallow'd e'en in these times of ours.

I've a pair of tireless pinions,
  Cleaving space and the shores that lie
Between us and the palm's dominions
  Under a golden Syrian sky,
  Oh, far away on these wings I fly
    To the land of the date and the citronelle;
    I see the desert's red veins swell,
    As the fiery breath of the fierce simoom
    Crimsons the firmament's brow of gloom,
    Like the molten seal that shall mark earth's doom!

I've a pair of restless pinions,
  Never weary of their flight,
Glittering up in the Day's dominions—
  Parting the heavy folds of night—
  And hovering over the fields of light

That Progress plants as she journeys on
Her upward path!   Oh never done
These sweeps of mine ; for I would pierce
The depths of the boundless Universe,
Could I its wondrous tale rehearse !

I've a pair of daring pinions,
  Drooped when human fowler's near—
But reaching to the stars' dominions
  When an angel's call I hear !
  Not a quiver or a thrill of fear
    Ruffles their plumage as they soar
    Over the din and the troubled roar
    Of Life's too treacherous sea, away
    Where rolling spheres grand anthems play
    On Nature's golden harp alway !

Oh shall I e'er have pearly pinions,
  Like a radiant, snow-white dove,
And furl them in the blest dominions
  Where never-dying, holy love
  Is eyried in the cot above ?
    Then no more flights from earth to air—
    No more swoops to dark despair—
    No false hopes or vain endeavor—
    No golden links for death to sever—
    But joy for ever and for ever !

THE CALL.

"COME! come! come!"
 Is the call from the far-off shore,
That the Poet hears from the starry dome
 Where angels watch evermore!
"Come! come! come!"—
 In cadences sweet and low,
Like strains of music once heard in home,
 That breathe of the "long-ago."
  "Come! come! come!"

"Come to our bowers of light!
 Come to the Morning land!
Dreary and dark is the baneful night
 That shrouds the world's cold strand.
'Tis suspicion and doubt and wrong
 That 'genders the earthly cloud—
But come to the bowers where faith is strong,
 And the sorrowing head's ne'er bowed.
  Come! come! come!

"Come, with the heart of youth—
 Come, with the pulse of fire—
Drink of the fount of immortal truth
 And quench each gross desire.
'Tis the glow of generous thought
 That, golden, lights our sky—
And love makes our music, melody wrought
 By the Spirit's harmony!
  Come! come! come!

" Come, with thoughts that breathe—
   Come, with words that burn—
And they'll spring into living flowers, to wreathe
   Thy Hope's now mouldering urn.
Lay down thy petty cares,
   Cast off thy sin's dark yoke,
And cool thy brow with ambrosial airs,
   Whose echoes grief never woke !
      Come ! come ! come !"

Alas ! that his wings are tied !
   Alas ! that he cannot soar
To the realms of light, on the other side
   Of Time's old wreck-strewn shore !
O child of the dreamy eye !
   Poet ! the earth is cold,
And heedeth not thy anguish-cry
   That swells o'er its brown old mould.

But not in vain that cry,
   For the angel-watchers hear,
And weave a new link out of every sigh,
   In the chain, where they've gemm'd each tear—
To draw thee upward, o'er clayey clod,
   To the Spirit's shining dome
In the golden city of our God,
   Where they ever are calling, " Come !"

19 *

THE MOMENTS.

TICK, tick—calling cheerily,
    Rosy moments in childhood gay,
Sunshine laden, dancing merrily,
    Speed on their joyous way!
Tick, tick—light on the summer wind,
Hopefully onward, casting no look behind,
    Time, without whip or spur,
    Proving no loiterer—
Speeds, while the morning of youth lights the way!

Tick, tick—louder in manhood's prime,
    Honor-crowned moments tell their proud tale—
Fame points the dial—Ambition rings the chime
    Thrillingly out on the gale!
Tick, tick—hark! how the roaring blast
Flaps its broad pinions, hurriedly sweeping past—
    Onward, with lightning wings,
    Wildly it rolls and sings,
Ringing its pæans o'er mountain and vale!

Tick, tick—faintly, in Life's decline,
    Wearied moments whispering flee—
Bat-like, flitting where Age and Want recline,
    Over a darkening sea.
Tick, tick.   List, while the sighing breeze,
Plaintively murmuring dirge-notes among the trees,
    Scatters the withered leaves,
    While a dun shroud it weaves,
Wailing a requiem so mournfully!

EVE-LAND.

L O ! the mystic fires are gleaming
    From the twilight's hall of amber,
Where the weary day is dreaming
    In her crimson western chamber;
And the panoramas olden
    Of the cloud-racks no more darkle,
For they're flooded with the golden
    Rain of sunset, all a-sparkle.

Up the shining ladder bending
    From the purple Eve-land brightly,
Go I with thought-angels, wending
    Starry labyrinths so lightly—
Onward, onward, pausing never,
    Past the ice-bands of Uranus
And the rings of Saturn, ever
    Singing glorious hosannas!

Cleaving all the sparkling stretches
    Of the stellar sea, that floweth
Its immeasurable reaches—
    And the whirling tide that goeth
With its planet waifs terrestrial
    Circling marches, that ne'er tire—
Till upon the strand celestial
    I can hear the seraph choir!

And I gaze upon the glory
    That blue ether veils from mortal—

Listen to the stars' sweet story
  At the arch of Heaven's portal.
(For the distant spheres all hymn it,
  Singing o'er the legend wondrous
Of a space that knows no limit
  Filled with worlds and systems pond'rous!)

See the golden pen Jehovah
  Sets on the blue scroll of heaven
And writes his mighty name all over
  The soft vellum page of Even!—
Hear the blessed benediction,
  " Peace on earth, to man good-will!"   Tho'
Mortals in each dereliction
  Flout the kindly message still so.

Linger till the fires grow paler,
  And the shining ladder's fading,
When earth calls me back—Old Jailer,
  All bright fancies rudely shading!—
Downward, downward, while the glory
  Of the sunset is departing,
Again to hearken Life's sad story,
  Where with sin and woe 'tis smarting.

DEATH IS THERE.

STEP lightly through the crowded street—
    See, floating on the dusty air
From yonder knocker, streaming crape
    Tells death is there!

It matters not if all unknown
  The shrouded form that coldly lies
With icy brow, white folded hands,
    And glassy eyes!

A brother Pilgrim has lain down
  His staff, to rest at close of day;
Step lightly—for your journey lies
    The selfsame way!

Though narrow walls alone divide
  His lifeless form from your bright eye,
They're wider than the gate which opes
    Eternity!

Though firm your pulse and springing step,
  Your boasted life hangs on a breath—
A paper screen is all that stands
    'Twixt you and death!

The nodding plume and tolling bell,
  The narrow house and couch of clay
Are thine inheritance—how soon
    May dawn the day

On which you'll claim them!   Think of this
  When passing by the coffined dead;
Death's next cold mandate may lay low
    Your stately head!

P

"IS THE EARTH GROWING COLDER?"

IS our planet growing colder?
  Asks the learn'd, the science-seeker;
Chills the heart when waxing older?
  Questions Nature's child, the meeker!
Has Time, with circling ages hoary,
  Grown cynical, and also bolder,
To breathe o'er worlds his withering story—
  That thus the earth seems growing colder?

Are yon bright-banner'd hosts above us
  Marching toward those chilly regions
Where we must go, and all who love us,
  To join the shrouded army's legions?
Must those deep fires that burn and sparkle
  On Heaven's blue heights grow dim and smoulder
A charred existence out—to darkle
  In a night still growing colder?

Ah! human love and generous feeling,
  Grief, fear and joy, their shadows blending,
Their lessons teach—still, still revealing
  The finite here must have an ending.
But there's a realm whose glow supernal
  In fadeless youth can ne'er grow older—
But warmer, brighter and eternal,
  The clime that never will be colder!

Between us and that land celestial
  There flows a viewless, icy river,

Through whose cold waves all things terrestrial
  Must onward to the great " For ever !"—
But o'er the curdling waters sparkling
  Comes light to gladden the beholder—
Warm light, o'erpowering Death's chill darkling—
  Then fear not as the earth grows colder !

THE DROP OF DEW.

YOU send to me a word of cheer,
  That falls as summer rain
Upon the fainting foliage near,
  To waken life again.
For tho' an olden thing to give
  It always seemeth new ;
A little thing—but flowerets live
  Upon a drop of dew.

And there's a flower which, Poet says,
  Blooms on a leafless bough ;
Such is my heart ; its cheerless days
  Are silver-petal'd through
By leaves of hope, that my poor lays
  May warm to life anew
Some trodden soul, to give God praise
  For the " wee drop o' dew !"

Your word of kindness bids me live—
  I'd thank, but not oppress you ;

For foes I have a " God forgive"—
    For you then, a " God bless you !"
You've bid the buds of feeling start
    Their tendrils forth anew ;
I'll treasure in my parchèd heart
    The kindly drop of dew.

AN EPISTLE

TO GEORGE D. PRENTICE.

WITHOUT a delay your kind letter,
    With welcome, came safely to hand—
And I think that I cannot do better
    Than answer its inquiries bland.
I am glad that you think I have genius,
    And with it can win a great name ;
But (this is no secret between us)
    A hard-trotting nag's that same Fame !

To begin, then : I'm just in my prime, sir,
    Of my age I shall leave you to guess—
That it's not a fit subject for rhyme, sir,
    Or reason, you'll surely confess.
My friends say (to please me), "I am pretty"—
    My looking-glass answers, " Nay, nay ;"
And tho' sometimes I strive to be witty,
    The effort still ends in a bray !

I am neither too short nor too tall, sir,
    But just the right height, if I reach

Your approval—and if not, I fall, sir,
    To low-water mark on Fame's beach.
My complexion was roses and lilies,
    But, alas! they have faded away,
And a full crop of young daffodillies
    Crowd out the sweet flowerets of May.

But down in my heart there are bowers
    All verdant with fragrance and bloom,
Like those bright-tinted groups of wild flowers
    That wreathe the cold sides of a tomb—
And when with the world I grow weary
    I enter this garden of mine,
To forget the old wilderness dreary
    Where " green spots" but sparingly shine.

And here you may enter with me, sir,
    And view what my fancy has wrought;
No sleepless old dragon you'll see, sir,
    To guard the gold apples of thought.
I know you're a jovial, good fellow,
    When the right hand of friendship you send—
Ah! the fruit of my Muse will grow mellow
    In the sunshine you freely extend.

New Orleans, *August* 27, 1859.

MOONLIGHT.

THE moonlight sleeps soft on the tide,
    The ripples kiss lightly the shore,
As, silver-linked, swiftly they glide
    The gold-sanded, pebbly beach o'er;

There's an odorous breath of the night
  Playing soft with the curls on my brow,
Then fanning the almond blows white
  Where they droop from their silvery bough.

Abroad is the spirit of dreams,
  Floating drowsy thro' heaven's soft hue ;
But merry thoughts twinkle in gleams
  From yon star-watchers in the deep blue :
'Tis the hour for their revels, I ween,
  And they twine in a mazy dance now,
Circling round their great centre of sheen,
  With a diamond crown clasping each brow.

Where the white-columned moonbeams uphold
  The azure-tipp'd roof of the sky,
The wandering zephyr so bold
  Is tuning his wild minstrelsy !
And fountains celestial are playing,
  In pearly drops trickling thro'
Their mist-fleecy basins, and straying
  To earth in a glittering dew.

O midnight ! thy moon-lighted glory
  More dear is than day's ruddy glare ;
 Tis a gentle and strangely sweet story,
  Thou breath'st thro' thy silver-hued air—
It whispers of peace ! Like life's splendor
  Paling out where the white tombstones gleam,
To tell us that death's message tender
  Has tempered the fire of the beam,

Which shines with a softened reflection
  From good deeds done in sunshine of life,

And with mildly moon-lighted projection
  Looks calm from the grave's conquer'd strife !
When the midnight of death o'er us darkling
  Is shrouding our spirit in gloom,
May remembrance of virtue come sparkling
  To gild with its moonlight the tomb !

SUMMER'S DEAD !

SUMMER'S dead !—
      Luna, with her silver sickle,
In the " moon of fallen leaves,"
'Mong the yellow blades of sunset
  Stood like Ruth amid the sheaves,
And saw her die ; the sand was falling
  Grain by grain, until the night
Showed empty glass—and blue-eyed Summer
  Closed her dewy orbs of light—
      Summer's dead !

      Summer's dead !
She who bore her blushing honors
  From her mother May's sweet side,
With fragrant dower of buds and blossoms
  To be the young June's rosy bride—
Has lived her hours of love and gladness,
  Has basked in Pleasure's fleeting ray,
And, like all lovely things, must perish,
  Fade, for ever fade away—
      Summer's dead !

Summer's dead !
There is a sighing in the woodlands,
　　Where the mourning wind now goes
Strewing blood-stained leaves, in anguish,
　　As he vainly breathes his woes ;
But no fragrancy replying
　　Comes from flowers that drooping lie
Where their gentle mate reposes
　　With cold lip and rayless eye—
　　　　Summer's dead !

Summer's dead !
Ay, Summer's dead, and soon forgotten—
　　Soon her rival's yellow eye
And flaming robe of crimson, flashing,
　　Will all fainter charms outvie.
Glowing Autumn, richly laden
　　With a crown of golden grain,
And singing harvest-songs, will banish
　　All of sorrow from the strain—
　　　　Summer's dead !

Summer's dead !
Yes, " dead," we cry, when bright things leave us—
　　" Dead !"—and drop an anguish tear ;
But the next gleam meteoric,
　　Lures us from the gloomy bier—
And our sorrow's evanescent
　　As the fickle wind's, which grieves
A while o'er Summer's faded roses,
　　Sighing 'mong the withered leaves,
　　　　Summer's dead !

" Summer's dead !"—
Then, when the cornstalk's yellow tassel
　Gleams in Autumn's tresses brown,
Flirting wind will lift the bauble—
　All its short-lived grief is flown !
Thus, with us ; and well it is so :
　Since our life's a summer's day,
Let's hail the sunshine or the shower,
　And try to smile the while we say,
　　" Summer's dead."

NELLIE.

HER soul is very beautiful—
　　I know not that her face
Is limned in perfect symmetry
　Of elegance and grace ;
She may sadly lack perfection
　To cold, artistic eyes—
But with me it is the gem,
　Not the setting, that I prize !

For the eyes, to me, are lovely
　That look back love to mine ;
The cheeks are very beautiful
　That modesty enshrine ;
The lips are saintly portals
　That only ope to truth—
And the heart that's filled with sunshine
　Makes perpetual youth !

Such my Nellie's heart : you'd know her
 If you only heard her laugh ;
Such my Nellie is : unto her
 A golden bowl I quaff!
If to spirit form is given
 In that land than earth more fair,
She'll be beautiful in heaven,
 For souls but enter there !

AN INVOCATION.

SPEAK to me, speak, O Spirit Voice !
 Moon of my night, arise !
Roll back the pall that shadows all
 The splendor of the skies !
The golden waves of sunset flash
 No glory o'er my brow—
I only hear the angry clash
 Of battle ringing now.

For, fiery Mars, the red-orb'd star,
 Sits in my house of life,
And bids the ruthless demon, War,
 Unsheath his glittering knife :—
No breathings soft of beauty steal
 My spirit's rose-leaves o'er,
My palsied senses only feel
 Blasts from the Stygian shore.

Ah ! once the blue-eyed June could call
 My soul from out her cell,

Where, nun-like, wrapped in serge and pall
  She loves to brood too well;
But now young Summer climbs the hill
  To kiss the morning's eyes,
And finds me torpid—not a thrill
  Responds to her "Arise!"

Ye gentle sprites that love the dales
  And banks where violets blow,
And thymy knolls and wooded vales,
  Where are ye wandering now?
No more ye float on moonbeams white
  Unto my casement lone,
'Mid softest visions of the night—
  Oh where, where have ye flown?

Come back—the thorn is on my brow,
  The veil upon my sight—
Oh lay the troubled spirit low,
  And let me dream to-night!
Come from the fragrant cowslip mead
  And sing the witching lay
I heard when June was June indeed,
  And life a summer day.

Lead me by hedgerows smooth and trim,
  And past the tuneful brook,
Until my heart has caught the hymn
  Paged on great Nature's book!
I weary of this daily strife
  Of bodily control—
Oh charm away the earth of life
  And let me see my soul!

Like the leashed hound that chafes the bight,
  My spirit feels the thrall
That wraps it in a dreamless night,
  Whose stars are hidden all.
Roll back, roll back, O sombre shade,
  And let the light shine thro';
For it my soul doth faint and fade
  As pines the flower for dew!

June 5, 1861.

WEARINESS.

WOULD I'd been born a country lass,
  In days gone by, when hearts were simple;
When honest name was friendly pass,
  And rustic jest woke rosy dimple.
The world, they say, has wiser grown,
  But knowledge oft brings melancholy—
Where ignorance is bliss we own
  Wisdom to seek is height of folly!

The fewer wants, the fewer woes—
  The bumpkin in a state of nature
Can never feel the feverish throes
  That agitate our legislature!
The rosy milkmaid, pail in hand,
  And blest with health—life's richest treasure—
The weariness can't understand
  That overcomes the child of pleasure.

Ah! happiness is what we want!
  (A mind contented dwells in bliss!)

The great round world's allurement can't,
  With all its boasts, ensure us this.
For happiness is Nature's child,
  And dwells with her in homely guise ;
She flies from crowds and tumults wild,
  And shuns the gaze of worldlings' eyes.

The petty strivings, gnawing cares,
  To seem to others what we are not,
But bring us wrinkles and gray hairs—
  And thus we toil for those that care not !
Oh, far from traffic, noise and strife,
  I'd flee away among the roses
That bloom to bless the happier life
  That in their quiet shade reposes.

"HOW LONG, O LORD?"

[Psalm xiii.]

HOW long, O Lord of Hosts !
  Before thy face I'll see?
Wilt thou thy smiles for ever hide
  Nor heed mine agony?
The words of counsel wise,
  My soul would whisper o'er,
Are faintly heard, when through my heart
  Such floods of sorrow pour.
How long shall cruel foes essay
To strew with thorns my weary way?

For foes I have a " God forgive"—
  For you then, a " God bless you !"
You've bid the buds of feeling start
  Their tendrils forth anew ;
I'll treasure in my parchèd heart
  The kindly drop of dew.

AN EPISTLE

TO GEORGE D. PRENTICE.

WITHOUT a delay your kind letter,
  With welcome, came safely to hand—
And I think that I cannot do better
  Than answer its inquiries bland.
I am glad that you think I have genius,
  And with it can win a great name ;
But (this is no secret between us)
  A hard-trotting nag's that same Fame !

To begin, then : I'm just in my prime, sir,
  Of my age I shall leave you to guess—
That it's not a fit subject for rhyme, sir,
  Or reason, you'll surely confess.
My friends say (to please me), "I am pretty"—
  My looking-glass answers, " Nay, nay ;"
And tho' sometimes I strive to be witty,
  The effort still ends in a bray !

I am neither too short nor too tall, sir,
  But just the right height, if I reach

Your approval—and if not, I fall, sir,
  To low-water mark on Fame's beach.
My complexion was roses and lilies,
  But, alas! they have faded away,
And a full crop of young daffodillies
  Crowd out the sweet flowerets of May.

But down in my heart there are bowers
  All verdant with fragrance and bloom,
Like those bright-tinted groups of wild flowers
  That wreathe the cold sides of a tomb—
And when with the world I grow weary
  I enter this garden of mine,
To forget the old wilderness dreary
  Where "green spots" but sparingly shine.

And here you may enter with me, sir,
  And view what my fancy has wrought;
No sleepless old dragon you'll see, sir,
  To guard the gold apples of thought.
I know you're a jovial, good fellow,
  When the right hand of friendship you send—
Ah! the fruit of my Muse will grow mellow
  In the sunshine you freely extend.

New Orleans, *August* 27, 1859.

MOONLIGHT.

THE moonlight sleeps soft on the tide,
    The ripples kiss lightly the shore,
As, silver-linked, swiftly they glide
    The gold-sanded, pebbly beach o'er;

20

'Tis a flower which, brushed, can never
　　Bloom as erst it did before thee!

Ah! then linger, gentle maiden,
　　Yet a while in bowers of childhood—
For, full soon thou wilt, care-laden,
　　Long to roam again its wildwood!—
Sing with birds and blush with flowers,
　　Coax gay butterflies unto thee—
Laugh away the rosy hours,
　　There's time enough for grief to woo thee.

THE MANIAC'S SONG.

MAD! mad!
　　When the thunder calls to the deep, I'm
glad!
When the storm's black bark unfurls its sail,
And Death rides out on the fearful gale,
　　I am glad! glad!

Sad! sad!
　'Twas to see my Willie drown! Too bad,
That the glittering threads of his golden hair
Should hold him fast in the Siren's lair—
　　Too bad! too bad!

Mad! mad!
They call me mad, when I am but glad,

As I shout his ever blessed name
To the lightning's telegraphic flame,
    I am glad! glad!

    Sad! sad!
No answering message comes back.   Too bad!
The lightning's chain in the surging seas
Breaks near the Hall of the Nereides—
    Too bad! too bad!

    Mad! mad!
There's a lurid light in the cloud!   I'm glad!
Yon sea of fog the stars will drown,
I saw the moon's white face go down,
    I am glad! glad!

    Sad! sad!
I shall be if no shipwreck's near; too bad
If there goes not a goodly company
To meet him under the stormy sea—
    Too bad! too bad!

    Mad! mad!
Hurrah! there's a crash!   I'm glad! I'm glad!
The wind's sharp plough turns up the deep,
And furrows the beds where the sea-gods sleep,
    I am glad! glad!

    Sad! sad!
Bound down like a felon!   Too bad! too bad
That I can't escape this torturing chain,
And join my love in the foaming main—
    Too bad! too bad!

Mad ! mad !
When I hear the whirlwind roar I am glad ;
For I hope that the Storm-king will hear my cry,
And clip these cords as he thunders by—
I am glad ! glad !

Sad ! sad !
His chariot wheels drown my voice—too bad !
I must wait for the tardy jailer, Death,
To close the gates on my trembling breath—
Too bad ! too bad !

ANNABEL MAY.

WHERE flag-lilies dip in the tide pearly chalices,
And blue herons skim to their wide crystal
palaces—
Where winds, flirting gayly, kiss the wave, flout the
willow
(With a crimson coral branch in a cave for a pillow),
And waters murmur sweetly thro' the long summer
day,
While o'er her flits the wild sea-mew, sleeps Annabel
May.

The old, old story—she loved too well, but not wisely,
And woman's shame or glory will her love tell concisely.
She was beautiful, alas ! and frail—oh dangerously
beautiful !
And easily, at Love's prevail, she left the dutiful.

But in that sleep that knows no waking—ah! well-a-
    day!
Where silver-crested waves are breaking lies Annabel
    May!

She wandered when the breeze mowed the willow's
    drooping tresses,
And saw the wild-winds toss the waves—(the billow's
    rough caresses!)
Watching for the sail to come, the sail that bore away
Her heart and duty from her home with him who led
    astray.
He came not, he came not, but the tide seemed to say,
" My blue arms grief and shame will hide—come, An-
    nabel May!"

Sing your gentlest lullaby, waves, in your play—
Billows, ripple softly by where she doth lay;
Siren, tune your sweetest strain—Halcyones, sweep
Your peaceful wings across the main, lest tempests
    rouse the deep!
Love for her spread angry skies—life a stormy day—
But now in death she calmly lies—rest, Annabel May!

LIFE-TIDES.

THINE, murmuring o'er golden sands
    Kissed by the sunrise,
Linked wavelets on amber strands
    Glinting 'neath bright skies—

Mine, swelling o'er rough rocks,
   Jaggèd and broken,
To scatter but foam-flocks
   As tearful token.

Thine, fanned by the zephyr sweet
   From his soft wooing
Where blue-eyed violets meet,
   And doves are cooing—
Mine, tossed by the tempest's might,
   Cleft by the storm-flash,
On the bleak shore by night
   Where breakers wild dash!

Thine, moulding the sand to each
   Whim of thy pleasure,
For the next wave to teach
   Fleetness of treasure!—
Mine, laving the gleaming edge
   Of some harsh experience,
To soften the barren ledge
   With Hope's effervescence!

Thine, singing blissful songs,
   Which the beach-fairy
In sweet, silver sound prolongs,
   Sportive and airy—
Mine, o'er the shattered wrecks
   On the strand lying,
Chants a wild dirge, and becks
   Phantoms still flying!

Both, hastening onward, still,
   Singing or surging,

That ocean vast to fill
To which is converging
Each human tide that strives,
Ebbing or flowing,
To round up our mortal lives
For heavenly growing!

CLOUDS.

LIKE to ships with graceful motion,
White sails swelling on the breeze,
O'er light ether's far-spread ocean
Summer clouds cleave peaceful seas.
Airy billows gently ripple
To the fragrant breath of June,
Piling foam-fleck'd crestings triple
On the blue tide's flooded noon,
While the pearly-hued armada
Parts the golden waves of day,
Leaving in its wake no shadow
Save a feathery, snowy spray,
Evanishing—and but remembered
As the gleam of waving wings
We catch, when pure souls are dismembered
Of dull matter's leaden strings.

Like to fiery chargers rushing
To the battle's revel red—
While the wind's shrill bugle's gushing,
Calling all "to arms!" o'erhead,

And the rocket-lightning's sending
  Its blue signal o'er the plain—
Storm-clouds (as war-steed, distending
  Nostril, shakes his streaming mane),
Swell their blacken'd fronts and clamor,
  Waving shaggy locks on high,
In their Jove-forged, thunder armor,
  Shrieking, neighing o'er the sky.
But, from warrings elemental
  Clearer atmospheres evolve—
So, self-conflict, if repental,
  Radiates a pure resolve !

Like to rose-leaves lightly lying
  On a blue lake's tranquil breast,
Cloudlets, when the day is dying,
  Veil the azure of the West!
Like, again, to sable banners
  Streaming o'er the realms of death—
When tempests shout their wild hosannas
  Wave cloud-pennons at the breath.
Yet each cloud has silver lining
  Tho' on us its dark side lowers—
We know the sun is brightly shining
  When deepest shadows mark the hours.
Vain were Pleasure's joyous being
  Did not pain and grief oft meet—
Thus earth's woes are for our seeing
  Heavenly blessings more complete !

WATCHING AND WAITING.

WAITING under the shadow
    Of the elm at the foot of the hill,
Gazing over the meadow,
    And along the path by the mill—
Watching and waiting for somebody,
    Somebody's waiting still;
Dreaming and longing for somebody,
    'Neath the elm at the foot of the hill.

Waiting under the star-beam,
    On the beach, where the emerald sea
Dots each wave with a white gleam,
    Like crocus buds on the lea—
Watching and waiting is somebody
    For a glimpse of the distant sail—
Hearing the death-tick for somebody
    In every sigh of the gale !

Waiting in the embrasure
    Of a darkly-curtained room,
To catch the first glimpse of azure
    Eyes, and to press the peachy bloom
Of a first-born's lips, is somebody,
    Watching and waiting still—
As parts Life's curtain for somebody,
    Disclosing good or ill.

Watching still, while the night rolls
    On its ebon wheels away

Till its knell the sexton lark tolls
  From the gilded spire of day—
Watching and waiting is somebody,
  As speeds the parting breath
That solves the problem to somebody
  Of the mystery called death !

Watching and waiting ever
  From life's dawn till its close,
For fancied good that never
  Comes—for a sweet and thornless rose,
Watching and waiting is somebody—
  Nor heeds the waning light
That closes for ever on somebody
  As falls each sombre night.

Watch ! O son of the earth-land !
  For you know not when the hour
Your bark will touch the cold strand
  Where the grave's chill glaciers lower.
Watch ! for the tide for somebody
  Is setting now to that shore—
Bearing still onward somebody
  For ever, evermore !

"I."

WHAT individuality,
  What embodiment of self,
That little personal pronoun has
  Above the mounds of pelf !

'Tis the stamp of man's divinity,
   The seal of higher life,
Which the great Life-giver gave, when He
   Ordained this earthly strife.

'Tis the pledge that ye shall know me by,
   When, free from flesh and sense,
My soul shall plume her pinions for
   A sphere above pretence ;
When naked, as on earth I came,
   That soul shall be re-born,
And every secret spring revealed
   That gave forth love or scorn.

Ye'll know me then, my friends, my foes,
   Ye'll know me as I am—
How much of right to bless in me,
   How much of wrong to damn !—
Ye'll know what immolation
   Of sordid self I've nailed
Upon the cross—what promptings
   Of earth-life I've impaled.

And whether in a shining garb
   Of white I shall be robed—
Or serge and sackcloth bind the wounds
   That man has deeply probed—
What matter? If for weal or woe,
   As lion or as lamb,
Earth sheltered me—in heaven ye'll know,
   Ay, know me as I am !

TO THEE.

TO Thee, my God! to thee
  The incense of a grateful heart shall rise—
A heart by sorrow purified;
Accept, O Lord! the humble sacrifice.

Thro' lowering tempests drear
My fainting soul groped struggling for the light,
  When lo! o'er storm and darkness broke,
Spanning the clouds, thy bow of promise bright!

Hail! holy emblem, hail!
No cloud so dark but faith can see thy rays!
  Look up, O grief-encompassed soul!
To heaven for comfort thro' earth's darkest days!

Ask, and ye shall receive—
Knock, and the door of heaven shall open stand!—
  A refuge from the wild storm sent
To draw thee nearer to the Better Land!

The World's alluring voice
Too loudly sings when Fortune's sunlight pours;
  It drowns the gentle angel tones
That plead for entrance at the heart's closed doors—

But when the sky's o'ercast—
When whirlwinds scatter friends and fortune far,

And night and darkness gather round,
Nor shines to cheer us one inspiring star;

Trembling and sore amazed,
We view the gathering gloom, and wildly cry
    For help—when soft the angel stands
On our heart's threshold, pointing to the sky!

Bend, bend, rebellious soul!
Nor spurn the proffered aid from God's right hand;
    Twill gently lead thee thro' the gloom
Safe to the bright, the far-off Promised Land!

PERFECTION.

"MARK the perfect man!"—says the Book
        Of books.   Alas! but where
Shall he be found?   In vain we look
    On earth,—he is not there!
Some God-like ones do walk this sphere,
    Less human than divine;
But not in mortal shape, I fear,
    Can full perfection shine.

"In God's own image fashioned," man
    Was moulded, still, of clay;
The spirit struggles in the span
    Of flesh, and owns its sway;
And soul and sense unequal war
    Have ever waged, and still

Must on Life's lyre discordant jar
  While swayed by finite will.

The brightest things our mortal eyes
  Are dazzled with, are not
Without their blemishes—the skies
  Grow dim, and many a spot
Yon monarch of light's golden realms
  Has on his glittering throne—
The diamond, first of radiant gems,
  Has flaws within its zone.

And lordly man, the last and best
  Of all God's works, will show
His weakness when there comes the test
  Of joy, or pain, or woe.
Temptation, too, in varied guise,
  Will spread her devious snares,
Until his charmed and dazzled eyes
  Know not the wheat from tares!

But spurn thou not, for this, one worm
  That crawls the earth with thee—
For in each shell there lies a germ
  That, in maturity,
Shall put forth hidden wings, to soar
  Beyond the reach of clay,
When chrysalis of life no more
  Shall clog the spirit's way!

Perfection's not a flower of earth,
  Although the blossom here
May bud—its fuller, purer birth
  Is in another sphere ;

And every seed of good, the soul
  In ripening has given,
Shall, when sin's bands no more control,
  Perfected, bloom in heaven.

DISTRUST.

ONCE she raised the veil from her heart
    That its depths my eye could trace—
It was as tho' I had found a rose
  Lifting its pleasant face
From a cleft in the rock—or a sunbeam caught
  Asleep in a shady place.

She was not always as you see,
  'With a shadow in her eyes,
Like a flaw in the diamond's crystal light
  To dim their sweet surprise ;
And a voice with a tone of unshed tears,
  Like Autumn's hopeless sighs.

But the silver cord was loosed that bound
  Her faith in the good and true,
And one by one fell the gems to earth
  She had garnered when life was new—
And memory's tablets are inky black
  That in rose-color she drew.

So, she wraps herself in a mantle dusk
  With nettles overblown,

22

To purge her heart of the ready faith
    That she in her kind has shown—
Alas! for the shattered golden bowl,
    For the trust of youth o'erthrown!

ADELA.

COME away, come away,
    Weep not o'er the senseless clay,
Tho' it held our Adela!

Clasp within the waxen hold
Of her pearl-tinted fingers cold,
One pale rose-bud—there! now fold

The fleecy muslin, virgin white
As is her spotless soul, alight
With purity's clear crystallite.

Twine her amber-threaded hair,
Like a golden glory, where
The marble of her forehead fair

Gleams, blue-veined, and penciled brown
Over white lids folded down,
Like snow-banks which the violets drown.

Make her couch where moonlight weaves
Silver network thro' the leaves
That form the wood-lark's emerald eaves.

Lay her where the clash of day,
Ringing peals in life's affray,
Will not reach her on her way—

She now treads the crystal floor,
Enters at the jasper door
Where the shining seraphs soar!

Thro' her sapphire eyes her soul
Went upward—where grand anthems roll,
And sin and death have no control.

Seal the casket that contained
Our gem, while earth its radiance claimed—
Without the stamp of woe:—unstained,

The precious jewel glitters now
Etherealized, where angels bow
Before His ever luminous brow!

God gave—and now he takes away—
As falls our night, bright breaks her day,
A heavenly dawn for Adela!

AUTUMN AND AGE.

THE summer days are fading,
  Passing away—
And Autumn's brown locks shading
  Her eyes' soft gray,

Droop, mingling with the tresses
  Of golden sheen,
With which the hazel dresses
  Its bough's bright green.

The maple leaf is browning
  In the deep dell,
Where yellow king-cups, crowning
  The grassy fell,
Lifted their golden chalice
  In merry May—
Which the fairies crushed in malice—
  Ah! well-a-day!

The spring with budding graces
  Is fair to see,
And summer's sunny places
  Gleam smilingly;
But Autumn's mellow glory,
  And falling leaf,
Telleth Life's simple story
  In lesson brief!

Youth in green valleys sporting,
  Is charmed with toys—
Manhood, ambition courting,
  Life's noon employs—
But softer the light shineth
  On Age's brow,
For ripened thought there twineth
  Its garlands now.

What tho' the faded tresses
  Have lost their brown—

Where every white hair presses,
  Wisdom hath grown!
'Tis like the crowning splendor—
  Soft Autumn's glow—
Painting with hue so tender
  The leaf laid low!

———

"THE DE'IL IS NAE SA BLACK AS HE IS PAINTED."

OH many sing of hopeless love,
  And broken hearts and blighted fancies;
And others string their lyres, to prove
  That glory lies where danger prances.
But, broken heart or wounded heel
  Will ne'er by me be sung or sainted—
My humble task's to prove the De'il
  Is not so black as he is painted!

A sooty subject, I will own,
  When hearts and darts and moonbeams quiver,
But all have fancies of their own—
  Some's from the brain and some the liver!
I know not whence the thought doth steal,
  It may be that my liver's tainted—
But this I'm sure of, that the De'il
  Is not so black as he is painted.

His name is bad—and that, you know,
  Is worse than hanging high as Haman!

The Quaker's dog proved it was so,
　　When all flew out if he but came in.
He might as well be mad, as feel
　　That people thought that he was tainted ;
But he, like many a luckless de'il,
　　Was not so black as he was painted.

Then let us pause, ere with the crowd
　　We lend our voices in declaiming
'Gainst those we know not, tho' aloud
　　Old Rumor's trump their deeds are blaming ;
Tho' sighs of holy horror steal
　　From lips of sinners newly sainted,
Remember always that the De'il
　　Is nae so black as he is painted.

WE TWO.

GO to !—I would not have you smile :
　　Your smile hath lost its light ;
It glares like charnel lamp, the while,
　　O'er dead men's bones at night.
Too well I've proved how false the gleam,
　　That it should still deceive me ;
Ah well ! we all must sometimes dream—
　　I've wakened now, believe me.

Pass on !—I would not have you speak ;
　　There's many a word unspoken

Printed upon the changing cheek
  As a deep burning token
Of what the lips could never frame,
  Or, framing, still dissemble ;—
I would not have you breathe my name—
  Then wherefore should you tremble?

We know the tide of time has set
  Its counter-currents near us:
What boots it, that a tricksy jet
  Should to each other bear us?
The rushing floods must onward flee—
  Take *your* course to the main;
For the wild waves for you and me
  Will never meet again.

AT EVENTIDE.

THRO' the purple vistas at eventide,
  When the golden waves of day
Are ebbing low, from their noon-flood pride,
  On the twilight strand away—
Up, on a rosy beam of thought,
  To my cloudland shore I fly,
Where never a tear from earth is brought
  But a gem is wrought on high !
And beds of pearl in that stellar sea
  I find, where my tears I hide—
And the crystal drops are bared to me
      At eventide.

'Tis a glowing strand whose fires ignite
  While the earth beneath grows gray—
A blending of sunshine and star-beams bright,
  From the mingling night and day;
And the farther along the golden shore
  My fluttering pinions play,
More faintly I hear the sullen roar
  Of Life's discordant fray—
Higher—up to the crystal bars
  That stem the current wide,
My soul would float to the silver stars
        At eventide.

Float on an ether sea of light,
  That the leaden eyes of earth
Are closed upon, in the falling night
  That gives my spirit birth.
One by one, as the stars peep forth,
  Do my aspirations rise,
Grasping south, east, west and north,
  The jewels of the skies!
Like to the fabled mystic words
  In the story of Eastern pride,
Comes the "open sesame," touching the chords
        At eventide.

Earth! my body to thee belongs,
  A bond and wretched slave
That never hopes to burst its thongs
  Till opes the welcome grave.
But sometimes will my soul look out
  Between its misty bars,

Seeking to find the hidden route
  Back to its native stars—
And glimpses of the path are given,
  When the sunset surges wide
Are setting ajar the gates of heaven
  At eventide!

A TRIBUTE,

TO THE MEMORY OF WALTER HOPKINS.

A TEAR, 'tis all I have to give—
  A tear and a blotted page, to thee;
A memory, lasting while I live—
  For thou wert kind to me!

Bright child of genius, sleep well! sleep well!
  Tho' far from thy home o'er the rolling sea;
There are hearts in this land that love to tell
  How much they honored thee!

An humble lyre shall breathe thy name,
  Whose tones were kindly borne by thee
Along the sounding aisles of fame
  To higher minstrelsy!

And a trembling hand shall touch the string
  Of a harp that tuneless but for thee
Had hung, a useless, broken thing,
  Upon the willow tree.

Not that its strain can tell the worth
    Of gems that centred bright in thee—
But 'tis the little all that earth
    Has given unto me ;

And sadly now the chord will trill
    A simple requiem for thee—
Tho' not attuned with master-skill,
    It hymns sincerity !

Farewell ! farewell ! should the wreath of fame
    Crown thy early tomb, this leaf let me
But add—my mite may be the same
    As greater meed, to thee.

'Twere wrong to mourn thee, for we know
    Stars set to rise again—and we
Would shrink before the dazzling glow
    Thy rising sheds o'er thee !

The morning hour was thine ! a ray
    Which by the night could not hidden be,
But melted away in the light of day,
    A glorious day for thee !

Its noon-light splendor far, far exceeds
    The light of ten thousand suns we see ;
And its glory halos the earthly deeds
    Of good once done by thee !

And while we worms, in our walls of clay,
    Lay thy empty shell 'neath the cypress tree,
On thy new-found wings thou soar'st away
    Where all, where all are free !

One form less to walk the earth—
  One ray more in heaven we see !
Mortal death and spirit birth
  Bring peace and joy to thee !

September 19, 1858.

HOPE DEFERRED.

WEARY, weary, endless longing—
  Heart-sick fancies ever thronging
In the wake of visioned joys !
Why do these dark shadows thronging
  Shut out my joys?

'Twas delusive hope, once sitting
By my soul, then sudden flitting
  Far away when nearest me ;
Like the bird in story, flitting
  From tree to tree.

And she swept from out my heart-strings,
With the rustle of her false wings,
  All their melody, and threw
Dark'ning shadows from her false wings
  There, as she flew.

Ah ! she trimmed her taper brightly
By my hearth-stone, trimmed it nightly,
  And I hailed it with delight—
But she ever bore it nightly
  Far from my sight !

When I heard her rushing pinions
Sweeping from the stars' dominions,
   Sprang my soul to meet her there !—
But she brought from those dominions
   To me a tear !

I grew weary, weary, weary,
Weary waiting—oh ! how dreary
   Roll the moments told in pain !
Falling cold and still and dreary,
   Like autumn rain.

As the moist breath of September
Plays o'er Summer's fading ember
   And puts out the feeble spark—
So delay pales Hope's faint ember
   Till it grows dark !—

And the heart, grown sick with longing,
Sees pale fancies, thick and thronging,
   Ghosts of joys in spectral train—
Wan despairs, in shadows thronging
   Thro' the craz'd brain !

HER SMILE.

LIKE the golden gleam that flashes
   Thro' the gray sky's dewy lashes,
When the day has spent in tears
A penance for the wasted years,

And seeks its stormy couch in sorrow,
With brighter promise for the morrow—

Was her smile, that touched the cloud,
Wont her azure eyes to shroud
In leaden pall—with inward glory,
Flashing forth a brighter story
Than her cheek's wan hue could say,
Where tears had washed the rose away.

Coldly beautiful, as death
Sealing fast an infant's breath,
Was she (or like that marble god,
Which maid, impassioned, vainly woo'd),
Until a smile broke o'er her face,
Like light in alabaster vase ;

Or like the beauteous summer lightning
Day's white ashes inly bright'ning
When its fires have smouldered low
And only left a fitful glow
On twilight's hearth, to gleam and flicker
Thro' the evening's starry wicker—

Then her features caught the glow
Gleaming o'er their moulded snow,
As rosy morning's beams will play
Upon the white mist-folds of day
In golden ripples—showing still
That sunlight lay beneath the hill

Of cold reserve her maiden pride
Had raised, her wounded heart to hide,

And coated o'er with chill distrust ;
But thro' the frosty, icy crust,
When broke the warm beam of her smile
You saw the fire beneath the pile !

As Hecla's mount is wrapt in snow
While deep within the molten glow
Of liquid lava seethes and burns
Or flames away in space by turns—
So many a heart's thus crusted o'er,
Whose fires burn inward as of yore !

LOVE AND THE MAIDEN.

A MAIDEN gazed from a castle wall
    Over a twilight sea,
Watching the wavelets rise and fall
    And dimple with playful glee ;
While the answering dimples in her cheek
    Told a merry heart had she—
And the glance of her bright eye seemed to speak
    That heart, as yet, was free !
And she sang a lay, a merry lay,
    "Oh ! I would a maiden be,
As glad and gay as yon waves at play,
    As joyous and as free !"

But waves, you know, will ebb and flow,
    And maidens lose their glee ;

There's a sly, sly foe doth bend a bow,
   And cunning aim takes he—
Tho' bound his eyes, the arrow flies
   And striketh speedily ;
Then off mirth hies, while quivering sighs
   Proclaim the victory !
And changed the lay, the merry lay,
   That tells of a young heart free—
" Ah ! well-a-day ! ah ! well-a-day !"
   Is the tone of the minstrelsy.

The maiden kneels by the altar now,
   And not alone is she,
For a manly form breathes a holy vow
   On lowly-bended knee !
And her sighs are stilled and her heart is filled
   With hopes, no longer free—
By another skilled its pulse is willed,
   And a different lay sings she :
" Oh ! never say that a maiden gay
   Is happier than she
Whose lips shall say, ' Love and obey
   Till death parts thee and me !' "

JUST MARRIED.

LAUNCHED on the bosom of the sparkling river,
   Thy little bark, love-freighted, seeks the tide ;
Onward the rose-hu'd wavelets leap and quiver,
   As toward the deep, broad ocean swift they glide.

But not more rosy-hued the bright waves gleaming
    Than thy young hopes, which paint with rays of light
The misty future, from dim distance beaming
    With radiance caught from thy fond fancies bright.

Cloudless the sky to thy ensanguined vision,
    The morn of love with soft effulgence beams;
No shadows darken o'er the hues elysian
    Which gild thy waking thoughts and light thy
        dreams.
Too trusting heart, that fancies bliss is real !—
    That scans not close the beck'ning phantom bright,
From whose gaunt form when fades the soft ideal,
    The flush of day gives place to gloom of night.

O venturous voyager on love's deep ocean,
    Trim well thy sails, and ply with skill thine oar,
Tho' soft the waves with coy and gentle motion
    Woo thee to leave the green and friendly shore,
Think not they'll ever whisper low to greet thee—
    That sunny skies shall always smile above—
The treacherous tide that sparkling springs to meet
        thee
    May ebb again, to strand thy bark of love.

The clouds of dark distrust may shade thy heaven,
    And tinge with green the rose-light of thy sky—
Brave not their rage, but heed the warning given
    When the first fleecy speck thou see'st on high !
For vainly wilt thou battle with the billows
    The demon, Jealousy, can raise at will—
'Twere better thou wert laid beneath the willows
    Than dare the storm, which roused, there's naught
        can still.

Let Reason take the helm, mild light distilling
    To guide thee safely thro' the passing gales
By Passion raised ; and when too proudly filling
    With Love's soft sighs, are spread thy yielding sails—
Still trust the sober helmsman ; he will moor thee
    In safest anchorage, by day or night ;
In every change of time or tide before thee,
    To Reason yield—he'll guide thy bark aright !

THE DROWNED MAIDEN.

WHERE rolls the green billow and kisses the
            sand
    Of an Eastern sea-girt isle,
There wandered a maid of a sunny land,
    Where the golden summers smile !
The glowing red of the ruby gleamed
    In her lips' warm, melting hue ;
Of pearl was her brow, and the sapphire beam'd
    In her bright eyes' deepening blue.

A Naiad sat on the rock's low side,
    Combing her long green hair
With a coral branch, and the silvery tide
    Served as her mirror fair—
When the maid drew nearer the rippling wave,
    The siren eyed the prize,
And murmured—" Deep down in an ocean cave
    I will steal her sapphire eyes !

23 *

" From her ruby lips I will drain the red
    To paint my car of shells—
  And I'll gather the pearl from her brow, to spread
    On the floors of my amber cells."
  Then she gently floated upon the crest
    Of a mighty billow near,
  And clasped the maid to her scaly breast,
    And laid her on Ocean's bier.

  But a wandering Peri of upper air
    Looked down with tearful eyes,
  When she heard the murmurs of wild despair,
    And caught the anguished sighs
  Of sorrowing friends ; and she softly stole
    To the watery couch of the dead
  And bore back the form—but ah ! the soul,
    The gentle soul, had fled !

  For Hope had stood, with her taper trimmed,
    On that sandy shore's bright side,
  And the spirit had wandered back, undimmed,
    From the rush of that sweeping tide.
  And now with Hope it onward flies
    To the shores of the peaceful river,
  Leaving earth's storms of tears and sighs
    For a calm that is broken never !

LIGHT AND SHADE.

'TIS the time when Spring, the rover,
   Wanders back to mead and down,
And bids the daisy lift her cover,
   Golden tuft and silver crown!

When crocus buds peep from the grasses,
   In purple yellow, white arrayed,
And apple blooms o'er leafy passes
   Shower paly stars beneath the shade.

'Tis golden eve—the young primroses
   Sudden leap from buds to flowers,
To watch the sun as he uncloses
   The gates of night in western bowers;

While in his track of fiery vapors
   The evening goddess mounts her car,
And with her wand lights Heaven's tapers
   With blaze caught from the signal star

That trembles on the purple banner
   Flung from Twilight's gilded tower,
Whose walls give back the glad hosanna
   Rising from folding leaf and flower!

An eve of beauty! Oh what wonder
   Young hearts and wandering feet should stray!
Such tempting skies—such green boughs under—
   Oh, love should never sigh by day!—

" Wilt thou be mine?"   The low words quiver
   Like Spring's soft sigh o'er ice-bound stream,
And at the breath the glad, wild river
   Dimples with smiles in day's bright beam.

But wooing Spring, with gentlest praises
   Ne'er brought to wavelet softer glow
Than paints the maiden's cheek, who raises
   Then quick lets fall her lids of snow.

In that shy glance her soul revealing;
   No need of words to tell the power
That mocks the effort at concealing,
   And bursts all bonds in Love's own hour.

Alas! that hour comes in a life-time
   But once: like fair Hybiscus frail,
That flaunts gay petals in the noon's prime,
   And the next hour droops withered, pale!

The Spring sang out her song of gladness—
   The Summer gayly caroled by—
But when the Autumn's wail of sadness
   Showered withered leaves—Love droop'd to die.

The peach-bloom faded to the lily;
   The tender flower that Love had nursed,
And Hope had ripened—shrunk, when chilly
   Cold Neglect upon it burst.

Now nipping winds wave lichens hoary,
   And crimson leaves shower all unheeding
Where shorn, bereft of all its glory,
   The stricken flower of Love lies bleeding.

THE LILY'S REPLY.

LILY, drooping lily,
    Tell us why so pale?
Why, with wan cheek waiting
    In the mossy vale?
Weaving fragrant garlands
    Thy sister flowrets near
Sport them in the sunbeams
    While thou sighest here!

Daisies freshly springing
    From the dewy grass,
Send their smiles of welcome,
    Sweet to all that pass!
Crimson-tipped anemones—
    Violets from the ground—
Heliotropes and mignonette
    Scatter perfume round.

Blushing in the sunshine,
    The conscious rose bends low
Beneath the bright, warm glances
    That o'er her bosom glow.
Is it that a rival
    Out-blooms thee in the vale,
Whose flushing cheek makes white thine own,
    With blighting envy pale?

" Ah! no ;" the lily sighed—" the sun
    With fond, impartial beams,

S

Smiles o'er the humblest floweret
   As on the proudest gleams !
But while they blush beneath his gaze,
   And plume their varied hue,
Thinking that 'tis their beauty bright
   That from him claims its due—

"I silent worship at the shrine
   Whence the bright beam and flower
Derive alike their light and tint—
   Their beauty and their power !
Undazzled by the glittering ray,
   Unwarmed by flattery's tale—
I wrap myself in Purity's
   Unspotted garment pale !

"It pains me not to see the glow
   By sister beauty shed,
If loveliness must be her dower,
   And Faith's be mine instead.
Beauty fast binds the mortal heart—
   To it earth's praise is given ;
But Purity's the better part
   That blossometh in heaven !"

THE HEAVENLY HOME.

FAR, far beyond this vale of tears,
   Beyond the reach of mortal eyes,
A heavenly mansion's dome appears
   Eternal in the skies !

No earthly tower for mould and worm
   To sap, and laugh man's work to scorn—
But on the Rock of Ages firm
   Its hold can ne'er be worn!

The living waters lave its base—
   'Tis sheltered by the tree whose leaves
Are healing balm—while God's own face
   Its light resplendent gives!

Its gates are never closed, for night
   Can come not in those blissful lands;
But Truth's pure rays illume with light
   The " house not built by hands!"

Within this mansion's walls are met
   The pure, the upright and the few,
Upon whose radiant brows is set
   The seal which stamps them true!

Oh early let thy footsteps roam
   To gates whose portals ope to peace—
" The Spirit and the Bride say, Come!"
   Thy earthly wanderings cease.

Behold! the bright, the Morning Star,
   Whose light shall guide thee on the way:
Oh when thou see'st its beam afar,
   Watch for the coming day!

Follow the light that calls thy soul—
   Thy 'nighted soul, tired of earth's race—
Oh haste! its glimmer speaks the goal
   That gives in heaven a place!

NEVER TOO LATE.

A S walks the kingly noon
   Where sang the morning stars,
I hear the rosy feet of June
   Beating the golden bars ;
And the pulse of the listening tide
   Throbs sweet to the tender tale
That the south wind tells, of the waves that glide
   Where the Nautilus hoists his sail.

A dreamy melody rings
   From the flowery belfry near,
A silken sound of invisible wings
   That we hold our breath to hear ;
And the yellow sunlight weaves
   In a gossamer mist the air,
And borders with tinsel the velvet eaves
   Of the wild bee's leafy lair.

Oh summer sits on the hill
   And sings to the lonely vale,
Till the dimpling face of the laughing rill
   Is flashing adown the dale ;
And Ocean old lays bare
   His brow, without a doubt
That her breath will toy with his silvery hair,
   And smooth his wrinkles out

Then, drooping human heart,
   Ope wide thy doors, and let

The sunshine in ! and buds will start
   From the fainting foliage yet ;
Sweet Summer beckons thee
   From her shining golden gate
Her regal state and stores to see—
   Murmuring, " Never too late !"

See where she smiling stands
   Flower-crown'd in the year's ripe noon,
And bids thee break from December's bands
   And list the voice of June,
The icy mantle rent—
   Lo ! bursting from the sod,
What starry eyes, what brows unbent,
   Look trusting up to God !

Why wrap thyself in doubt
   And shut out every ray,
Girding a frosty belt about
   Such a sun-loving day ?
Oh let its genial smile
   Thaw thro' the ice of fate,
And lead thee to Hope's summer isle,
   Murmuring, " Never too late !"

CALEDONIA'S· WILD HARP.

O HARP of the hills ! oft I hear thy wild numbers
   Upon the deep breath of the mystical night,
When o'er the dim vaults of my dream-haunted slumbers
  Arises in glory and grandeur and might,

The bright star of Caledon, radiantly shining
  With knighthood's fair crest, while the Bruce led the
      day,
And Wallace's deeds in their lustre were twining
  Their rich scintillations around its bright way.

And low in my dreaming ear, over Time's ocean,
  Fall symphonies resonant still of old fame,
That rouse in my bosom the wildest emotion
  To echo the refrains for Douglas and Graeme !
Wild harp ! has thy wizard note ceased its vibrations?
  Or is it the strain (when no longer I dream)
That the storm-spirit sings to the clouds, when libations
  He pours to the gods in a crystalline stream ?

Ah ! gone are the days, they live only in story,
  When wild border-minstrelsy thrilled on the gale ;
But sometimes I see the McGregor in glory,
  With spear, sword and battle-axe sweeping the
      dale—
Clan-Alpine's blue bonnets and tartans are waving,
  The while the war signal, the red-cross, flies on ;
And harpists are telling the dangers they're braving—
  I look once again and the pageant is gone !

The centuries drop a deep curtain between us—
  The old harp is hung on the willow to rest ;
But out of the mist rises Albin's blest genius,
  With a lyre wreathed with daisies clasped over her
      breast,
And down where sweet Ayr to the green braes is
      singing
  A lowly love-ditty with musical turns,

The bright-pinioned spirit the gold lyre is bringing
　To lay at the feet of the shepherd boy, Burns!

And now, too, hath passed that sweet vision—all broken
　The chords whose wild melody spake to the heart,
Whose depths they have sounded by many a token,
　And bade from its rock feeling's rivulets start.
Oh where is the hand now to call forth new numbers,
　And sound for Old Scotia a soul-stirring strain,
Till her ancient harp vibrates thro' all its deep slum-
　　　bers—
　Oh where is the harpist to wake it again?

APATHETIC.

PUT your cup of sweets away,
　　Summer!　I have drained the lees
From the honied foam of May
　To such tasteless dregs as these,
Lying like the withered leaves
　In the hollows bleak and bare—
So my heart no longer grieves
　When your roses fade in air

I have seen the crocus born,
　Yellow-tressed, from out the snow—
And the sunshine kiss the morn
　Till her cheeks were all a-glow ;
Seen the hawthorne's scarlet hood
　Proudly donned, when winter gray

Fled with his white-bearded brood
　From the flowery hosts of May!

Seen the brilliant daffodil,
　And the star-eyed daisy rise,
Shaking off December's chill
　When sweet April trod the skies—
Heard the wild, melodious tune
　Which the wandering breezes play
'Mong the chiming leaves of June,
　Beating rhythmic time alway!

Seen a softly golden haze
　Veiling forest, mead and down,
When the Autumn's dreamy days
　Slumbered on the hillside brown;
Heard September's fretful tides
　Break upon the silver sand—
Seen October's crimson ides
　Glowing o'er the burnished land;

And I've seen them pass away
　To the sombre churchyard shade—
Red-lipped Morn and blushing May,
　Down where chilling graves are made!
Not a bud of hope that blooms,
　Not a leaf of trust that waves,
But will wither 'mid the tombs,
　Fade within unpitying graves!

All my sweet faith now is dead;
　So my heart no longer grieves

When the Summer hides her head
   Underneath the fallen leaves.
For my soul hath conned the page
   Time and sorrow only teach,
That 'tis useless, all, to wage
   War with things beyond our reach !

MAD MADGE.

THE wailing winds mourn thro' the glen,
   The cloud-racks smother the moon ;
A frightened star peeps now and then
   From its covert, but hides it soon !
The leafless branches toss and rattle
   Like murderers' bones in the blast—
The spirits of air are doing battle,
   And their war-steeds hurry past.

A hooting owl from yonder height
   Screeches his omen dread—
And flitting bats thro' the dusky night
   Are wheeling overhead ;
While whirling along to the deafening shriek
   Of the reckless, crazy wind,
The withered leaves in a mad, mad freak
   Their dance of death have twined.

On yonder gray rock's barren ledge
   What ghostly form gleams white?
Come nearer, see ! 'tis but Mad Madge,
   She sits and sings thro' the night.

24 *

Deep down in the glen her lover's bones
    Have battened the wolf in his lair—
'Twas a night of storm heard his dying groans,
    When his rival laid him there !

Oh, Madge was the pride of our village green,
    Our dainty blossom rare ;
No flower that bloomed 'mid the summer's sheen
    Could with our bud compare ;
And each one sought to pluck the prize
    To wear on his manly breast,
But one found favor within her eyes
    Above the rival rest.

The hour drew near for the joyful rite—
    The day had risen in gloom
And rolled along till a stormy night
    Spread for it a wild, wild tomb—
And Madge, with her maidens, arrayed in white
    Awaited the tardy groom ;
·"Where lingers he on his bridal night?"
    Was her thought in that flower-deck'd room.

Oh nevermore, oh nevermore
    Will the sound of his welcome feet
Make music around that cottage door
    Her listening ear to greet.
The moon looked down with a whitening cheek,
    On his life-blood's sanguine flow
That painted the sod with a crimson streak
    Where the path thro' the glen wound low.

'Twas the lightning's glare that showed his form
    To the searchers in the glen,

That thro' the dashing, blinding storm
  Sought for the bridegroom then;
And a pale, pale cheek on his gory breast
  Was laid with a shudder wild—
Poor Madge! when they raised her from that rest,
  She was simple as a child.

And now she wanders, a helpless thing,
  Her favorite haunt the glen;
On its rocky sides she will sit and sing
  When storms hide the moon, ye ken;
She will tell you her lover's cheek so white
  She sees in the murky cloud
Where the veilèd moonbeams tint with light
  The edge of the sable shroud.

And when the red lightning flashes free,
  She will scream, " See there! see there!
'Tis the crimson blood of his heart I see,
  That flows o'er his bosom fair!
Oh he rides the storm on a snow-white steed,
  I but linger till he hath passed—
But if he beckon me, then indeed
  I will follow him at last!"

A harmless wight is poor Mad Madge,
  Tho' her words are strange and wild:
'Twere cruel to bind in a prison cage
  Warped Reason's gentle child!
Her feeble step and paling cheek
  Show the strand of her life's undone—
Let the pearls drop silently, nor seek
  To crush with a harsh step, one!

EPITAPH!

DARLING Nannie sleeps beneath—
  A bud just leafing in the gloaming,
When angels twined it in their wreath,
  And now it blooms where they are roaming!

BOYHOOD.

OUT upon a croaker,
  A fault-finding dame—
Who tries with bit and curb
  A bright boy to tame;
Who looks for threescore's wisdom
  In curly pate of ten!
(Inoculating babies
  With the gravity of men!)

Who thinks a child's requirements
  Are compassed by a school—
A bed and board and clothing warm,
  And all things done by rule;
Forgetting, in her zealous care,
  The proverb which doth say—
That work a dull boy makes of Jack
  Without a little play.

Give me a noisy, joyous one,
  Whose ringing laughter clear

Speaks youth's bright sunshine in the heart,
  Undimmed by sorrow's tear.
An oasis in the desert,
  A flower on rough rock wild,
In this weary, wasting world of care
  Is the glad face of a child!

Then leave, oh leave to childhood
  Its all-unconscious joy;
And chide not for his mirthfulness
  The merry-hearted boy!
Full soon the clouds of manhood
  Will throw their shadows grim
Athwart the golden-tinted sky,
  And all its splendors dim!

FLIRTATION.

SHE said she would meet me at twilight
  By the buttonwood tree in the dale—
I held her soft hand while she promised,
  And gazed 'neath her lashes' dark veil;
Her brown eyes looked dewy and tender,
  Her little hand trembled in mine—
Oh say not a part she was acting
  To lure one heart more to her shrine!

She came—when a crescent of silver
  The moon in the west hung so light—

And I sprang thro' the clover to meet her,
  When lo ! an astonishing sight !
By her side was a six-foot protection,
  A thing of shirt-collar and hair—
Whom she named, with a cool self-possession,
  And I hailed with a stupefied stare !

For a moment we stood like two canines
  Undetermined to bark or to bite ;
Then wisely forbore to do either,
  And talked of the beautiful night !
That moon had scarce rounded to fullness,
  When orange-buds graced a fair brow ;
The bridegroom was gouty, but wealthy,
  And six-foot and myself heard the vow !

TO "LEANDER."

IN REPLY TO HIS LINES—

"A request I would make, Millie ;
  It simply will be this :
If affixed to your name, Millie,
  Is that little word—Miss ?"

'TIS not a-*miss* that you should make
    A laudable endeavor
My brain-*mis*-shapen foolscap folds
  Of *mys*-tery to sever ;
But do not *mis*-interpret, pray,
  My motive—'twould be grievous,

If while I vow I'll not *mis*-lead,
  You label me *mis*-chievous!

If " Miss" were tacked unto my name,
  It would be no *mis*-nomer,
For *mis*-construed I've often been,
  And *mis*-judged by each comer.
And *mis*-improved, I fear my time
  Is often *mis*-employed
In scribbling *mis*-erable rhyme
  And *mis*-cellany void.

These *mis*-ty products of my muse
  Are often, sir, *mis*-printed,
(But that's the printer's fault, you see,
  When lamp and eyesight's stinted !)
I seldom am *mis*-ruly, sir,
  Tho' oft I send a *mis*-sile,
'Tis harmless (as *this* specimen)
  As down from off a thistle.

And for my name—*Mis*-fortune 'tis,
  For every hope's *mis*-carried
(But do not from this *mis*-conceive
  That I have been *mis*-married).
I do affirm I was *mis*-born,
  And *mis*-appreciated
Still remain ; and better so
  Than hapless be *mis*-mated.

And yet I am no *mis*-anthrope,
  Nor scarcely *mis*-affected ;

And *mis*-allied, I've shown I'm not—
  I'm only *mis*-directed !
And now, brave *Miss*-issippi's son !
  I hope your faith's unshaken ;
'Twill be thro' no *mis*-statement, sir,
  If you should be *mis*-taken.

THE WITCH-HAZEL DELL.

SHE wandered in the gloaming
    In the witch-hazel dell—
Ah ! she waited for the coming
  Of footsteps cherished well ;
November's sighs of sadness
  Around her wailing fell,
But her heart knew naught but gladness
  In the witch-hazel dell.

Not long had she to linger—
  For her ear soon heard a tale,
And a ring pressed on her finger
  With its motto—" Do not fail !"
Told she willingly had listened
  To the honeyed tones that fell,
And with tears her eyelids glistened
  In the witch-hazel dell.

Ah ! knew she not that vows breathed
  Where blooms this mystic plant,

Were frail as curling smoke wreathed
  Where twilight's pale beams slant?
The plant that flowers when leaves fall,
  But bears not fruit as well*—
Shrouds lovers' hopes with a dark pall
  In the witch-hazel dell.

When in her garb of beauty,
  Her robe of emerald green,
Young Spring, as bound in duty,
  Tipped all the buds with sheen ;
When o'er their mountain passes
  The sparkling streamlets fell,
And when waved the scented grasses
  In the witch-hazel dell—

In the gloaming still she wandered,
  But weary and alone,
Her heart's best feelings squandered,
  Her household gods o'erthrown !
Vainly binding up the gashes
  That on her spirit fell
When her love-fruit turned to ashes
  In the witch-hazel dell.

* The witch-hazel flowers in the autumn and perfects fruit the next
summer.

A PICTURE.

THE chequered sunlight, peeping
  Thro' the leaves of the old oak tree,
Turned to diamonds the dew-drops sleeping
  On the green and flowery lea ;
It lighted with merry dances
  On the brow of Childhood fair—
And shone with its gleesome glances
  On Age's silvery hair.

With his chin on his shrunk palm resting,
  The old man looketh on,
Where playful children jesting
  Remind him of days that are gone.
He sits at the cottage portal,
  An aged pilgrim gray,
At one end of the chain that's mortal—
  At the other—those children gay !

Oh back o'er its links he wandered,
  In thought, to those joyous hours
When moments were freely squandered
  In Childhood's happy bowers—
Till his manhood's toils and heartaches
  Fade from his fancy wild,
And he joins in their merry outbreaks,
  And seems again a child !

Like the breeze of autumn sighing
  Where leafless branches sway,

Or Echo's voice replying
  From ruins, old and gray ;
Or the curfew's chime of sadness,
  That tells of the daylight gone—
There came no strain of gladness
  In his voice's feeble tone.

As well might December's snow-wreath
  Boast of the bloom of May,
As the quivering voice of Age breathe
  The shout of Childhood gay !
The old man looks around him—
  The merry group has flown ;
Gone is the spell that bound him,
  And he is left alone !

And back o'er the rusty links roll
  The memories that seldom sleep ;
Awakening the past in his sad soul,
  Till he cannot choose but weep !
Comfort thee, aged mortal !
  For near is the summons mild
That will call thee to heaven's portal
  To be again a child !

MORNING.

THE skylark has caroled his warning—
  The gate of the Orient opes,
As the light aureola of morning
  Reflects from the dewy-gemm'd copse ;

And above, o'er the billowy ridges
   Of ether's cerulean sea,
The rosiest amber-propp'd bridges
   Are spanning the realms of the bee.

A wan cheek the moon has with waiting
   From earliest fall of twilight
Till dawn, peering thro' its gray grating,
   Blows out the bright candles of night—
And unfurls o'er the ramparts of crystal
   A banner of saffron ; which shows
But a lone star, like lamp of a vestal,
   That with purity's radiance glows !

And see now the goldenest granules
   Of dust, o'er the arches that span
With pearly and sapphiric pendules
   The emerald palace of man—
Roll up ; and the fiery trappings
   That harness the steeds of the sun
Shine out, as the sombre-hued wrappings
   Of envious night are undone.

Away with bright pennons all streaming
   Of amethyst, ruby and gold,
Is the chariot of Morning now gleaming—
   Its clear scintillations retold
In each mirror of ocean or lakelet,
   Each silvery fountain or rill,
Each dew-embossed leaf in the brakelet,
   Each rain-drop-spray'd twig on the hill !

The horn of the beetle is sounding,
   The pipes of the bee droning hum—

And the forest is gayly resounding
  With the woodpecker tapping his drum ;
The sentinel mock-bird now hushes
  His challenge, as shrilly away
Thro' the camp of the morning, blithe gushes
  Old Nature's untaught reveillé !

Up, up where the cloud-tents' white awnings
  Are flecking the measureless plain,
And down where the gilded adornings
  Of tassels wave o'er the bright grain—
Thro' the glossy green plumes, gently bending
  Where the woodland's gay standard appears,
Floats the matin of earth, that is lending
  A chord in the anthem of spheres !

THE LAST SLEEP.

" I must sleep now."—*Last words of Byron.*

REST for the throbbing heart and fiery eye,
  The fevered pulse and wild, unconquered will !
From the Eternal came the mandate high
  That hushed the storm and murmured " Peace ! be
    still."
  Hate and contentious strife that once did fill
His heart with desolation, and did roar
  Their notes discordant thro' his soul, until
The strains Elysian, which his lyre would pour,
Caught their harsh tones and with their bitterness ran
    o'er.

25 *

No more their vexèd tides shall round him lave,
  Chafing his restless spirit in their hold ;
No more he'll seek in elements that rave
  Companionship and brotherhood most bold !
  Dreamless the sleep whose low descending fold
Wrapt in its chilling panoply his soul.
  Child of the universe ! within his hold
The mountains high, the stars that o'er them roll,
But playthings were to his most reckless, daring soul !

" After life's fitful fever he sleeps well !"
  No dreams of hopeless love or fiercer wail,
Thro' the lone chambers of his heart now swell
  And unto caves and rocks breathe forth their tale
  Of bitterness ; spring decks the mossy vale
With verdure, and the summer's noontide heat
  Paints with its warm, rich hues, the fruitage pale ;
Autumn's and winter's howling tempests beat
Alike in vain—they cannot pierce the grave's retreat.

But may we not, with seer-inspired eye,
  View the illimitable fields of space,
And mark his transit o'er the realms on high ?
  His progress thro' their starry wonders trace ?
  As his freed spirit standeth face to face
With worlds his eye had peopled from afar—
  Now 'scaped from clayey clods, its onward race
Thro' Nature's mysteries, there's naught can mar—
As in its upward flight it speeds from star to star !

The thunder's mighty secret now revealed—
  The lightning's subtle essence analyzed—

Naught from the clear-eyed spirit's gaze concealed,
  But all that heart of bard had idolized—
  The wonders of creation, eulogized
In earthly verse—made comprehensive, plain!
  Angelic harps, to his well harmonized,
Celestial wonders trill in rapturous strain,
Till all the Poet's soul renews its fires again!

Who envies not such sleep—when life no more
  Glows with the freshness of its early hour?
Who 'mongst us can with cunning hand restore
  The bloom and tint to rudely-rifled flower,
  Or paint with noontide rays the twilight hour?
Who would not lay his weary head to rest
  When cold Reality asserts its power
And stifles Fancy's dreams within the breast?
O grave! then ope thine arms and leave to God the
      rest!

ALWAYS REMEMBERED.

FAR o'er Life's surging sea
    Wind and tide bear me on—
Far, far from love and thee
    I am gone!—
Gone from the home of years—
    Parted in sorrow—
Dimly, thro' blinding tears,
    Dawneth the morrow!

Say, was it well in thee,
  Was it well to heed them—
The fiends who counseled thee?
  Didst thou need them?
Coldly their work they've done,
  Rudely to sever
Hearts that else had beat as one,
  Ever, for ever!

Not such my love for thee—
  Swayed by each passing breeze
Of envy or calumny—
  Oh, not by these
Could doubts of thy truth be sown
  In my heart;
Hastening the hour on
  That bid us part.

Oh can the love of years
  Thus lightly stifled be?
Those who have wept our tears
  And joyed to see
Our smiles—oh say, can they
  Turn with altered brow
Coldly from us away,
  And spurn us now?

Alas! for human love,
  And friendship's vainer term—
Words traced in sand will prove
  As truly firm!
Scattered by passing gales
  The sand sweeps the shore,

So Malice breathes her tales,
　And love is o'er !

Well, well then be it so,
　Since thou hast will'd we part ;
'Twere best from thee I go,
　Though swells my heart !
I do not claim the right
　To force thy will—
I only ask to be
　Remembered still !

———

PSALM CXXXVIII.

WITH my whole heart, O Lord of Light !
　Before all gods thy praise I'll sing ;
Unto thy holy temple bright
　My grateful praises, Lord, I'll bring ;
For when with anguish sore oppressed
　My feeble heart for help did cry,
Thou strengthened my o'erburdened breast,
　And hushed my sad and trembling sigh.

The kings and princes of the earth
　Their homage yet to thee shall bring !
When from thy lips they learn thy worth,
　Their songs of praise they'll joyful sing !
Yet tho' thou, Lord, exalted art,
　The lowliest may to thee draw near—
'Tis but the proud and stubborn heart
　That stands aloof in doubt and fear.

Tho' clouds of grief around me roll,
　Thy smile of love shall chase the gloom ;
Tho' treacherous foes would pierce my soul,
　Thy strong right hand shall ward the doom !
My faith's unbounded, Lord, in thee !
　Thou wilt perfect what thou'st begun :
For ever flows thy mercy free—
　Thou'lt not forsake thy work ere done.

HOW TO PRESERVE YOUTH.

WOULDST know
　　The secret, child of clay,
How, Hebe-like, the steps of Time
Thou ever mayst delay—
　Twining thy brow, thro' life's long hours,
　With chaplets of unfading flowers?

　　Wouldst have,
As roll the years away,
　Thy heart renew its youthful fires,
Nor know nor feel decay?
　Then list—the secret's easy told,
　How thou may'st keep from growing old.

　　Arise !
Shake off the deepening gloom
　Which clouds thy soul with hues of night
And murmurs from the tomb !
　A selfish sorrow, we are told,
　Indulged in, soon will make us old.

So live
That each day's setting sun
　Will close upon some good resolve,
Or worthy action done !
　Thus keep thy heart from getting cold,
　And fear not that thou shalt grow old.

Old friends
Whom thou hast proved and tried,
　Whom good report or evil word
Found ever at thy side
　Still true, to thy fond bosom fold !
　Such friendship's always young—'tho' old !

Ne'er turn
With cold, averted eye
　From child of want, who in thine ear
Breathes poverty's sad sigh.
　Relieve !—his thanks, worth more than gold,
　Thee shall ensure 'gainst growing old.

Ne'er sit
With silent lip and eye
　When calumny, foul whelp of ill !
A friend doth vilify—
　The sneering whisper check ere told ;
　By listening such you'll soon grow old !

And when
The beldam, Rumor, 'round
　With trumpet tongue and brazen voice,
Some scandal doth resound—
　Help not the tale of slander told—
　An evil tongue soon maketh old !

Be kind
To all who o'er your path
  With wandering steps may chance to stray ;
Kindness a power hath
  Most potent in its spell to hold !—
  The heart which owns it ne'er grows old.

Turn not
From him whom others slight,
  Because he wears a seedy coat ;
Your conscience will feel right
  If needy virtue you uphold—
  By doing so you'll ne'er grow old.

Laud not
With honors rare and high
  The moneyed villain who with wealth
Can hide iniquity !
  Help not to cover crime with gold—
  No surer way to make you old.

But keep,
Through every change of life,
  A firm resolve and purpose high,
Prepared to meet each strife—
  A conscience that cannot be sold ;
  And Time will fail to make you old !

THE WIND AND THE SHOWER.

HARK to the wind's low wail,
As with sobbing voice to the flying clouds
It murmurs its plaintive tale !
The sorrowing moon her white face shrouds
Beneath a misty veil ;
While the cloudlets a moment pause and listen,
And soon with soft tear-drops their fringed lids glisten ;
Heaven's starry eyes, with pitying gaze,
Grow dim and shed but watery rays—
For the sad, sad wind, with breathings low,
Whispers a tale of long, long ago—
When the infant earth, in its Eden bloom,
Rosy and bright
In its early light,
Knew naught of sinful gloom !
When the new-born zephyr with dallying wing,
Fanned the young buds to blossoming
Or kissed into life the opening flowers,
To grace with sweets those primal bowers—
And had never breathed o'er a guilty world,
And fierce, defiant mutterings hurled.

Ay, grieve, thou moaning Wind !
And tell to the stars thy sorrows wild :
Thou ne'er again canst find
The careless joy of the happy child,
The innocent peace of mind,
As when free and unfettered thou danced along
To the joyous music of childhood's song,

And the maddest freaks of thy wayward will
Were to curl in soft wavelets the sparkling rill ;
Or to lift from the face of the blushing rose
Its leafy veil, and its sweets disclose ;
Or to steal on a beam of the setting sun
　　　To the evening star,
　　　From whose dewy car
Thou'd shower the bright drops thy sighs had won !
Woe for the hour when thou turned away
From the happy light of youth's glad day,
And fiercely o'er manhood's stormy path
Poured out thy bitter vials of wrath !
Well may all Nature drop pitying tears
When thou wail'st forth thy plaint of early years.

GOOD AND EVIL.

NOT all of evil nor all of good
　　Is thine, O Man, below !
Nor thine to question the wise decrees
　Of Him who made it so !
There's an undercurrent we cannot see
　That wends with life's stream along,
Bearing the waifs on the tide that float,
　Whether for right or wrong.

The beautiful glowing sunset clouds
　That have charmed us so at even,
Have held the fierce lightning's scathing shaft
　That the stoutest oak hath riven.

The silvery leaves of the almond bough,
  And the kindly fruit it bears,
Hide a deadly poison that lurketh low,
  As among the wheat lie tares.

But, Man, in thy Maker's image formed,
  Thine in the God-like work
To find the bright grain of good—and where
  Each evil seed may lurk,
To crush it down with an iron heel
  Tho' it spring in thine own heart,
And hold aloft the golden flower
  That blooms from the weeds apart.

Thy heart deep down in its shady nooks
  Hath many a slender shoot,
That only waits for some kindly hand
  To water its tender root
To spring into tropic glory bright
  And tell of the genial soil
That under a sterile surface lies
  Awaiting the needful toil.

We know that the wayside weed will grow
  Apace in the meadow rank,
But the gardener's hand must prune the tree
  And trim the flowery bank
To forms of beauty and grace, to charm
  The critical eye of taste—
Then why not prune the flowers of the heart?
  Nor let them run to waste.

Not all of evil nor all of good,
  Is awarded each mortal's lot,

But his the fault if he fails to find
 In his heart the genial spot
Where kindly culture may bring to light
 Some little leaf, to show
That a ray of sunshine has pierced the sod,
 Tho' all seemed dark below.

MY ENEMY.

OUT in the churchyard she sleeps to-night
 Under the cold-eyed moon ;
And the will-o'-wisp is dancing light
 To the night-wind's hollow tune,
Where the white stone stands with its letters bright
 To tell of her clouded noon !

She was mine enemy—alas !
 That the eyes of Day look down
On human enmity—but I pass
 That page without a frown ;
There is no life, I ween, but has
 Such a dark leaf folded down !

I said, " mine enemy"—but still
 She met me with song and wile ;
The world, when it saw her the goblet fill,
 Ne'er dreamed of lurking guile—
But Judas kissed his Lord with a will,
 And betrayed him with a smile !

And now she lies in her narrow bed,
   All helpless for weal or woe ;
This life hath its hollow lustre shed,
   And the grave is dark below !
Poor white lips closed !—Their ire all fled—
   What more can they harm me now ?

This little heart's-ease sprang from the sod
   Where she lies in her dreamless sleep—
Perchance it proclaims her peace with God !
   And no bitter feelings creep
Toward a fellow-worm who hath sorely trod
   The path that she helped to heap

With the poison-thorn and prickly brier
   Of unjust calumny.
I would I could lift my vision higher,
   And see what she now doth see,
When the sting of death and each low desire
   Is swallowed in victory !

But I may not stand by the sea of glass
   That laveth the golden throne—
I can only kneel on her grave as I pass,
   And my free forgiveness own,
And weep as a mortal must weep that has
   Such a dark leaf folded down.

26 *   U

"BE STRONG IN THE LORD."

[Ephesians vi. 10.]

BE strong in the Lord, in the power of his might,
And clothed with his armor stand forth for the
right,
When wickedness rules in high places, and sin
Casts the die for the rulers of darkness to win—
Be ye strong in the Lord!

His safeguard, the breastplate of righteousness, wear,
The girdle of truth wrap around thee with care,
And sandal thy feet with the gospel of peace
(Jehovah will give in the harvest increase);
Be ye strong in the Lord!

Stand forth with the sword of the Spirit, his word!
And pray in the spirit—thy prayers shall be heard,—
That evermore thou shalt be able to stand
When the spirit of evil stalks forth thro' the land,
And be strong in the Lord!

TELEGRAPHIC.

"A bark in sight—bound in."

" A BARK in sight, bound in"—
So runs the swift despatch;
A bark bound in from stormy seas,
Where tempests brew and hatch.

A bark bound in, with a freight
  Of human hopes and fears ;
A bark that has bravely battled with
  The great deep's smiles and tears.

A bark bound in ! Oh we know
  How many a venturous sail
Spreads snowy wings o'er Ocean's caves
  And dares the treacherous gale,
Lured by the wooing breeze
  And kissed by the mad-cap wave,
Till down in the dreadful dark abyss
  It sinks where whirlpools rave.

" A bark in sight—bound in !"
  Oh, out and hail her now
Clap hands as she throws the sparkling spray
  From off her cleaving prow !
For she is a wondrous thing,
  Endowed with life and light,
And comes to us laden with messages
  From the land where is not night.

For she says, when we cast adrift
  This coil of life, and steer
For the vast unknown, if our hulk is strong
  No tempest can make us fear—
If we have but stanchions fast
  And rigging and rope and spar,
And trust to the faithful Pilot Star
  That points to our home afar—

Right royally we'll sail
  By the lighthouse flashing bright,

Thro' boiling wave and surging foam
  And dark cloud-ridden night;
Right royally we'll fling
  Our pennons to the breeze
When past death's stormy cape we glide
  Into celestial seas!

O bark of life, we know
  Thou must battle with the waves
And sink or float, as thy strength holds out,
  Or thy trust in the Hand that saves!
But joyfully thou'lt thrill
  When the sweet seraphic din
Echoes the heavenly telegram—
  " A bark in sight—bound in!"

"OUR FATHER."

" And because ye are sons, God hath sent forth the Spirit of his
Son into your hearts, crying, Abba, Father."—GAL. iv. 6.

FATHER, Creator, thy Spirit is here—
  Lo! when the Word was made flesh, full of
    grace,
Then the true light by thy will did appear
  Shining and bright in a desolate place.
    Father, Creator, we welcome the light,
    Guiding us out of the gloom of the night,
    Help us its brightness more perfect to see—
    Father, Creator, we lean upon thee!

Father, Creator, we lean upon thee
  In the deep darkness—as children in sleep
Feel that the mother is bending the knee
  And o'er them her vigil doth wakefully keep.
    Father, Creator, bend down from above,
    Loving us still with a motherly love,
    With the Christ-heart that has borne human pain,
    Father, Creator, look on us again !

Father, Creator, look on us again—
  Tho' we are erring, thy children are we ;
Scourge us and chasten, if only by pain
  We can be brought to the penitent knee.
    Father, Creator, thou gav'st thine own Son
    To teach how the heavenly goal may be won—
    Oh when we faint 'neath the cross, then bend down,
    Father, Creator, and show us the crown !

DREAMS.

WHENCE come ye, dovelings of the night !
    Is it from some starry height
Ye flutter down on noiseless wing
And in the soul's deep chamber sing?
Piercing the mists of sleep—as thro'
The rifted vapor smiles the blue—
Ye come, like the bright gleams of heaven
When the cloud-pall's dark fold is riven !

Dreaming?
          Ay, " 'twas but a dream !"
I saw thine eyes with fondness beam,

O friend of other days! on me;
Coldness hath come 'twixt me and thee—
But to the dream-land I may hie
And meet thee there, nor shun thine eye;
Its veil of scorn is flung aside—
The cold, dark folds no longer hide
Thy heart, but in its depths I see
The mirror faithful still to me!

When at the voice of sleep, my soul
Escaped the body's harsh control,
It sought thee in the silent hall
Of dreams! Thou camest at my call;
Methought a mask thy features hid,
All save thine eyes; beneath each lid,
With the old look I joy'd to see,
They shone—oh fondly shone on me!
And thro' those windows of the soul
I read thee, as I would a scroll.

Masked we all are—but to me
Thine transparent is; I see,
Not only in the dream-light now,
Tho' curled thy lip and cold thy brow—
Down thro' the misty veil, a place
Thou can'st not if thou would'st erase,
Within thy heart—where still enthroned
The love is which thy lips once owned.
Ah! if I've read the dream aright,
Not vain these visions of the night!

REST.

DING! dong! dell!
    Hark! 'tis the chime of a passing bell—
What does the iron-tongued messenger tell?
    Rest! rest! rest!
A pure, pale brow on the green sod press'd,
And meek hands folded o'er icy breast!

    Ding! dong! dell!
A deep tone speaks in the tolling bell
As its hollow voice sounds the parting knell:
    Dust! dust dust!
Mortal, return to it thou must—
'Tis written so by a Being just!

    Ding! dong! dell!
Thro' the hushed air, with a billowy swell,
Comes the solemn voice of that old church-bell!
    Life! life! life!
What is it at best but a ceaseless strife,
With warrings of soul and body rife?

    Ding! dong! dell!
Oh when those sounds for me shall tell
The last of earth, may all say, " How well!"
    Death! death! death!
'Tis but the stopping of this faint breath
To win a bright immortal wreath!

LYRA.

" There Lyra, for the brightness of her stars,
  More than their number eminent ; twice seven
  She counts, and one of these illuminates
  The heavens far around, blazing imperial
  In the first order."

WHEN the ripened Summer's golden
    Twilight paints the western portal
Of that palace where the olden
  Constellations dwell immortal,
And the dusky night is flitting
  In and out her starry bowers,
Ere with crown and sceptre sitting
  She holds court thro' darkness' hours—

Comes sweet cadence, softly trilling
  Plaintive air and heavenly measure
From a golden harp's strings—filling
  All the spheres with rapturous pleasure !—
Orpheus' lyre—now constellated—
  (He who wrought in Dis a pæan—
In gloomy realms of Pluto—fated
  To leave his head in Sea Egean !)

Lyra ! group of matchless splendor !
  Music's deified, pure essence !
Flooding with thy stars so tender
  Midnight's halls with iridescence—
Beauteous constellation ! art thou
  The recipient celestial

Of the sweetest strains which part now
    From the nether shore terrestrial?

Soft, persuasive echoes, blending
    With the melodies of Eden
Like repentant sighs, and lending
    Earth new beauties—while they lead on,
Over sin's dark night victorious,
    Over death, despair, and madness—
Tell us, may not music glorious
    Change earth's woes to breathing gladness?

" Yes !"   Thine eyes with brightness glowing,
    Scintillate reply celestial ;
Telling—cadences sweet, flowing
    Upward from the realms terrestrial,
Are messengers that speak to heaven
    With angel tongues, tho' earthly pleading !—
And error e'en may be forgiven
    When such blest sounds to good are leading.

Lyra—golden harp immortal,
    At the gate of Eden trilling !
Speak to man ! and say, That portal
    He may gain, by ever filling
Full his heart with all harmonious
    Notes of sweetness, and discarding
Envy's discord harsh, erroneous—
    . Which his upward flight's retarding !

27

THE SPIRIT OF THE PAST.

JUST as the golden gate of sleep vibrated
　To my calm'd pulses' even-tempered flow,
And blest forgetfulness o'er all that grated
　Upon my heart-strings, came to soothe my woe—
Soft from the silent hall of dreams, a spirit
　Glided, with moonlit robes and shadowy brow:
A mark was there—the seal which all inherit
　Who've found their idols clay, and air each vow !

Deep in its misty eyes were tombed wild fancies,
　The painted bubbles youth delights to blow—
And flashing lights were there, and dreamy glances
　That gleamed upon the heights of " long ago !"
And there were blended hues of deeper feeling,
　Loves and remembrances now faded, gone—
Or wraith-like, thro' sleep's ivory portals stealing
　To chant a dirge and tell of pleasures flown.

Within its hand a wand of fairy lightness
　Parted the curtains of the solemn night,
And flashing o'er the gloom, with radiant brightness,
　Came the long-lost but fondly-welcomed light
Of early days—with amber-tinted glory
　Gilding the edges of each warning cloud
Gathering to tell Life's stormy, wrathful story,
　In low, deep mutterings, or thunders loud.

Back from the bower, the happy bower of childhood,
　Floated a mother's voice, so soft and low,

It seemed but echo sending from the wildwood
  The sounds it caught and treasured long ago ;
Snatches of song, the early loved and cherished,
  Blending with prayers my infant lips were taught
By her, true friend ! who but untimely perished,
  With love had chased the gloom by falsehood wrought.

Sweet were the tones, more tangible, more real,
  They came to cheer my heart in midnight's gloom—
" Live !" spake the voice—" live in the bright ideal ;
  'Twill smooth thy lonely passage to the tomb !
Phantasmagoric, life at best a dream is,
  Gilded to some, to others darkly drawn—
That is a happy heart where but one beam is
  That struggles with earth's clouds for brighter dawn.

" Forget the present, with its dark surroundings—
  Backward o'er Memory's ocean steer thy bark
And moor it in the mirrored Past's aboundings,
  Lighted by holy Love's undying spark !—
Thus may'st thou call thy treasures back, and borrow
  From Fancy's loom a mesh to deck the rod,
That purifies with every earthly sorrow—
  And for thy future, trust it to thy God !"

It ceased—that holy voice ! Perchance a ripple
  Broke o'er the waves of ether where they roll
Thro' space—parting the spirit-links, the triple
  Chain that bound the dim Past, my mother's soul
And mine, in sweet communion, pure and lonely,
  In midnight's solemn hour, the deep, profound !—
And now my heart, cheered by remembrance only,
  Paces the Past's all-hallowed arches round !

THE WORLD BEYOND.

"In the beautiful world beyond."
MRS. SOUTHWORTH'S *Island Princess.*

NO waif of humanity, cast on Life's ocean,
　To breast its dark waves or float light 'neath its
　　smile,
But has rested a while from the billow's commotion
　Upon the green breast of a magical isle—
An isle in the sea of futurity sparkling,
　Where each as a sovereign may rule without wand ;
Whose shores 'twixt the sunrise and sunset lie dark-
　　ling,
　And shut out the beautiful world beyond !

Oh who, in the visions of youth's sunny morning,
　Has not longed for a glimpse of that mystical clime
Which the veil of uncertainty hides—while adorning
　Its myth-peopled realms and air-castles sublime?
And who when the shadows of age o'er them stealing
　(Reality's shadows, that darken hopes fond)
Has not sighed that the curtain was e'er drawn reveal-
　　ing
　How false were the hues of that far world beyond?

O Pilgrim ! whose footsteps have wearily measured
　Earth's broad aisles in search of green pastures of
　　rest—
Who hast lost by the wayside each object once treasured,
　And buried each hope in despair's chilly breast—

Look up! see yon heaven, with its wide arms en-
   folding
The shores of the sunrise and sunset, so fond ;
Then pass thro' Death's portal, in rapture beholding
   The goal of thy dreams in that bright world be-
   yond !

ODD FELLOWSHIP.

Written for the celebration, in New Orleans, of the Fortieth Anni-
versary of the Independent Order of Odd Fellows in the United
States, April 26, 1859.

THE chimes of Eighteen hundred years
   Have circled thro' the rolling spheres,
Since angels over Bethlehem's plain
Hymned a sweetly solemn strain :
" Peace on earth, good-will to men !"
And wingèd winds have harped since then
The hallelujahs deep, that rang
As when the sons of morning sang !

Eighteen hundred years have sped—
And from the thorns that bound His head
Who bleeding hung on Calvary,
Have sprung the buds of Charity—
The flowers of Friendship, Love and Truth—
The bloom of Hope's perpetual youth—
The silver leaves of Faith's white tree,
To wreathe the brow of Unity !

27 *

Brave workers in a noble cause,
True unto God's and Nature's laws,
Have wrought a mystic chain to bind
Earth's family of human kind—
For while Odd Fellowship abides,
O'er stormiest swells of sorrow's tides
The golden links shall stretch, to save
Each brother from the threatening wave.

The widow's tearful eyes shall speak
The thanks denied her utterance meek—
The orphan's grateful prayers shall swell
The " songs of praise" the angels tell !
And when the reaching chain has grasped
The world's wide bounds, and nations clasped,
Then shall we see that glorious birth
Which prophets say awaits our earth !

Then hail ! the blessed trinity
Of Faith and Hope and Charity !
Hail ! the links, dropp'd from above,
Of Friendship, Truth and holy Love !
Angels hailed the golden morn
When the Prince of Peace was born !
Angels may unite again,
And echo o'er our deep amen !

THE ODD FELLOWS' MISSION.

[Written for the same occasion as the foregoing.]

TRUE pioneers of right, we stand
  In armor staunch to-day ;
And proudly o'er our native land
  Behold our happy sway.
Not subject to the despot's nod
  To circumscribe our span,
Our golden faith is, " Love of God
  Includes the love of man !"

We may not claim the conqueror's wreath,
  The hero's gory crown—
Our task's the wreaking sword to sheathe,
  And turn to smiles the frown !
And tho' the storm-fiends may be proud
  Who wake the tempest's din—
'Tis much to lift the sable cloud
  And let the sunshine in.

The earth is gray, the earth is old,
  And time's a passing breath ;
But hearts where Love is never cold
  May conquer grim-brow'd death !
And deeds of mercy rising high,
  Above old error shriven,
Make golden ladders to the sky,
  On which to mount to heaven !

THE ANGEL CHILD.

" COME with me, mother," the angel child
　　Whispered, with eyes that strangely smiled—

" Lonely and drear will the journey be
　　Thro' the misty dark, if I go without thee.

" Come! I will guide thee to bowers of bliss!
　　'Twas angels that sent me to tell you this—

" I come from a bright and smiling band
　　To lead you to their happy land!"

　　And the mother closed her eyes, with faith
　　In her angel guide thro' the gates of death!

THE MORNING COMETH.

THE morning cometh—the heavenly morn
　　That ushers in the glorious day
When kindreds and tongues and nations born
　　From darkness, shall bask in the sun's bright ray.
The Sun of Righteousness!—widely his beam
　　Shall pierce the depths of the deepest gloom—
Shall glow in Ganges' unhallowed stream—
　　And warm the desert to life and bloom!

The morning cometh—the blissful morn !
  'Tis singing now on the hill-tops near ;
Far over the rolling ocean borne,
  The heavenly anthem ringeth clear !
The wild floods hear and clap their hands,
  The heathen isles shake off the night—
While the glad warm earth, new-mantled, stands
  In garments of redeeming light !

The morning cometh—its Herald Star,
  The Star of Bethlehem, points the way !
The clouds of darkness are fleeing afar
  Before the bright, all-perfect day,
Which prophets and saints of old foretold—
  When Messiah's name shall illume each clime,
Shall pierce the gloom of Idolatry's fold,
  And eternal day chase the night of time !

The morning cometh—awake ! arise !
  Shake off the dust from thy garments fair,
O Captive Daughter of Zion !   Sighs
  No more shall echo thy heart's despair !
And thou, Jerusalem—loose the band
  That has bound thee long to the night's dark side—
Redeemed, thou shalt stand, like the Promised Land
  That smiled o'er Jordan's golden tide !

The morning cometh—the holy morn !
  When radiant upon Zion's hill
Are the feet of him with good tidings borne,
  Who to Zion saith—" Thy God reigneth still !"

v

The watchmen shall in unity
   Lift up their voices in wrapt accord,
And joyful sing, " Oh blessed is he
   That cometh in the name of the Lord !"

EVENING.

WEARY Day, its course nigh run,
   Distanced by the fiery sun,
Paler grows and longs for rest
In the chambers of the West—
Breathes a low, expiring sigh,
Closes up its round red eye,
   And, like the faithful Indian bride,
   Dies because its mate has died.

See the timid evening star,
O'er the sunset heights afar,
   Trembles as the dancing ray '
   Ignites the funeral pyre of day.
While the twilight's bark of blue,
Rimm'd and barr'd with silver dew,
   And rosy pennons floating free,
   Skims along a purple sea.

Up the slanting bridges bright,
That span the gulf 'twixt day and night,
   Fair Dian's crescent's silver sparks
   Light the chase in starry parks

Where the crystal fountains play,
And the vagrant zephyrs stray
  Kissing open the bright eyes
  Of the glow-worms in the skies!

Eve with rosary of stars,
Like a pale nun thro' the bars
  That lattice in her convent cell,
  Gazes over grove and dell;
Faintly sounds the vesper bell:
As the sweet notes sink and swell,
  The drowsy cattle slowly come
  From hill and dale to sheltering home.

Now the cloister's curtain falls—
Night opes wide her ebon halls;
  Lights her alabaster lamps;
  Scatters far her dew and damps
Wanton winds in revelry
Shout their wild hilarity—
  Pensive nun in revery
  Seeks her couch and breviary!

THE EAGLE AND THE DOVE.

GOLDEN bronze as a lion's eye,
  Or amber drops in a sea-bird's lair,
Or flashing topaz from Araby,
  Is the sunny dash of her nut-brown hair.

Sparkling jewel, the queenly Clare!
  But her rich red lip is wreathed in scorn—
Coral and pearl are gleaming there,
  Like the berry and bloom of the poison thorn.

Ye would not give one dreamy glance
  Of the violet eyes of Maud, sweet Maud,
For all Clare's haughty looks, that dance
  Like soulless rays from tinseled gaud—

Maud, the chaste and tender flower,
  Timid mimosa, sensitive, shy—
Knowing not the wondrous power
  Veiled 'neath the lash of her downcast eye.

Maud, the gentle, of simple race,
  Who ne'er owned a rood of greenwood bower—
Maud, whose wealth is her own sweet face:
  Never maid hath a richer dower!

Lady Clare hath acres broad,
  Vassals serve her on bended knee;
But one hath kneeled to the humble Maud,
  Who bows not to the proud ladye—

One who claims from mother earth
  The heritage only Nature gives—
Not lands that are his right of birth,
  But a heart of truth that truly lives!

Ah! Lady Clare, you boast your share
  Of this world's wealth, but it cannot buy
The jewel you secretly pine to wear,
  Tho' you curl your lip and flash your eye.

No glittering ray from your richest gem,
　Tho' prison'd sunbeams gleam from the gaud,
Can halo you with the diadem
　That love has wrought for the brow of Maud!

And ever the bells ring merrily—
　Merrily forth from the belfry old;
And the Lady Clare sits scornfully
　Braiding her tresses like threads of gold!

Braiding her tresses with costly pearls—
　For the bells peal forth for the bridal day,
And the village girls wreathe Maud's bright curls
　With the pouting blooms of the early May.

And Clare must give the bride away—
　Every chime from the old church tower
Ringing, singing, seemeth to say,
　" Maud will be lady of Glenwood bower !"

Ye've seen the lurid light that gleams
　In the folded cloud when the tempest's nigh?
Ye've watched the red electric streams
　Flashing athwart the mist-wrapt sky?

But what are these to the flaming eye,
　Burning beneath its lid of snow,
Of Clare?—as the fatal hour draws nigh
　To stamp her life with the seal of woe.

*　　　*　　　*　　　*　　　*

" Thine for ever !" is whispered low,
    And Maud is Lady of Glenwood now !—
" Never ! never !"—a shriek, a blow,
    A crimson tide, a ghastly brow—

And village maidens with roses wreathed,
    And priest in sacerdotal stole,
Rise with the prayer on their lips half breathed,
    As the old church rings with a maniac howl—

" In the dark valley go seek your bride,
    My Lord of Glenwood !—ye spurned my prayer,
Ye cast to the winds my maiden pride,
    And ye reap the stormy revenge of Clare !

" Ring, old bells, ring out again !
    Peal me a merrier, happier lay—
Tell of the dusky burial train,
    The narrow house and the couch of clay !

" The spectre bridegroom waits to-day
    He clinks his bones in his noisome cell—
Ring, old bells, ring a roundelay,
    I've given the fair bride with him to dwell !

" I've pledged her deep in ruby wine,
    See ! it stains the bridal robe of snow—
No bursting pulse from the purple vine
    E'er throbbed with life like its crimson flow.

" Ho ! knight and squire and page, ho ! ho !
    Fill high, fill high to the fair ladye !
Not Lady of Glenwood—no, no, no !
    But queen of a greater realm is she !

" Bride of the king of terrors!   See!
    And her wide domain, the grave !—ha ! ha !
  'Tis a green retreat where no rivalry
    Save with the worms, there'll be.   But ah !"

And the burning eye took a softer shade,
    The quivering lip a sadder tone,
As the scarlet cheek began to fade,
    And the pulses faint, of the maniac one—

" Ye'll never know, poor gentle Maud"
    (She kneeled by the pallid corpse the while),
" When your head lies lowly beneath the sward,
    What 'tis to pine for a loving smile—

" What 'tis to worship some golden ray
    From a sunny heart, that is not for you—
As the wrecked mariner sees away
    O'er the wide waste of waters blue,

" A snowy sail that tells of home,
    Of hope and rescue from perils drear ;
Then fades away in the ocean foam,
    Nor heeds the wretch that is perishing near !

" Ye passed away while your life was love,
    And rosy sweet will your dreamings be
In the mossy nest—poor, harmless dove !—
    That my wild hand has given thee.

" And is there not a nook for me ?
    I come from my eyrie in the clouds
And lay me down all pantingly,
    While thy snowy plumage my brow enshrouds ;

" Room, for the wounded bird to die !"—
  The writhing limbs have ceased to move ;
A quivering lid—a low-drawn sigh—
  And the eagle lies at the feet of the dove !

AN EXCUSE FOR RHYMING.

'TWERE pleasant could we clothe in verse
    Our daily thoughts, and speak in rhymes ;
And poetry is none the worse
    For ending in these pleasing chimes.
A happy thought cannot be spoiled
    By smoothly giving it a finish ;
Tho' captious critics long have toiled
    The Rhymster's merits to diminish.

The Rhymster may not be a Poet—
But when 'tis so we soon will know it ;
For words that burn will make their mark—
The lightning's bright electric spark
From heights empyrean claims its birth,
While grosser fires are chained to earth ;
The lark that carols from the sky
Is known from birds that lowlier fly !

But deem it not an idle thing
For Nature's worshiper to sing ;
To seek in Rhyme's soft, flowing measure
A tuneful vent for harmless pleasure.

For verse is melody divine,
When pleasant thoughts harmonious chime—
'Tis like the setting of sweet words
To music's softly thrilling chords.

Unlike the tender swan (that pours
  Her life-breath in a rapturous lay
And dies, in telling she adores
  The golden hours that throne the day)
Are hearts whose gushing harmony,
  Like the young bird, must find a wing,
And flooded with sweet melody
  Must give it vent—must die or sing !

SELF-COMMUNING.

COMMUNING with myself, I ask
  My heart the reason why
I love as well the ashen cloud
  As the blue, stainless sky?
And why the cheerless autumn days
  Have still for me the charms
Of Spring, all blushing, when she clasps
  Young Summer's outstretched arms?

I know not. But I think my soul's
  A waiflet of the mist—
Born when our mother, Nature, kept
  A blessed eucharist—

28 *

And left a wayside foundling at
  The trembling gate of tears,
Where Heaven's own bow of promise still
  Its radiant circlet rears!

For when I think my life is vain—
  I cast my eyes abroad
Upon the fields of golden grain
  Fed by the smile of God!
The virgin lilies, clothed with grace,
  Who toil not, neither spin—
And then I ask myself, which race
  Hath the best boon to win?

For surely if the Father's love
  Is poured on flower and tree,
His "last, best work" must claim a share
  E'en from Divinity!
For what He does He doeth well,
  And I, His wayward child,
For some wise purpose have been sent
  To tread Life's desert wild.

And I am thankful to the power
  That's given unto me—
The eye to pierce the darkest cloud
  Its silver side to see;
For in the stormiest sky I trace
  The hand of Love Divine,
Pouring with ever gracious palm
  The sacramental wine!

And thus, communing with myself,
  I feel the cheerless days,

The burden and the heat I've borne
The steep and thorny ways
My weary feet have sorely pressed,
I still must fainting plod,
If I would share His grace who hath
The burning ploughshare trod!

A STORMY SUNSET.

THERE was a hush on leaf and flower—a pause
Of terror, which foretold the coming storm.
The crimson curtains fring'd with gold that hung
Above the couch of Night were closely drawn
To shield the sun, that hid his sleepy face
An hour too soon!

        Behind the battlements
That wall'd the North, an inky fortress of
Misshapen clouds arose, from whose dun towers
A thousand gayly-painted banners waved
Fantastic folds, as parting rays of light
Changed their gray gauze to rainbow-tinted hues.

High where the zenith reared its stately dome,
Chaotic darkness hung a leaden shroud
Which laid a funeral pall on Day's blue eyes,
And with unearthly sighs and mutterings told
Of desolation. One by one, the fires
Round Sol's bright car of light expired—and forth

The spirit of the storm sped on his wild, wild work!
Huge bombs, hurl'd downward by demoniac hands,
Exploded, and their burning fragments cast
Now near, now far: the fiery rocket flew
From cloud to earth, and with it brought dismay;
The mad winds raised their voices, howling forth
Fierce anthems of exultant rage!

     Oh wild
The revel of the elements!   But now
Their mother, Nature, heard the angry clash,
And parting the dark curtain of the clouds,
Look'd out upon her warring children; then
Bow'd low her head and wept!   Tears, copious tears
Stream'd forth upon the earth—and, at the sight,
Her guilty children, one by one, retired.
Stilled in each fiery bosom the fierce rage
That thus could draw from parent's eyes such drops
Of blinding agony!

     Her grief was hushed!
She stayed her gushing tears, and raised her eyes
In thankfulness devout; then, as still hung
Upon her fringèd lids the pearly drops—
The sun arous'd from his siesta light
And sent a stray glance upward, which just touch'd
Those glittering drops with many color'd dyes,
And bound her forehead with a rainbow crown!

A SOLEMN MARCH.

LO ! 'tis the conqueror, Death !
    With his captives wan he is marching on
The path he has trod since creation's morn—
    His is the victor's wreath !

His sweeping scythe lays low
The parent trees in our household groves,
All that the heart most clings to, loves,
    With his shrouded army go !

Far over mount and vale,
The phantom train are hurrying fast,
For Pestilence rides the wings of the blast,
    And brings its trophies pale.

The hoary brow of Age,
And Manhood's locks in their ebon flow,
Are bowed in the van of the conqueror, low—
    To his power there is no gauge.

Away ! away ! away !
He sweeps from our homes their budding flowers,
The clinging vines from our cherished bowers—
    The beautiful ! the gay !

See the fair bride now pass
From the ivied church, with a merry train—
The archer aims his dart again,
    And turns his empty glass—

Another victim's placed
In his sheeted ranks, and the bridal wreath
Is laid at the feet of the tyrant, Death,
    That Love's brow should have graced.

A mother shrieks, " My child !"
He has torn the babe from her quivering breast
(Oh ! where will it find so pure a rest ?—)
    And mocks her anguish wild !

He ranges the earth's broad dome,
And he tramples kings 'neath his icy feet
As he does the outcast in the cold street
    Dying for want of a home !

Ermine or beggar's garb—
'Tis all the same, so a human heart
Quivers beneath, as his fatal dart
    Wounds with its poisoned barb.

But an angel of mercy, he
To the sorrowing comes, the sorely tried
Who long to soar—but their wings are tied—
    To the land where the spirit's free !

Then softly come, O Death !
When the weary would fain lie down to sleep,
And the faded eyes would cease to weep—
    Come with a gentle breath,

And blow out the tiny flame
That flickers and glares in the socket so,
And keeps the poor body in fretful glow—
    Come ! and we'll bless thy name !

THE MAGICIAN.

NO lean, wrinkled necromancer,
    Quaintly garbed—
Nor weird Hecaté, witch-dancer,
    Adder-barbed—
Neither good Old Mother Fairie,
    Gift-laden—
Nor spectral hobgoblin, nor airy
    Elf-maiden—
Nor sprite, nor fay, that drew the veil Elysian—
But sweetest sorcerer and holiest Magician!

Choked by the dark tares of sadness,
    Each bright seed
I'd dropped on my wayside's gladness
    Sprang a weed!
Sharp thorns grew where fairest roses
    Should have bloomed—
As sack of honey-bee discloses
    The sting it tomb'd!—
While Hopes glad beam flashed only meteorical,
And truthfulness in aught seemed fable allegorical!

Yet in this, my darkest midnight,
    Dawned a ray
Bright'ning to broad, perfect noonlight—
    Glorious day!
All the misty vapors rolling
    From my brow,

And with golden pen there scrolling—
    " Blest art thou !
Who, groping in the labyrinth of fell sorrow,
Hast met the sibyl, Faith, to gild each coming morrow !

THE GREATEST IN THE KINGDOM OF HEAVEN.

" At the same time came the disciples unto Jesus, saying, Who is the greatest in the kingdom of heaven?"—ST. MATTHEW xviii. 1.

HE took a little child, and in
    Their midst He sat him down, and said :
" If ye that heirdom seek to win,
    Turn from the devious ways ye tread
With vaunting—for, unless ye be
    As humble as this little child,
And with such faith believe in me,
    Ye cannot share my kingdom mild !

" And woe to that man who offends
    One little one that on me calls ;
He'd better lie where sullen wends
    The dark, deep sea thro' crystal walls—
For these are they whose angels see
    My Father's face, which is in heaven !
Then one of these despise not ye,
    Lest ye in turn be unforgiven !"

So spake He ; and when face to face
    With conscience and with God we stand,

And He who died for us, in grace
  Sits at Jehovah's strong right hand!
Not ermined state or sceptered power,
  Nor knightly fame of high degree,
Will be to thee as rich a dower
  As lowly-born humility!

For 'twill not then be asked the line
  Of kings thou hast descended from;
The right to heritage divine
  Lies in the good to man thou'st done!
Thy nightly prowess may have rung
  And blazoned in high heraldry,
But deeds of mercy will be sung
  Above the deeds of chivalry!

And earnest faith—the childlike faith
  That lowly bends the reverend knee,
And looking thro' the darkness, saith
  " Our Father," in sincerity—
Is all that is required to make
  The greatest in that land divine!
Accept His word, and fearless take
  The hand that's bent in love to thine.

ACCORDING TO THY GIFTS.

ACCORDING to the grace
  That by the will Divine is given thee,
Whate'er thy calling, do it faithfully
  According to thy grace.

Let love be without guile—
Thy honored part, to give thy brother place
When thine by right of precedence the race—
  Thus, love is without guile !

Open thy larder wide,
And share thy crust with him whose need demands.
The widow's cruse was filled by angel hands—
  Open thy larder wide.

Rejoice with them that joy.
Tho' fortune may not smile just then for thee,
'Twill solace thee another's bliss to see—
  Rejoice with them that joy !

And weep with them that weep.
How soft from Friendship's eye the tender tear
Falls on the heart !   Sweet sympathy is dear—
  Oh weep with them that weep !

Seek not earth's titled ones,
But condescend to men of low estate—
He that is least on earth, in heaven is great !
  Seek not earth's titled ones.

Bless them—bless and curse not—
Which persecute thee ; for thou sow'st a seed
That beareth sweeter fruit than cursing's weed
  And thorn.   Bless, and curse not !

According to the gifts
Thou hast receivèd at thy Maker's hand,
Thy stewardship must be within the land,
  According to thy gifts.

But whether great or small
The trust reposed in thee, thou still canst find
Some chord responsive in thy brother's mind,
  Whether he's great or small.

Then seek the trembling string,
And touch it with the tender hand of Love—
You'll hear it echo from the courts above,
  If you but touch the string!

JEAN INGELOW.

"Jean Ingelow is twenty-eight years old, unmarried and homely!"
—*Newspaper paragraph.*

HOMELY? Ah, me! the diamond hath
    A dark encrusted shell,
But lapidaries know a gem
  Is hidden there full well.

The purest pearl that ever graced
  A queenly diadem,
Was incubated where the rocks
  Old Ocean's wild waves stem.

The luscious fruits of tropic climes
  Have rough outsides, but there
The honey of Hymettus finds
  Its own sweet hiving rare.

The violet and the mignonette
　Are " homely " little flowers,
But summer hath none sweeter in
　Her dew-bespangled bowers.

Ah ! would we only know the worth
　Of spirit-beauty, then
We might select the beautiful
　Of women and of men.

But now we through a glass but see
　Too darkly to do this ;
But when as soul to soul we stand
　We shall achieve that bliss.

Then, sister Jean, my " homely " one,
　How glorious thou'lt shine
Where cherubim and seraphim
　Shall hail thee all divine !

NOTHING TO LOVE.

" Alas !" said she, " I have nothing to love."—*Extract from a letter.*

NOTHING to love?　With the arching skies
　　Bending above thy head,
And looking love with unnumbered eyes
　That o'er thee radiance shed?

Nothing to love?   When the beauteous earth
  Lays her emerald crown at thy feet—
And holds to thy lips, at each floral birth,
  Her perfume-chalice sweet?

Nothing to love?   With an eye to see,
  And a heart to feel?   Not so ;
For Nature's breast has a pulse for thee
  That ever will ceaseless flow.

Nothing to love?   Why the world is fill'd
  With the lovable, the pure ;
And the chords of thy soul must have sometimes thrill'd
  When angels have swept them o'er !

Nothing to love?   Oh a loving breeze
  Is kissing now thy cheek !—
There are myriad things that the true heart sees
  To love, if we only seek !

A voice comes up from the flowery heath,
  A tone from the dancing wave—
And Love is the whisper of every breath,
  And the music the billows lave.

And Love is the theme that the seraph choirs
  Are hymning now thro' the stars—
And we catch the strains from their golden lyres
  When our soul lets down its bars !

Then say not that you have naught to love
  And none to love you—when
Ye know there are links from the chain above
  Clasping the sphere of men !—
    20 *

But love all things, for He made them all !
   And you near his throne above
When you love His works—the great and small—
   For God himself is Love

"THY FAITH HATH MADE THEE WHOLE."

[St. Matthew ix. 22.]

'TWAS not the glory shining from His brow,
   'Twas not a magic in His garment's flow
That healed the stricken woman kneeling low

To kiss His robe ! "Thy faith hath made thee whole,"
He said. And down the centuries still roll
The words of cheer to many a fainting soul,

That, groping in the dreary depths below,
Would blindly stumble, knowing not where to go,
But for the light within, whose steady glow

Christ's hand hath kindled and his breath hath fired,
To lead us thro' the darkness all untired,
Up where the golden pinnacles are spired !

For we are voyagers who gayly sail
Away from land unwitting of the gale
That perdu lies within our very "hail !"

But Faith's our pilot when the storm beats fast,
And all our sails are riven from the mast,
Our bark of life a plaything for the blast,

And Hope, our anchor, wrenched from out its stay—
While on the rock of sin the breakers play
And treacherous undercurrents lead alway.

But, steady! see, our Helmsman good has spied
A little glimmer o'er the boiling tide,
And toward the friendly lighthouse on we ride,

O'er lashing wave and wrecking billow, on!
Past low Despair's dark-surging Phlegethon,
Until the wished-for, heavenly goal is won,

Where shines the crystal lamp whose silver flame
Comes rippling down Time's tidal sea—the same
The lowly Nazarene hath given to fame!

LIFE'S MISSION.

POOR hands, scar-stained with labor,
    Soft palms uplifted high,
Ye ask a benediction
    From the Ruler of the sky—
Whatever these hands findeth
    To do, use all their might;
'Tis thus the great Creator
    Has armed us for the fight.

Has given us god-like reason,
    A strong enthronèd king,
That we with mind may govern
    Each sublunary thing;

May crush from out our natures
    The animal and low,
And give with loving kindness
    A kiss for every blow.

And bravely to the battle
    Go armed with truth and love,
Our banner, the branched olive
    Brought by the weary dove,
Who stemmed the raging waters
    And battled with their strife,
(Just as poor human bipeds
    Breast the wild waves of life)

And passing all the whirlpools
    That led to Ocean's cave,
Found the green leaf Earth offered
    From out the watery grave;·
And we may also find one,
    However tempest-beat,
If with unflagging pinion
    We seek the mercy-seat,

And learn Life's mission truly,
    And trusting, look on high,
And ask a benediction
    From the Ruler of the sky !
Poor hands, scar-stained with toiling,
    Soft palms, in prayer upraised,
If ye've learned to labor truly,
    God's name ye've truly praised.

EPICEDIUM.

[DR. E. K. KANE, OBIIT, FEB. 16, 1857.]

A STAR has fallen!   From the empyrean heights
    An orb of light has set in depths profound!
A while it shone o'er space, a beacon blaze
To guide to mighty deeds; a shining mark,
Which with a startled glance we upward gazed
To contemplate—and lo! it was no more.

A nation mourns, a hero is laid low!
Not his the glory purchased with the wild
And anguished widow's cry—the orphan's wail—
The bloody fame won o'er the reeking corpse,
The gory, headless trunk and mangled manes
Amid the carnage of the battle-field,
Where men like demons hew God's image down,
Till more like work of foulest fiend it seems—
The impress left by Deity, to stamp
His work divine, defaced and blotted out
By seething, boiling passions, and desire
For what the world calls glory!

                His the meed,
The nobler meed of fame—the laurel wreath
For conquest over self! that shadow huge
Which darkeneth our best resolves, and comes
Between us and our duty. But with firm,
Unflinching soul, that looked far, far beyond
The narrow confines of a mortal's span

Of life—man's little hour!—he freely gave
His all of life to benefit mankind.

His country's pilot, he!   And when the stars
And stripes shall fill with Arctic breezes, and
Unfurl their glories 'neath the Polar star,
Which from the zenith shall look down upon
Its sisters which the spangled banner grace,
Then shall a Nation's heart with proudest throes
Swell earnestly and high, and long and loud
The name of "KANE" shall ring from pole to pole!

Peace to his hallow'd manes!

                    Not only on
The marble cold his epitaph engrave—
But on his country's heart, in words that burn,
We'll trace, " He gave his life, a stepping-stone
For Fame to sound his country's triumphs to
The world!"

          Train o'er his sepulchre the bay,
As tribute of a Nation's grateful heart,
And watered by a Nation's sacred tears!
  New Orleans, *Feb.* 24, 1857.

THE EARLY DEAD.

"It was among the loveliest customs of the ancients to bury the young at morning twilight ; for as they strove to give the softest interpretation to death, so they imagined that Aurora, who loved the young, had stolen them to her embrace."

BEAR forth the early called, to rest 'neath the grass,
While the garments of morning brush the dew as they
    pass—
Bury them when the first beam that steals from the
    skies
Trembles in the depths of the violet's blue eyes.

Let no wail of sorrow break forth o'er the beds,
With their downy moss coverlets, where ye rest their
    young heads—
'Tis no crumbling, dark sepulchre, with its foulness and
    gloom,
That will cover them with mildew and the blight of the
    tomb—

But a soft couch of roses, where the glad voice of morn
Will call them from slumber to sport with the dawn
In the crystal-columned palace that rises in the East,
With its many colored windows, thro' which the day is
    pressed.

Oh lay them where the glow-worms will light up the
    grass
As the dark-browed night with its shadow doth pass—

On their grave's green sod let each lark build its nest,
And soar upward with their spirits when the dawn is
       in the East.

Oh mourn them not as those whom Death's cold clasp
Hath severed from your love to languish in his grasp—
A soft voice came whispering, which you could not
       hear,
At its call their souls listened with a smile and a tear ;

It came o'er them stealing like the low sweet hymn
That their infant spirits heard ere heaven's light grew
       dim—
The melody of Eden, ere their souls had lost their
       wings,
Or the stains of earth had darkened their angel lyres'
       strings !

Oh wonder not they listed those tones from on high
That ever called, " Come, come away !"   It was not to
       die
That they followed the windings of that soft, mystic
       horn
Across the golden bridge to the pearly gates of morn !

Oh rejoice that the sorrows and regrets of age
Will never leave a blot on their memory's pure page—
That from earth they have passed in their spring's
       green hour,
Ere withered was a leaf or faded was a flower.

Oh gem their graves with daisies whose silver crowns
Will shine with a glory o'er the soft green downs

Where their spirits when they hover in the morning
    hours
Will touch with their pinions the golden-tufted flowers.

Oh lay not the early called 'neath the cold stones
Where the sad willow weeps and the wild wind moans,
Where the churchyard's gloom with its skeleton eyes
Will look a reproach at their spirits in the skies—

But write o'er their graves, with God's own flowers,
A hymn of thanksgiving that they've passed to the
    bowers
Where sorrow cannot enter—where night has passed
    away—
And morning has ushered in eternal noonday.

THE STAR OF JUDEA.

" And lo ! the star which they saw in the East went before them
till it came and stood over where the young child was."—St. Matthew ii. 9.

GLIMMERING down from far-distant spheres,
    Thro' the long arches where multiplied years
Slowly and solemnly file to the shades—
Ray upon ray twinkles, brightens and fades ;
World upon world and sun upon sun
Flash out existence !   Which is the one
Whose quivering beams led the men of the East?
Star of Judea, where shineth thy crest?

30

In the mild spring-time, when green leaves again
Send their bright promise of seed-time and grain—
In the warm summer, when valley and hill
Tell of the vintage their sweets can distill—
In the dun autumn, when the fruit-laden bin
Groans with the spoils of the year packed within—
O'er yon blue ether, in season, each star
Rolls to its throne in the deep vault afar.

Leo, rampant, with his bright train appears,
Just as he's done thro' centurial years;
Arcturus, hounding the Bear, still drives on
His bruinish trade, as 'twere just but begun;
Virgo still weighs out the nights and the days
With justice, which crowneth her heavenly ways;
And Scorpio lashes his fiery tail
Thro' summery skies, as a farmer his flail.

Lyra attuneth her lyre, as of old,
Capricorn enters the Zodiac's fold—
Aquarius, Pisces and Aries appear,
And Taurus and Cancer, as year upon year
In the wide field of creation takes part.
Star of Judea, wherever thou art
In the great galaxy, point us thy place!
Let us not lose thee, tho' jostling the race.

We know from yon heaven hath silently passed
Orb upon orb of the many that glassed
The sparkling cerulean;—thine, too, perchance,
In its bodily light, may have sent but a glance
O'er the hills Oriental—and so, passed away;
Implanting the germ of the all-perfect Day

That, breaking in glory from Zion's bright brow,
Shall gladden the waste places desolate now.

Star of Judea, if mythic thou art,
Viewed by the erring and weak human heart
Which seeth so dimly thro' eyes mortal blind—
Thy mission, mayhap, is but illy defined;
Teach us thy meaning—we ask for more light!
By thy beams we are led to the manger to-night:
There thou standest still! Is thy duty fulfilled?
And must we solve the problem—tho' sadly unskilled?

Star of Judea, a faint dawn appears
Just where the gray shades are tombing the years—
Each, as 'tis sepulchred, points to the sky,
Where brightly thy splendors shine out to Faith's eye!
Over the manger and Babe lowly born,
Past the rough cross and the crown made of thorn,
Till merged in a flood-tide of glory, its light
Fills the city celestial where cometh not night!

Star of Judea, immortal! shine on,
Till all of the crown by the cross we have won!
Guide us o'er hill-top and valley and plain—
We bring, as the Wise Men, our offerings again;
Not myrrh and frankincense, but penitent sighs
And prayers that are voiceless and suppliant eyes!
Step by step lead us to Jesus' care,
Star of Judea, then pause with us there!

JUDGE NOT.

WHEN thy fellow-sinner weighing
　In the balance, look within,
Down in thy heart's mausoleums
　Where thou'st buried many a sin;
Tear away the mould and mosses
　Which have gendered, year by year;
Let there be a resurrection
　Of the dry bones gathered there:
In the silent, white-faced spectres,
　In review thus passing on,
One may rise whose cold hand hideth
　All thy brother may have done.

One may rise, who, with wan finger
　Pointeth to a nameless mound
Where thou thought to hide for ever
　Some transgression under ground;
One gaunt skeleton may rattle
　All his fleshless limbs, to show
Where thy heedless feet have stumbled
　In the life-path here below;
One may turn his empty sockets
　With an awful questioning stare,
Asking, " How thy fellow-mortal
　Thou to judge shalt boldly dare?"

How shalt thou, of flesh the offspring,
　Dare condemn what flesh may do,

When the great Incarnate Spirit
   Sits in judgment over you?
For the judgment ye shall measure
   Shall be measured you again,
When Death's harvest-time shall open
   All the stores of joy or pain.
Oh be merciful! the erring
   Trust to the Almighty hand—
For thou gainest naught, condemning
   What thou canst not understand.

BORN.

PAUSE, Pilgrim, pause! and ponder on the word—
   The little word that on the threshold stands
Of our existence, and the spirit calls
Forth from the unknown mist, to act its part
In Life's uncertain drama!—Born!
For what? As heir to Man's inheritance,
His gilded hopes and loves—his hates and pains!
Launched on Life's turbid ocean, with its waves
To war, and "sink or swim" as fortune rules
The tide. Born—but not buried! "there's the rub"
('Twere well did we but oftener think on it),
For none can tell what threads are wove by Fate
To trip our heedless feet while wand'ring o'er
The winding path that circles to the tomb!
Oh! let us not, with pride-inflated hearts,
Boast of our strength, and think by it alone

To stem the whirling pools that eddy to
Destruction—oft it fails us in the time
Of need, to show us of what flimsy stuff
'Tis made!   But let our prayer still ever be,
Oh lead us not into Temptation's path,
But from all evil, Lord, deliver us!

ARISE!

A RISE!
   The light-voice messenger of Morn
Breathes o'er the poppies' eyes,
And softly whispers 'mong the waving corn;
  Sweet Fragrance wanders with her perfume cup
Amid the bowers where rose and jasmine twine
  Their leaves; the lark is up
And hymns a lay; the Orient's jewels shine—
     Arise!
Nature lifts up her great heart to the skies!

    Arise!
The golden noonday sun pours down
  His yellow rain, his eyes
Of fire pierce the round acorn's cup of brown
  And draw the tender sapling from the sod—
So, when the beams of Truth upon the heart
  Fall from the mount of God,
They warm good seeds till their dark shells they part
    And rise
In stately trees that tower to the skies!

Arise !

Eve whispers it unto the stars !
  They raise their sparkling eyes,
And showering radiance, mount their silver cars
  To breathe their nightly messages of love
To mortals groping in the dreary dark—
  Bidding them look above
When shades of earth obscure their hope's bright spark :
" Arise !"
They murmur—" All is brightness in the skies !"

Arise

Above thy sorrows, child of clay !
  Lo ! faith is born of sighs,
As from the night's dark side springs glorious day !
  The stately ship that ploughs the pathless deep
Would never reach its port did calms prevail—
  And thou, when dark woes sweep,
Art borne the nearer heaven on the gale !
Arise !
The phœnix from her ashes seeks the skies !

Arise !

Thro' Heaven's court seraphic din
  Fills all the echoing skies,
When thro' the gates of death a soul goes in !
  Oh folded hands !   Oh closed and rayless eyes !
Why do we mourn thee—we that linger here?
  When peace so calmly lies
On thee—and angels call around thy bier,
" Arise,
O soul redeemed from earth, to fadeless skies !"

THE CONVERSION OF ST. PAUL.

" And he fell to the earth and heard a voice saying, Saul, Saul, why
persecutest thou me ?"—ACTS ix. 4.

STRICKEN blind by the dazzling light
   Which from the clouds shone o'er him,
Prone on the earth he trembling lay
Under the Syrian palms, that day
   That brought his sins before him.

He saw poor murdered Stephen rise
   With eyes of loving kindness—
He heard the words from Christ's own lips,
That from his soul rent the eclipse
   Of more than mortal blindness.

And in each mangled form his hand
   Had given to be martyred,
He saw Christ crucified again—
He felt the passion and the pain
   Of all his soul had bartered.

And, groveling in the dust, he plead—
   " Lord, teach to me my duty !"
Oh humbly, with him, let us pray
For light to guide us on our way,
   That we may see its beauty.

For, like to Saul of Tarsus, we
   Still lend a hand in stoning

Some helpless Stephen—tho' the grace
Of God shines in his anguished face,
  That pride forbids our owning.

We wrap us in self-righteousness,
  And thank the God that formed us
Of common clay—that we are not
As yon poor Publican, whose lot
  Is far from that that warmed us.

Oh smite us blind! if from the blow
  Our inner vision waketh—
That we may see how Jesus died,
And feel that all the crucified
  His heritage partaketh!

LOVE ONE ANOTHER.

"These things I command you, That you love one another."—
St. John xv. 17.

CLASP hands, pilgrims, sore benighted
    In the darkling mists terrestrial—
There's a beacon, heaven-lighted,
  Shining from the heights celestial,
That will guide ye upward ever,
  When, as brother unto brother,
Ye resolve, with true endeavor
  And God's help, to love each other.

'Tis a rugged way we travel,
  Here a slough and there a brier—

And the farther we unravel
  Its dark depths, the more we tire;
But a little lamp of brightness
  Each can trim, to cheer another
With its holy, heavenly whiteness—
  'Tis to truly love each other.

Love not only them that love thee
  (This is but thy self-love feeding),
But, as He loved who above thee
  From high Calvary bends bleeding,
Love the hand that's raised to scourge thee
  By thy fellow-worm, thy brother!
Thus, and only thus, thou'lt purge thee
  Of all pride—thus love each other.

Love, through direst persecution;
  All thy foemen are but mortal,
And must make thee restitution
  At Death's surely leveling portal;
Where, if proven thou hast ever
  Hate and Falsehood tried to smother
By sweet Truth—ah! never, never
  Can it be said, "Ye loved no brother!"

Hatred cannot bud and blossom
  If by love 'tis softly grafted;
And the seed within thy bosom
  Still will show whence it was wafted;
If the soil is barren, never
  Will ye harvest reap; then smother
All thy littlenesses, ever
  Thinking how to help a brother.

THE OLD WOMAN TO THE YOUNG ONE.

OH deem it not, Jeannie, an idle task
    To give what lies in your power
To poor old grandma, who asketh to bask
    In your sunshine one little hour.
For it comforts the agèd heart to see
    Its own dear lambkins play,
And to think of the world as it used to be
    When life to it was May-day.

In my cheek, where ye see a wrinkle now,
    A dimple once lay hid—
And toss as ye please the curls from your brow,
    And roll up the fringed eyelid—
Ye are coming to this, my dear, my dear—
    Your beauty is coming to this,
When Time on your brow sets his stamp of care
    And seals youth's fountain of bliss.

Then, looking back, Jeannie, upon the past,
    Ye too will learn how much
Life's venturous voyagers have cast
    In its sea of promise !—and such
Ye'll know yourself to be, my dear,
    When wreck after wreck floats by,
That once bore freightage of goodly cheer
    And flaunted gay pennons high !

And then, when ye roam on that barren strand
    And hearken the moaning tide

As it ebbeth away from the darkened sand,
  Bereft of its silvery pride,
Ye'll search with a quivering hand, my dear,
  For each little wave-washed shell,
And list with an eager, trembling ear
  To the tale that its pink lips tell,

Of other climes and of sunny seas
  Far away in the golden land,
That has musical whispers in its breeze,
  By angelic pinions fanned !—
The land, my Jeannie, you live in now,
  My darling, my pink-lipp'd shell
To whose tuneful cadence I bend my brow
  To dream 'neath the magical spell.

MY NEIGHBOR.

OVER the way I've a neighbor,
  A peering, inquisitive she,
Who leans over her balcony scanning
  My poor little garden and me ;
I've planted a few simple flowers,
  To brighten my home with their bloom,
And to waft me at even a dream-thought
  Of Araby steeped in perfume.

But this neighbor of mine sees no beauty
  In green leaves, unless underneath

A pea-pod or bean lies maturing,
  Or sugar-corn in its silk sheath ;
And thinks that my time I am wasting
  In watering and tending with care
My rosy-lipp'd pets, and deploreth
  Because I've of brains such small share.

I know that I am sadly deficient
  In many things, " brains" 'mongst the rest,
And find a delight in small pleasures,
  And relish with infinite zest
The trill of the song-bird at twilight,
  The chirp of the cricket so shrill ;
The whispering breeze 'mong the myrtles,
  The music of fountain and rill.

And tho' I am awed when the storm-king
  His wind herald sendeth abroad,
And calls the red lightning to aid him
  With its flashing electrical sword—
Yet, trembling, I still stand entrancèd
  This versatile Nature to see,
That can launch forth the thunder and whirlwind
  Or sport with the buds on the lea !

And only because I love roses
  Much better than cabbage—why she,
My critical neighbor, deploreth
  The want of good sense in poor me !
But God made the flowers, my dear lady—
  You say, " He made cabbages too"—
Well, leave me my roses, I'll freely
  Give all of the cabbage to you.

31

THE WEDDING GARMENT.

"Many are called, but few are chosen."—St. Matthew xxii. 14.

MANY are called to the marriage-feast,
   From the highways and byways to enter there—
He that is greatest and he that is least,
   The penniless and the millionaire ;
The saint, the sinner, the simple, the wise—
   And the fatlings and the oxen are killed ;
And the hungry guests may feast their eyes
   On the sumptuous board with dainties filled.

But the King has spied, 'mongst the motley crowd,
   One with no wedding-garment on,
And unto his servants he calleth aloud
   To cast him out and bid him be gone !—
Out in the darkness, to moan and weep
   And gnash his teeth in vain despair,
For the folly that bade him blindly creep
   Where his garb proclaimed he had no share.

It was not a robe of purple and gold,
   This wedding garment, so chaste and fair,
But a mantle white, in whose every fold
   You might read a ready obedience there
To come, when the King saith, " The feast is spread !"
   Then come from the highways and byways, all,
With a simple trust and a reverend tread,
   When the Lord of the feast doth on you call.

Enter ye in at the open gate,
  Lo ! it stands by the wayside now—
There ye may sit where Jesus sate
  And preached to the crowd from the mountain's
    brow ;
Out where the broad bright smile of God
  Lightens the earth and touches the heart,
Till the stubborn knee is bent to the sod,
  And the fountains of feeling their waters start ;

And the upturned rays of the eye of Faith
  Acknowledge the Father's protecting power—
Tho' the trembling lip no utterance hath
  In deep contrition's sacred hour !
Yet think ye that ever the loudest prayer
  Of the hypocrite, breathed in the temple, is heard
Above the sweep of the golden hair
  Of the Magdalen's offering without one word ?

Nay, nay ; for she sat at Jesus' feet,
  And he pitied her, for " she lovèd much !"
Your wordy devotions may sound complete,
  But in charity, ah ! have they lessons such ?
Nay, nay ; again, a thousand times nay ;
  That Man of Sorrow ye never knew—
From your cushioned footstools Him ye slay
  And His crucifixial pangs renew !

The lessons of mercy He gave His life
  To inculcate, where, oh where are they ?
Lost in the vortex of human strife
  In the pomp and pride of man's little day !—

Lost in the toil of pitiful worms
   For butterfly wings to sport in the sun
Of worldly favor—forgetting the germs
   That their earth-life faintly has begun.

Many are called to the marriage-feast,
   But few remain; oh be thou one
Of the favored few! Then haste, oh haste
   To put the wedding garment on!
And when thou'rt bidden, go freely in;
   The trusting ones are the pure in heart—
To the Lord of the mansion confess thy sin
   With truth, and He'll bid thee not depart!

"THE LOVE THAT PASSETH UNDER-STANDING."

SING, O my soul! in the morning,
   When golden the Orient gleameth,
Sing a glad song with the dawning—
   Sing of the love that there beameth
In flashes of beauty, expelling
   The mists that the dark night doth gather,
And join all the angels excelling
   In strength, in the praise of the Father!

Sing of the love that surpasses
   The love of the soft heart of woman;
The greater than any that glasses
   The soul's depths when linked with the human;

The infinite love the Creator
  Bestows on the creature inglorious,
And sends a Divine Mediator,
  O'er sin, death and hell all-victorious,

Who taketh away our transgressions
  That we may His kingdom inherit;
Who tramples all evil oppressions,
  To make us like Him in the spirit!
Oh greater than any that glasses
  The soul's depths when Life's bark is stranding
Is the infinite love that surpasses
  Our fallible, weak understanding!

THE BEGINNING AND THE END.

THE Alpha and Omega,
  The beginning and the end;
King of kings, and Lord of lords,
  Whom angel hosts attend—
Lo! in clouds He cometh
  With power and glory great,
And every eye shall see Him—
  Yea, they that on Him spate!

And men's stout hearts shall fail them
  With fear for what shall come,
For the heavens shall be shaken,
  While earth lies prostrate, dumb!—

31 *

Whilst He, with Truth's strong-bladed,
  Two-edgèd sword shall thrust
Each bosom's deep recesses,
  Despite of mortal rust—

And make of each a temple
  Ecstatic with God's praise—
Like those archived in mystic
  Old apostolic days.
Where, by the angel keeping
  The sacred record bright,
He stands in glowing vestments
  And loudly calleth, "Write!"

These things saith He that holdeth
  The stars in His right hand:
" To him that overcometh
  Shall be given the fruitage fann'd
By Eden airs eternal,
  Blown on the Tree of Life
That stands in God's own garden,
  Where sin comes not, nor strife.

" For he that overcometh
  And is faithful to the end,
The second death shall hurt not—
  And unto him I'll send
A new name which none knoweth
  Save he to whom 'tis given ;
And he the hidden manna
  Shall eat that grows in heaven !

" His name, before my Father
  And his angels, I'll confess ;

And from God's book not blot it,
　But in golden letters press ;
And a pillar in his temple
　He ever shall remain—
For I am He that openeth
　And no man shuts again.

" To him that overcometh
　I will grant to sit with me
Upon my throne in glory,
　And share my ministry."
These things saith He that holdeth
　Of hell and death the key :
He comes !　He comes in glory,
　And every eye shall see !

THE SUFFERING.

YE'VE suffered—yea ! and suffering, turn
　To Him who suffered more—
For he will take your pains and give
　Them to the cross He bore !
Then faint not when the petty cares
　Of earthly toils annoy,
But look above to Calvary
　And change your woe to joy.

For Life is such an empty show
　That vanisheth away

When death lets in the morning beam
  That brings all-perfect day,
That we, as children waked from sleep,
  Will wonder whence have fled
The phantom shapes that filled our dreams,
  And hollow mockery shed

O'er time, with all its changeful tides,
  And fitful calms and storms,
And magnified this poor frail flesh,
  Made to be food for worms;
Until, with pride-inflated brows,
  We'd strut our little hour,
And chafe at every threatening cloud
  That brought us wind or shower.

But as from earth we cleave away
  From star to star, and see
How glorious are the golden streets
  Lost in infinity—
Mayhap we'll find a little gleam
  Shining for us apart,
And by its light we'll read a page
  That earth wrote on our heart

When storm and darkness seemed to spread
  Between us and the sky;
When, if we knew, we might have heard
  A message from on high!
That God's own hand had sowed a seed
  Of anguish in our breast,
To bear immortal flowers when we
  Should walk the paths of rest!

For what is life, and what is wrong,
  That we should grieve at aught
We find upon our daily rounds
  Springing like tares unsought?
We may put out an eager hand
  To grasp some wayside bloom,
But it will vanish—as will grief—
  On this side of the tomb.

But yet, each little roadside bud
  Some lesson will impart
If with a child-like faith we lay
  Its unction to the heart;
For leaf and blossom, each doth point
  Unto the full-blown flower,
Which only springs perfected from
  Grieved Nature's tearful shower.

O fellow-pilgrims, who with me
  Do tread this vale of tears,
I would your eyes could pierce the haze
  Where the Dark Valley rears
A skeleton to fright the weak,
  Who think this world is all—
I'd help you shake the old dry bones,
  And lift the darksome pall,

To find a glorious light within
  The rank sepulchral gloom;
And then ye'd magnify the Power
  That doomed ye to the tomb,

And sent pain, sickness, sorrow here
  As ministers to lure
Us from these evanescent scenes
  To climes where all is sure.

THE INFANT TEACHER IN THE TEMPLE.

HE sits among the Elders
  And rulers of the land—
Twelve summers' suns have kissed His cheeks,
  Their airs His temples fanned ;
But in their golden glances
  He sees the rays divine,
And reads His Father's messages,
  Whether in shade or shine.

Grave, learnèd men attend Him,
  And bend the reverend ear
To catch the pearls His infant lips
  Let fall, both pure and clear !
Blind leaders, they, unconscious
  Of the honor that is theirs—
Just as in life we entertain
  Oft angels unawares.

For, from the mouths of sucklings
  And babes, comes wisdom forth,
And lordly man may turn to these
  To learn what life is worth ;

For fresh from heaven cometh
  The oracles of youth
Unstained by earth, their purity
  Flows from the fount of truth !

O little children, bless ye !
  For Christ has bidden ye " Come !"
So pure from Eden, sinless still,
  Ye leave the heavenly home,
That tho' your feet have trodden
  A while this mundane sphere,
Still, holy thoughts upwelling from
  Your soul's depths cometh clear—

Such thoughts, that we poor pilgrims,
  Scarred in the fray of life,
May ponder on and profit by
  When mingling in the strife ;
We may be learnèd doctors,
  And deem ourselves profound—
But a little child can questions put
  Which grayheads may confound.

"ONLY A JEW."

[AN INCIDENT OF THE EPIDEMIC IN NEW ORLEANS, SEP-
TEMBER, 1867.]

Passing along —— street, I saw a shabby-looking, dingy hearse
standing before the door of a little shop where all sorts of " notions"
had been exposed for sale only the day before. In such trying times
as these were, it mattered not whether rusty moreen and badly-painted

pine boards, or silver-mounted ebony and cut glass enclosed mortality's
poor remnant; our heart (if we have one) must give a few sympa-
thetic throbs in unison with the mourners around some desolate
hearthstone.   Stopping, I accosted a woman who sat upon a door-
step on the opposite side of the street (I was walking on that side)
with the question, "Who is dead over there?"   With an expression
impossible to describe in words, for it "out-Heroded Herod," she re-
plied, "*Only a Jew!*"

"ONLY a Jew!" from Christian lips
    Came the "blood-for-blood" reply—
As tho' Christ had never died for us,
    To teach us how to die—

And how to live; that His life and death
    Might bring "God's chosen" home
Along the thorny, blood-stain'd track
    His Son was doomed to roam.

Only a Jew—of them that scourged
    And crucified our Lord,
Who, hanging on the cruel cross,
    Prayed for them unto God!

"Only a Jew"—as tho' some dog
    Had yielded up this life—
And not a fellow-being, born
    To brave with us its strife.

Ah! wayside woman whom I met,
    Who "Christian" claims to be,
Perchance that Jew you scoffing spurned,
    May brighter shine than thee,

When that great book is opened, where
    The good seed sown on earth
Will show a golden tropic bloom,
    In a celestial birth.

" Only a Jew !"—O Saviour, King !
    When we shall come to die,
" Only a sinner"—on our lips,
    Shall wait thy sweet reply

WHO ARE THE BLESSED?

NOT the haughty, who their fellows
    Spurn as raised of coarser leaven—
But the poor in spirit, humbly
Seeking grace, though lowly, dumbly,
    Theirs the kingdom of high heaven !

Not the joy-crowned one, whom never
    Sorrow touched with blasting fingers ;
But the mourner, worn and weary
Of this earthly race, so dreary,
    Who beside some white stone lingers.

Not the Shylock, who exacteth
    Pound for pound—but he who ever
Weighs his fellow-man by human
Weaknesses, as born of woman,
    And from flesh can ne'er dissever—

32

He, the merciful, shall ever
  " Twice bless'd mercy" reap, rejoicing !
And the pure in heart, God's features
Shall behold, where cherub creatures
  And seraphic hosts are voicing

Hallelujahs, deep and tender,
  As when sang the sons of morning !
And the peace-makers are blessèd,
They God's children stand confessèd,
  All the walks of life adorning.

But thrice bless'd are ye, when falsely
  Men shall persecute, revile ye
For Christ's sake !—Their taunts unheeding,
Rejoice ! and be ye glad exceeding,
  For their tongues can not defile ye.

Great is your reward in heaven—
  For 'twas thus that they oppressèd
God's evangelists, before you—
Let no dark dismay come o'er you,
  For you're numbered with the blessèd !

Who are blessèd?   All who sorrow,
  All who are in tribulation,
Bearing still their cross in meekness,
Laying at Christ's feet their weakness,
  Are the heirs of His salvation !

"FOLLOW ME."

[St. Matthew ix. 9–14.]

SO Jesus spake to him who on
   The shore of Galilee
At the receipt of custom sat—
   " Arise, and follow me !"
And he arose and followed where
   The many sat at meat ;
The publican and sinner there,
   The outcast from the street.

And lo ! among the wretched herd
   The Lord of life sat down ;
While round about the scornful word
   And Pharisaic frown
Went curdling from lip and brow :—
   " Why doth your Master eat
With publicans and sinners?   How
   Takes he so low a seat?"

But Jesus heard, and answered quick—
   " They that are whole and well
Need no physician—'tis the sick ;
   Know ye the secret spell
Of what that meaneth?   I will have
   Mercy, not sacrifice !
'Tis sinners I have come to save—
   Repentance will suffice !"

And Jesus speaketh now, as then,
     Upon the crowded mart,
Where traffic weighs the souls of men
     And petrifies the heart:
" Come from your grasping, toiling strife,
     Heirs of eternity !
Lay down the petty cares of life,
     Leave all, and follow me !"

And Jesus seeketh now, as then,
     The wretched and forlorn,
The outcast and the scorn of men,
     The vile and lowly born—
Saying, " Poor sin-stained hands and feet,
     No more for refuge flee
Where quicksands lie and whirlpools meet ;
     Arise, and follow me !"

AN OBITUARY.

ANOTHER spotless angel stands
     Beside the great white throne,
A golden harp within his hands,
     His Saviour's love to own,

Who saith to little children, " Come,
     And share my kingdom pure !"—
Then weep not that your child has reached
     Unharmed the heavenly shore.

No load of sin, no earthly stain,
　To mar his upward flight,
But, passing on and on and on
　Unto the realms of light,

That glimmering afar had caught
　His eager, searching gaze,
That ever seemed to look beyond
　This life's obscuring haze.

Yes, little Tommy, thou hast pierced
　The veil; and on thy brow
Is set the seal God's hand imprints
　On those who early go.

The intellect that lit thy face
　With more than childish thought,
Shall brighten with angelic grace
　When time shall be as naught.

The love and tenderness that sprang
　Spontaneous in thy soul,
Will blossom with perennial flowers
　When years no more shall roll.

Then, father, mother, cease to weep;
　The early called are blest—
Escaped the turmoil and the strife,
　Theirs is the heavenly rest!

"DAISY WOMEN."

[TO "PEARL RIVERS."]

"So men of the Sunflower notion,
    Seeking the wide world through,
Mate with the Daisy Women—
    Simple and sweet and true."—*Pearl Rivers*

O SWEET Pearl Rivers,
    You are a Daisy Woman,
With the spirit of a flower
    And a heart that's very human—

But I would not have you mated
    With a tall Sunflower,
For he'd crush you with his greatness,
    And spoil your pretty bower.

For you, Pearl Rivers,
    Were made to bloom with roses,
When the fay-man of the garden
    Its tenderest buds uncloses.

Now, what would you be doing
    In a Sunflower palace,
Like a little meadow Violet
    In the halls of Borealis?

Oh never wed, Pearl Rivers,
    A man of "Sunflower notion,"
For you surely would be stranded
    By his uprising ocean—

And you'd miss the cozy brookside
  Where you dreamed away the hours,
Amid the whispering leaflets
  And the gossip of the flowers;

Where the butterfly was flitting
  Over every dainty blossom,
And the honey-bee was resting
  In the sweet acacia's bosom—

And the lilies of the valley
  Hushed their silver bells' soft ringing,
And all, with ears uplifted,
  Were hearkening thy singing.

Why, the humming-bird would never
  Seek you in your glittering raiment,
And poor, lost Robin Redbreast
  Would feel he was no claimant

On Lady Sunflower's bounty,
  Though she once was little Daisy—
Oh spurn the golden offer
  Lest you set the wildwood crazy;

And be, indeed, a Daisy,
  An unpretending flower
That is happier in the greenwood
  Than in a gilded tower.

For your men of Sunflower notion
  May stoop a while to dally
With the blossoms they have gathered
  In some green and happy valley,

But when Fame's trump is pealing,
   And Ambition calls " Arise !"
They, like the Sunflower, turn them
   To their idol in the skies—

And forget the wee wife-daisies
   Who, pining in the shade,
Lock their sorrows in their bosoms
   And in silence droop and fade.

THE NATIVITY.

FROM lands where rose the sacred fire
   (The Magian's simple rite)
Above the Orient's glittering waves
   Unto the source of light—
From lands where God's own starry skies,
An open book, before them lies,
In which they read, " A King shall rise,"
     A glorious King shall rise—

Came Wise Men to Jerusalem ;
   Led by the Herald Star
That o'er fair Persia's sun-kissed hills
   Had guided them afar—
While frankincense and myrrh they bring,
And golden gifts, as offering
To Him, the Prince of Juda ! King !
     Born to be Israel's King !—-

While shepherds in the distant field,
  Guarding their flocks by night,
Were startled by the passing wings
  Of angels in their flight;
When lo! the angel of the Lord
Came down with reassuring word—
" Fear not!" said he ; " but list th' accord—
        Th' angelic choir's accord !"—

" *Gloria in Excelsis !*" sang
  The host o'er Bethlehem's plain ;
" *Gloria in Excelsis !*" rang
  The sphere that caught the strain !
" *Gloria in Excelsis !*" still,
  In echoes from Judea's hill,
" Peace on earth, to men good-will !
        To men good-will ! good-will !"

" For all ! for all !" the angel said,
  Came tidings of great joy—
That in a manger low was laid
  A new-born, baby boy,
Of David's line—a Saviour ! King !
" *Gloria in Excelsis !*" sing,
  O earth ! while heavenly echoes ring !
        While heavenly echoes ring !

  And sing, O man ! the sacred strain
    That angels sang thee then ;
  Let sweet " good-will" be the refrain,
    And peace must come to men !
  For all, for all, the angel said,

The tidings of great joy were spread—
And for us all that Saviour bled,
　　　　For all, that Saviour bled !

For you, bold scoffer in your pride,
　Was he thus lowly born ;
For you, poor child of sin, He died,
　For you, whom sinners scorn !
For all, for all, He came that day—
To all He pointed out the way—
For all He gave his life away,
　　　　He gave His life away !

Gloria in Excelsis sing
　Unto the Prince of peace !
Let earth with hallelujahs ring,
　And strife and discord cease.
For all, for all, good tidings came—
Sing, all ye ransomed, in His name,
Sing hallelujah to the Lamb,
　　　　Hosanna to the Lamb !

"ARISE AND WALK!"

[St. Matthew ix. 6, 7.]

SEE the poor paralytic, numbed and trembling,
　His quivering limbs all useless at dissembling—
Stretched pallid, feeble on his couch, is calling
· Master !" and hears the words of comfort falling— .
　　　" Arise and walk !"

" Be of good cheer, thy sins are all forgiven !"—
Poor helpless one, by simple faith thou'rt shriven !
The Master bids thee use thy stricken members,
And tramples out thy sin's low smouldering embers—
" Arise and walk !"

Arise and walk ! Lo ! Christ the Lord hath spoken !
The bands of dark-brow'd sin and death are broken—
For He, the God of mercy, sees thine anguish ;
Afflicted one, no longer need ye languish—
Arise and walk !

Arise and walk ! The Son of Man hath power
To loose thy burden in the darksome hour
When in the " Slough of Despond" thou art falling ;
His help is near—His voice is ever calling,
Arise and walk !

Walk in the meadows green His hand hath planted,
He'll gently lead thee through the ground en-
chanted,
And thence unto the glorious city golden
Where dwell the Lamb, the saints and prophets
olden—
Arise and walk !

MY FAITH.

"Except I shall see in his hands the print of the nails, and put my finger into the print of the nails, and thrust my hand into his side, I will not believe."—St. John xx. 25.

I PLACE my hand confidingly
　In Christ's right hand stretched down,
And stand erect, as tho' my brow
　Were circled with a crown !

I ask not leave to touch the wounds
　That tore his side ; nor feel
The imprint of the nails that pierced
　His holy palms !—I kneel,

As kneeled the publican of old,
　And with a contrite sigh,
Pray, Christ, on me, a sinner, look
　With mercy from on high !

And oh, within my heart of hearts
　I feel His presence near ;
He counts each anguished pulse that throbs,
　And treasures up each tear,

Oh how I wish that I could put
　In words the faith that's mine—
That feels the keenest earthly grief
　Is sent by love divine,

Some wondrous mission to fulfill
　Within the stubborn soul—
The prophet's rod to break the rock
　And bid sweet waters roll !

I know not wherefore comes this faith—
　'Tis simple as a child's ;
But it a beacon-light will prove
　Through many dreary wilds

That lie between me and my home,
　Where surely I must meet
The suffering—and lay my cross
　At the dear Saviour's feet !

I would not give this humble faith
　For all the wealth of Ind,
For it will light my path when earth
　And care I leave behind.

I place my hand in Christ's right hand,
　And know he'll lead me through
The fiery furnace, and whate'er
　He wills I shall pursue.

"THE LORD OUR RIGHTEOUSNESS."

IN His days Judah shall be saved,
　And Israel in safety dwell ;
The Lord our Righteousness His name,
　Of whom the olden prophets tell ;

He shall with judgment execute
  Justice in this poor sinful earth,
Where disobedience flourishes
  Now, as in man's primeval birth ;

Where serpents still coil under flowers,
  And Satan evil counsel brings
To blast full many Eden blooms,
  And leave a blight, like creeping things.

But He, the righteous Branch, shall raise
  His crownèd head unto the sky—
And Sin shall cower its brazen front,
  And loving kindness multiply !

And all the faithful shall bring forth
  The fruit of their good works ; and Peace
Shall spread her snowy pinions wide,
  And War's red hand its slaughter cease.

The Dayspring from on high shall dawn
  Of which the seer inspired saith,
" The light shall come to them that sit
  In darkness and the shade of death !"

For God His people shall redeem—
  The Lord our Righteousness His name !
Be joyful in Him, all ye lands,
  And all ye nations sound His fame !